A Real Charmer

by

Iona Morrison

A Blue Cove Mystery

A Real Charmer

Cover Art by *Lisa Dawn MacDonald*

The Wild Rose Press, Inc.
PO Box 708
Adams Basin, NY 14410-0708
Visit us at www.thewildrosepress.com

Publishing History
First Edition, 2026
Trade Paperback Print ISBN 978-1-5092-6396-7
Digital ISBN 978-1-5092-6397-4

A Blue Cove Mystery
Published in the United States of America

Dedication

Dedicated to my husband Rob Morrison who recently passed away. Because of him I have lived my own sweet love story that rivals any that I have read. I will miss his loving presence, wonderful big smile, and the sweet companionship we shared for many years.

Chapter 1

Peyton yanked her hair into a ponytail, frowning at her image in the mirror. She bent down and tied her tennis shoes and headed for the front door. "I'll be back before you leave, Madi," she told her sister and closed the door with a bang.

She stepped out into a hazy, chilly November morning with the early fog still rolling in from the bay. The dense cloud of tiny water droplets hovered near the ground like a thick carpet hiding the trail in its swirling mist. Beautiful in its own eerie kind of way, the scene made the woods more unnerving today. All she hoped for was the cool air would clear her head.

Her morning had started out well enough but went downhill quickly after an argument with her sister. Well, argument might be too strong of a word to use—tiff might be better.

Either way, she needed space to get over her hurt feelings and let her sister do the same. No matter how much she cajoled, Madison didn't even want to talk about a move to Blue Cove. She loved the city and her job at the hospital. If she were honest, she had once felt the same way. Peyton's best option was to let her sister be and get away from the house. When Madison dug in her heels, no amount of words could change her mind. A lot like someone else she knew.

She castigated herself for being in such a rush to get

away. Was it her feet that had betrayed her or her head because she had definitely not made a smart choice. She couldn't have been in the right frame of mind. *Running away was your first mistake, girl, followed closely by choosing to run this way.* What had prompted her to run toward the wooded area this morning? Preoccupied would be her sad excuse to anyone who wanted to listen to her mournful complaint later on.

Her cousin Jessie had recently shown her the trail on one of their weekly runs together. Together was the optimum word and not alone. Why she went this way instead of the ever-popular path to the marina with the ocean view and other joggers, she would never know. On any other day the beauty and solitude of this trail invited you into the tranquil almost cathedral-like canopy of trees, but today the atmosphere felt more spooky than peaceful. "Well, you did it this time." She shook her head as the shivers skipped up and down her sweaty back like tiny spiders marching double time across her skin, leaving her with no doubt this wasn't one of her best ideas ever.

Alone with her thoughts and the rhythmic sound of her feet striking the ground, she kept running forward under the dark cover of the trees. Deeper in was the quickest way out, or she would turn around right now. She picked up her pace with a sense of urgency. Something wasn't kosher. With a quick glance over her shoulder, she forced down the panic that threatened to overtake her, screaming at her to run for her life. There was no threat that she could see, but her heightened senses told her a different story.

Her mind was no help as it played back in vivid detail a story her cousin once told her. Jessie had run through these same woods with a serial killer in hot pursuit. The memory didn't do anything to soothe her anxious sense of alarm. *Get ahold of yourself, girl. Your imagination is running wild.* When she rounded the corner, she realized it wasn't. A foot peeked out from the low-lying bushes. Any questions she had were answered and even more when she saw the girl's ghost standing by the tree watching her. Fate had stepped in. Someone needed to be found, and another case had pulled her in whether she wanted to be in or not. Darn, she was hoping to get a pass for a few weeks, but time wasn't in the cards. She would have her own story to tell about her run through the woods.

She pulled her phone out of her pocket and made the dreaded call, pacing back and forth, waiting for someone to answer. Body tense, she listened for the sound of a snapping twig or rustling bush because she didn't want to be caught off guard.

"Blue Cove PD. This is Joe. May I help you?"

"Hi, Joe, this is Peyton Reynolds. I found a body." She gulped as she forced the words out. There wasn't an easy way to tell him. She went on to explain the location in the woods down from the inn.

"Can you see the whole body?"

"No, only a foot. The rest is hidden in the bushes. From the size, I think you might be looking at a woman or a small man," she told him.

"I'll get a team right out there. Keep your phone on so we can track your exact location."

"I will. I'll stay put. I know the protocol." She took a deep breath and tried to compose herself for what was ahead.

"I'm sure you do by now, Peyton. Stay alert. The

killer could still be in the vicinity."

"You know I will." Joe's statement did nothing for her nerves while she waited. Every noise made her jumpy, and what appeared to be eerie silence only a few minutes ago was now alive with an abundance of magnified sounds. She leaned against the nearest tree trunk and remained for what seemed an eternity for the crime unit to arrive while her every move was observed by someone she couldn't see but could sense nearby.

****

He had lingered in the same exact spot most of the night and morning since lugging the girl's body to the perfect spot under the cover of night. Strange how even a tiny person's body can become heavy. Dead weight, isn't that what they call it? He smirked. Careful to cover his tracks, he had placed her tenderly where she rested. He had even arranged her dress to perfection and made sure her tiny foot could be seen if someone happened to come along. He snapped a picture for his collection. There were too many spread out over the years to recount. He found joy in glancing through his book of conquests. Some were his own artist renderings. His brothers would be proud and maybe his deliciously wicked momma too. Hopefully, his exploits would impress his brothers. They cast a big shadow over him.

Before he went to his hiding spot, he swept away his footprints and the area around which he placed her. He was nothing if not meticulous. Even knowing he'd cover his steps, his body tensed as he killed time. He grinned at his pun and shoved his hands into the pocket of his jacket. No one came. He glanced at his watch. Maybe he should've placed the body in a busier location. Discovery was part of the game he played. He didn't want to be caught of course, but he wanted each victim to be found. They were his legacy. He liked to think of himself as a real charmer. At least he had been called that often enough by his two brothers, and his momma when she found the time to talk to him. He was the handsome one and the baby. But a disappointment of sorts in comparison to his brothers. He tried hard and always left his calling card. Although, no one had uncovered his identity to this point or at any other time for that matter. Why he would never understand—he left enough clues. The time had come to reveal his genius again with each of his special offerings. He wanted the notoriety. The idea made him hopeful that his brothers would hear and come to see he was following in their footsteps.

Someone was coming. He crouched lower to the ground and stilled himself. The sound of shoes striking the dirt path was music to his ears. His body vibrated with anticipation, even before the person came into view. Aww, she was worth the wait. He perked up. "Bless me," he mocked, placing his hand over his heart. She not only saw the foot, but she posed for him quite nicely by the tree. Glowing and wet from sweat, she was beautiful to behold, and she stood there long enough for him to take his fill. A strong force surrounded her, which made him shudder. Memories of past defeats flicked through his mind, which he pushed aside but not before the sudden chill hit him. This could turn out to be an amusing game of cat and mouse, he thought. *My wits against hers.* She seemed familiar. "Impossible." He shook his head. And yet there was something…

He had a wide selection of pretty playthings to choose from, but it might be exciting to watch this one dance. He switched on the device in his pocket. When he pulled the piece out to have a look, numbers lit up the screen. The device worked just like the web site promised. If she played nice, he might choose to let her live and maybe even let her ransom another's life. He listened, waited, and knew the moment he needed to slip away before the police arrived.

****

Dylan, the acting police chief while Chief Parker was gone, was first to arrive on scene. "I guess with your cousin on her honeymoon you're the lucky one. What are you doing running alone in this area anyway? I'm only asking because you know Jaxon will ask you the same question."

"I'm sure he will. I've asked myself the same thing many times this morning. But after finding her, I believe I was meant to run this way. An amazing change of heart even for me." She forced a smile. "Although I admit I told my cousin more than once before she left I didn't want to deal with any cases while she was on her honeymoon. I knew I was hoping for the impossible, but you can't blame a girl for trying," Peyton told him. She watched as more team members arrived and got to work. Branches were lifted with care to reveal the body of a young woman. She couldn't stop herself from looking at the girl lying there as though sleeping. Her hair spread around her pretty face. She was young.

Kip crouched down to get a closer look.

Peyton listened while Kip called out the first visuals of the victim with a brief description. "We have a young female victim. Her mouth is taped shut, and eyes are shut. I can see multiple contusions on her neck. Our victim is placed on her back. She has on a pink dress and has a single white rose with some kind of charm or talisman attached to the stem arranged in her folded hands. This was no rush job, placing her in this spot. The scene is neat, almost as if he wants us to believe that he cares. The victim appears to be in her late teens or early twenties." He lifted the charm wrapped around the stem. "Unusual, I wonder if it has a meaning."

"I'm sure that it must," Peyton replied as she saw the girls spirit hovering over her body.

"How?" one of the officers asked.

"In some cultures, a charm is supposed to hold magical properties and bring the owner good luck. But not in this case obviously."

The longer she listened to their conversation, Peyton found herself holding back the sobs rising in her throat. Soon all pretense was gone, and the tears ran freely down her cheeks. No one should have to go through what this victim went through. Her sorrow was soon replaced with anger. The girl's poor parents and family. Glancing at the spirit, she could see the sadness reflected in the spirit's expression.

Kip placed his arm around Peyton's shoulders. "I know where to find you if we have any questions. Why don't you go home? This is hard to take for all of us, and we're trained."

"Thanks, I believe I will." Peyton took the tissue Evan, Matt's brother, handed her. He was there to photograph the crime scene. "Kip, do you think Evan can take a close-up picture of the talisman? I want to research its meaning. I won't show the picture to anyone else except for Jeremy. Your department has worked with him many times."

"I'll run your request by Dylan."

"I'd appreciate it. Maybe Jeremy can help me

discover info on its origin."

"Officer Harrison will escort you home," Kip said.

"Thank you." Peyton was grateful for the new officer's chatter as they walked. As soon as her cottage was visible, she told him goodbye, rushed the rest of the way home to get ready for work at her cousin's bookstore, and to see her sister off. An event she was dreading. She wouldn't tell Madison what happened. Peyton loved being with her sister, and she wasn't ready for their time together to end. Especially after this morning. She may have spent a good portion of their childhood protecting her little sister but seeing that young woman earlier brought home the fact that she couldn't protect Madison from everything. She was a grown woman. The time had come to let Madi fly.

Chapter 2

Peyton moved a few feet to her right, away from the door, and sighed, wiping at the tears spilling down her cheeks. She forced herself to move and almost made it to the book table before she stopped again. She had no idea how long she had been standing in the same spot, staring out at Main Street. Long enough to follow her sister's car as she drove out of town until she couldn't see the bumper anymore. Resolved to let her sister fly didn't mean she wouldn't cry. But no amount of standing at the window or busy work could wipe the image of the girl's body she discovered earlier from her mind. She hadn't told Madison, or her sister would be begging her to come live in the city again.

Women didn't fare well sometimes as she knew all too well. Had it not been for some miraculous intervention, her and her sister could have been victims themselves. They were abused, and she was finally free enough to acknowledge their abuse. Therapy had helped her let go of the anger and now was helping her to let go of the need to protect her younger sister. Although, if the morning was any indication, she might need a few more sessions on the subject.

She noticed a few cars pull into the church parking lot across the street. At least there was a bit of activity somewhere because there wasn't much going on here. She glanced around the empty store and at the clock on the wall that seemed to be ticking louder than normal. Of course, the store wasn't open yet, and she wasn't doing her job to remedy the situation. "Pardon me if I can't get motivated. I have a good excuse," she muttered.

With her cousin Jessie on her honeymoon, and Molly who owned the connecting shop on maternity leave, the usual lively store seemed empty without their presence. The whole sense of something bad happening that appeared to be linked to the body in the woods didn't help either. She may not have wanted to see another case, but the case found her. Darn, life in Blue Cove was a tad more unpredictable because she never knew when some uncanny event would sneak up and pull her or her cousin into another mess. This morning, she had felt anxious, and at least now she understood one of the reasons why. "Procrastinating again," she muttered to herself. Who was the murder victim? Was she local? No more stalling. She would have to find a way to muddle through on her own or chat long distance with her cousin.

"Time for a pep talk, Peyton. You've got to look for the positive, as Grandma Sadie has told you many times."

She glanced at the stairs. Their semi grumpy ghost and guardian was still standing watch, and the ever-faithful Audrey would be here later to help close the store for the evening—both a positive to her way of thinking. Of course, there were plenty of books to keep her company and customers to help her stay busy once she opened. She needed to gear herself up for the police interview that she knew would be coming.

She began the routine she had helped her cousin do many times since moving here. Starting at the book display table, she straightened books and ran the feather duster over them. Dust particles flew into the air with each pass of the feathers and were captured in the sunlight—mimicking tiny golden sparkles as they floated back to Earth and landed who knew where.

Her cousin's wedding was less than a week ago, and it had been quite the event. Jessie made a stunning bride, and Matt had never let her out of his sight. The look on his face when he saw her for the first time was over-the-top romantic and it still turned her insides all mushy when she thought of the moment. The entire event had been a blast. In more ways than one. Getting Jessie to the wedding in one piece along with Matt was a whole other story. Between gunshots, a botched abduction, and a few bomb threats, their wedding was one to remember and drew a large crowd of both seen and unseen guests.

There was no way her cousin's wedding could be a simple affair after the year she had lived through in Blue Cove. Simply perfect is the way Reba their friend had described the day. Peyton might have added a few choice words to Reba's description, but she opted to keep her mouth shut. A first for her. Her mouth had gotten her into trouble more than once. Grams warned her often, "Think before you speak and then keep it to yourself." The problem for her was if the words didn't come out through her mouth, they often did on her facial expressions. Jessie was stubborn and could argue with the best, while she said the first thing that came to her mind, appropriate or not. Defiant was the word Grams used to describe her.

Peyton swiped at the single tear rolling down her cheek. Was she having a pity party? A strange sensation to her, since she was the practical one. Still, there was the body. She couldn't simply unsee what she had seen.

Tears were threatening to spill down her cheeks

again, and she hardly ever cried. That was Jessie's department. She had learned early in life never to let her parents or anyone else see her cry. Never show them a weakness was her motto. She rubbed her cheek.

Her cousin was counting on her.

"Well, here goes nothing." She turned the sign around and opened the doors into Joe's. Time to do the great customer service thing her cousin always did. At the moment she wasn't feeling the whole happy thing, but maybe the day would turn out better if she tried. Plastering a smile on her face, she was determined to overcome her gloominess.

"Good morning, sweet girl." Reba, Jessie's mentor and, since seeing her first ghost, Peyton's too, came through the doors with two cups of hot tea in her hand. "I come bearing tea and goodies to get your day started."

"Let me help you carry those." Peyton took one of the cups and followed Reba to the table. Lord knew she could use a bit of happy sunshine this morning.

"It seems a bit strange not seeing our lovely Molly behind the counter." Reba shook her head. "I find change hard, don't you?"

"I was thinking the same thing this morning." Peyton sat in the chair next to Reba. "I miss seeing Molly and my cousin too."

"Of course you do, but change is inevitable, it seems. Besides, the nice young man working there promised to bring in our goodies. He told me his boss said to treat me well. That sounds like the dear girl."

"Molly is thoughtful." Peyton reached for a lemon bar that the young man placed on the table in front of them.

"What's your name?" Reba handed him a generous

tip.

"Jonathan, ma'am. I'm Molly's cousin." He turned to leave.

"Thank you, Jonathan." Reba smiled at him. "I will tell your cousin when I see her again what a fine job you're doing."

"I'd appreciate any kind words on my behalf. I've been a big pest to her most of my life." He chuckled.

"I find that hard to imagine," Reba said softly to Peyton. "But then again boys can be onery when they're young."

"Yes, they can." Peyton smiled. "I have a few in my class that give me a run for my money."

"Now, my dear, for the real reason I'm here." She reached for Peyton's hand. "I swear I see that fella crack a smile every now and then. At least his mouth turns up at the edge, and that's a good beginning." She pointed at the guardian floating above the stairs. "You girls are a good influence on him." Reba pursed her lips. "I get distracted way too easy some days."

"I sometimes do the same." Peyton wiped the powdered sugar off her lips with the napkin. "I wished he could talk and tell me his full story. I'm sure it would be interesting," she muttered beneath her breath.

"Now, now, you're way too young for getting distracted. Anyways the reason I'm here is to brighten your day. I thought you might be feeling a bit sad with both your cousin and sister gone. I'm offering you my ear to listen." She patted Peyton's hand.

"Your timing is always perfect." She gulped. "It was hard to say goodbye to Madi today, but that wasn't the hardest part of the morning." She swiped at the pesky tears starting again. Who was she this morning?

"Peyton dear, what's wrong?" Reba reached for a tissue in her purse.

"I found a body on my run this morning. I'm still reeling from that."

"Oh, goodness, of course, you are, dear. Where?" Reba tucked the tissue in Peyton's closed hand.

"In the woods down from the inn. I went for a morning run, and there she was." Peyton shivered.

"Oh, my dear girl, that must have been a shock." Reba patted her hand.

"Maybe a bit but not entirely," Peyton told her. "I sensed something was up but didn't want to face it. I think it was easier to blame my angst on my sister leaving." Peyton lifted the tissue and dabbed at her eyes.

"I can see how the emotions could get jumbled in you this morning. I would feel the same way. I would love my sister Barb to move closer to me. But distance has not stopped us from being the best of friends, and it won't hurt your relationship with your sister either."

"I know you're right, but in my heart I want Madison to move here. Is that wrong?"

"Not wrong, but maybe it's not right for her. I remember another girl who didn't want to move here at one time too. Do you remember what it took to convince you?" Reba's brows rose.

"Yes, don't remind me. It took being shot and recuperating at my cousin's with all the amazing town folks to help out. I fought the idea of needing any help. Believe me I don't want that for Madi." Peyton took another sip of her tea.

"She doesn't have to be hurt to make the decision, if this is where she's meant to be. She needs to find her on path without you. Things have a way of working out the way they're meant to. For now, Madison is supposed to be right where she is. Working in the hospital's ER and caring for the folks who come in there. And if I don't miss my guess, you'll realize that truth soon enough. When or if her time is done there, she'll know, and she'll decide to make the move on her own or not."

"I know you're right," Peyton said. "But I would love to help her along the way."

"You know life doesn't often work out the way we plan." Reba shook her head.

"I know, but one can wish." Peyton sipped her tea.

"Now to get to another reason for my visit this morning. You asked a question of Jessie not long ago about if your premonitions could be used to see things before they happened and prevent them. My answer is you're about to find out. One person may be saved, but others have already been lost. As you found out this morning. There is a connection you will understand in time. You'll need to listen to your heart. People and words will not be as they seem. You'll be sifting through lies that appear as truth and truth that seem like lies. You are only responsible for what you know or can discover." Reba dabbed at her lips.

"I hope I can't get in trouble for what I don't know. The truth is, I didn't want to deal with any of this until Jessie returned. I need to bounce things off of her." Peyton popped the last bite of lemon bar into her mouth.

"Oh, silly girl. Life doesn't work that way. Wouldn't it be a nice convenience if our plans did? Highly unlikely, but nice. You have me, of course, to talk to and Jaxon. You two must learn to work as a team. This may be a time of learning for the two of you." Reba smiled. "He's a keeper, you know. Not at all like your dad so stop comparing them."

"I'm on record to whoever is listening—I'd rather not deal with any of this stuff, thank you." Peyton jumped up when a customer walked in. "Time for me to get to work. But just so you know, I believe Jaxon is the best. I'm coming around slow and steady."

"I'll sit here for a while and finish my tea. I hope you get what you want, dear, but this morning told you already that you won't."

Peyton ended up having a busy morning with several new customers who had recently moved to town. She found enough downtime to walk Reba to the door and hugged her when she was ready to leave. But being busy hadn't kept Peyton from overthinking Reba's words to her. How had Jessie put up with the ghosts and premonitions on her own in the beginning? Of course, Jessie had Reba to guide if not confuse her. Her warnings at times were perplexing at best. Especially, if you didn't want to hear what she had to say. And that would be her at the moment.

She wrote out orders for customers requesting books that weren't in the store. Some were new titles, and others were popular books which sold out as fast as they were placed on the shelf. Especially with the fall bus tour groups descending on the store and holiday sales picking up.

After lunch, Peyton had time to scroll through her phone. Jaxon had texted her about dinner with him. Yes, please. Kip, good to his word, sent her a picture of the charm on the rose and told her to make sure no one but Jeremy saw the photo. He also wanted her to send any information she learned. She had seen a similar charm somewhere on their trip, which made her think that it was

Celtic in origin, which seemed about right considering her ancestors.

She no sooner had sent her reply to Jaxon and opened the photo of the talisman than the atmosphere around her was charged with an unknown presence. At least new to her, and she had plenty of experience with the strange and unusual. A hush descended over the store with not a sound to be heard, not even from Joe's.

What started out as a faint voice crying out for help grew louder and stronger until Peyton covered her ears. Through a dark haze around her, Peyton saw the young girl tied to a chair with duct tape covering her mouth. The girl's fear palpable, the shadow that moved around the young woman reminded Peyton of the demons she once fought each of those nights in the closet many years ago. Peyton knew she would do anything she could to save the girl.

"I'll find you, I promise." Peyton wiped the tears from her eyes. The gray tape covering the young woman's mouth reminded Jessie of the girl this morning. Maybe Reba was right—the two were connected somehow.

As quickly as the vision had come, the store returned to normal. The bell above the door rang, and another customer walked in with Audrey right behind her. It was as if nothing had changed, and yet for Peyton everything had. She was no longer on the sideline but ready to go to battle. She glanced at the guardian who watched her. Nothing from him?

Chapter 3

As soon as Audrey arrived, Peyton left for home. Her mind raced with thoughts about the vision she had seen earlier. Jaxon needed to know, of course. Maybe he would be aware of a missing girl in the area. She didn't doubt for a moment that the girl was real and not simply a figment of her imagination. She often second-guessed her premonitions in the beginning, but she wouldn't make the same mistake now. The girl's life was dependent on her belief in what she saw. A fact that wasn't lost on her if she wanted to find the girl alive. Reba reminded her earlier Jessie's gift had been used to save more than one person's life. It was easy to forget that fact among the ghosts and strangeness of the past year.

Peyton got dressed for her evening out and went through her messages before Jaxon arrived. Her favorite email was from Jessie saying married life was great so far. She was sure they had visited their fair share of Irish pubs and loved all the lively Irish music. Jessie promised more information when they settled down for the evening. Her hunky cop was a great traveling companion with fringe benefits. Peyton sent her a quick note back telling her she couldn't wait to hear more about where they were staying. She tried to imagine Matt and her cousin strolling hand in hand down the streets of Dublin.

She opened the door when she heard his knock.

"Hi," she said when Jaxon walked in.

"Seems like a long time since we've had a night out alone. I'm looking forward to it." He kissed her cheek and then pulled her into his arms. He leaned his chin on the top of her head. "I've missed you."

"I've missed this most of all." She snuggled against him. She pulled out of his arms and handed him her jacket.

He chuckled. "I take it you're hungry. I am too." He held her jacket for her to put on. "I never had a moment to stop for lunch today. My team was busy all day."

"Where we going?" She locked the door on her way out.

"Dylan told me about a nice place a few miles outside of town. He said the food is good and it's a great place for a quiet dinner."

"Sounds perfect. Dylan seems to know a lot of great places to eat."

"You tend to find them when you're single and rely on eating out. Now that he's married to Katie, I doubt he goes out near as often."

"Why would he? Katie is an amazing cook." She slid in the passenger seat of his awesome car. "You know your car is cool, don't you?"

"She's a beauty. My one splurge since receiving the money from Elliot Dawson. I never dreamed he would leave me all that money. How we developed a close friendship through the antics of his son EJ, I'll never know. I spent most of my time with Elliot going over EJ's run-ins with the law. I had to be a thorn in his side." Jaxon turned onto the highway and drove the few miles up the road to the restaurant.

Peyton leaned her head back against the seat and let

her mind drift. Her mind rushed through the events of the day. She couldn't forget the look of fear on the girl's face or hearing Kip describe the murder scene.

****

Jaxon kept glancing at Peyton. He couldn't tell if she was sleeping or simply being quiet. Either way she was beautiful. Matt's wedding had put thoughts of marriage in his head. Maybe hopeless dreams or at the least too early to initiate. He wanted to have a family, but he wondered if his job was conducive to family life. A thought uppermost in his mind ever since the last case when two agents were hunted down by a suspect and shot. One in front of his son. Even Matt told him the bureau was too intense for him. Not that Matt's job in Blue Cove had been a piece of cake lately. No doubt about it, the Reynolds girls had changed both of their jobs. In some ways the cases were harder, but in others they were better.

When they were close to the restaurant, Jaxon glanced at Peyton. "Am I boring you?" he asked.

"Sorry, I'm lost in thought. It was a different kind of day." Peyton turned to look at him. "You are never boring."

"That's nice to know." He smiled at her. "I was beginning to wonder if I had lost my charm." He slowed down and moved into the turn lane. "Here we are, but before the evening is over, I want to hear all about the day you described as different."

"Don't worry, you will." She glanced at him as she slipped her phone into her purse.

After he parked the car, Jaxon walked around to open her door. He took her hand and didn't let go until he pulled out her chair for her once they were inside.

Dylan knew all the best places to dine in the area. He would thank him when he saw him again.

"This is nice." Peyton took the menu the waiter handed her. "I'm not sure what to order. There are some great choices." She glanced at the waiter. "Do you have a suggestion?"

"You can't go wrong with a steak, but one of my favorites is this grilled chicken specialty." He pointed to the place on the menu.

Peyton read the description. Grilled chicken topped with tomatoes, mozzarella, basil pesto, and a lemon garlic sauce. "This sounds perfect." She smiled at him and thanked him.

Jaxon grinned at the waiter's reaction to her while becoming more annoyed by him. He'd been the nonexistent guy observing the young man's reaction to her smile that made the guy speechless. How well he knew that sensation. He couldn't hold a coherent thought in his head when he saw her walk out the door at the resort in Arizona. He fought the Peyton effect until he couldn't resist any longer.

"I'll have the steak." Jaxon broke into the awkward situation with the fawning waiter by reminding him of his presence. He had found it funny until he thought the young man had carried it too far by leaning over her shoulder to point to a dessert item on the menu. Enough was enough.

As soon as the server left, Peyton took Jaxon's hand. "Thank you for running interference for me."

"Any day." He rubbed his thumb across her hand. "To be truthful, I wanted to push his hand off your shoulder, but I controlled my caveman tendencies. I didn't want to embarrass you."

"Thank you on both counts."

They made small talk while they ate their meal. The evening had been perfect, but still Jaxon sensed something was weighing on Peyton's mind. She laughed at his dumb jokes, told him stories about her time with her sister, and yet she seemed distracted. He knew Peyton well enough to know something was bothering her. Once or twice, he thought he saw her eyes glistening. Were those tears? Early on, he discounted what his gut told him when it came to her, blamed it on those beautiful green eyes. Sometimes they looked like the dewy green hills of Ireland, and when she was mad, he'd seen them turn a stormy grayish green like the seas. He had the same problem Matt had with Jessie. He was smitten.

"Are you ready to leave?" she asked Jaxon after he paid the check.

"Yes." He held her jacket for her to slip into. "We need to talk about what's bothering you. You can tell me when you're ready."

Jaxon waited for most of the drive home for her to even talk, but hey, he was a patient man. He had shared more than a few sparring rounds with her since they first met. Those first few weeks had been quite a test of wills. He had won a few rounds but so had she. One thing he knew, Peyton was one strong woman.

Chapter 4

"I'm not ignoring you," she said softly. "I have a question before I tell you though."

"Ask away." He glanced at her before he pulled out onto the highway.

"Do you know of any missing girls in the area?"

"There are always a few missing persons that come across the wire. Why do you ask?"

"This would be recent. Did Dylan tell you I found a body on my run this morning?"

"I hadn't talked to Dylan today. Where did you find the victim?"

"In the woods near a path that Jessie and I sometimes run. I saw the foot sticking out from the bushes." She scrunched her lips together.

"That's the first I've heard about the body." He glanced at her. "Is that all?" There always was more to the story when she was involved. He had seen her abilities more than once.

"If only that were all." She frowned and then told him about her vision of the girl earlier. "I think someone is looking for her. At least that's what I sense. She's afraid, and the person guarding her seems to come and go, but her fear doesn't."

"Damn, Peyton. I wonder if there's a connection," he mused. "We need to talk. Something happened today, and Maxwell put me on a new case to investigate. First, a ground crew at the college found a hand sticking out of the compost pile, and the body of a young woman was extricated. The lab is working on identifying and notifying the next of kin. But that's not all. Later on, one of the students' fathers went to the college with a gun, threatening one of the professors with claims he had abducted his daughter. The professor vehemently denied his accusation, but it didn't stop the father from pistol-whipping him. When I interviewed the man, he told me this professor was the last person his daughter had been with. He was tutoring her because she was struggling in his class."

"Was there a rose with a charm involved with the murder victim?" she asked.

"I can't answer that question yet. I still have to go over the file on the crime site tonight."

"Have you talked to the professor?" she asked.

"I can answer this one." He merged onto the Blue Cove exit. "I interviewed the professor who is recovering in his hospital bed. The professor and later his assistant said the girl left his office very much alive. He had what seemed to be an ironclad alibi." He stopped at the red light on Main Street. "Did you mention a charm? What kind of charm?"

"Kip sent me a photo, which he told me not to show anyone. I will research its meaning, which reminds me of one the symbols I saw on the artifacts. Some call it a charm—others who believe in magic might call it a talisman. I believe it has Celtic roots. I'm sure Dylan will show you. But you already have your hands full with another investigation." She reached for her purse. "Did I sense a but in your statement somewhere with his alibi?" Peyton glanced at him.

"Not anything that I can put my finger on. I mean personally, there's something about the professor that bothered me, but then so did the girl's father. The good prof seemed too calm almost calculating. His words were measured and careful. He didn't want to press charges against the girl's dad. While the dad was filled with rage, which I can understand. He needs someone to blame for why he hasn't seen her in days. The poor guy's worry is off the charts. I have no evidence to support my feelings about either of the men. The professor is an upstanding part of the faculty. He's tenured and is a part of the great science program at the college. He's well respected among his peers. The students we've interviewed love him along with his aides and assistants. And the other man is simply concerned about his girl. Neither has a record. I'm at square one."

"Go with your instinct until you prove either one wrong or right. At least, that's what I've been told by this wonderful handsome detective that I know."

"Wonderful, handsome hmm." He grinned. "I'm going to interview some more of the students who are in the professor's classes or have taken them in the past. If Tom approves, I'd like you to come with me."

"I'm open if it doesn't interfere with my work schedule." She chuckled. "Are you the same man who told me to stay away from his investigation in Arizona?"

"I'm the same guy but a little smarter. The last few months have taught me that you, my sweet lady, are the good guys' secret weapon." He grinned. "And much better looking than the guys I work with daily." He frowned. "The thing is, the professor could be the guy plain and simple, but I doubt it. Since you are involved, there is bound to be more to the story."

"Probably. For now, the girl I saw is still alive, but there may be others who aren't. Something is going on at the college. If you have a photo of the missing girl, I would like to see what she looks like. I wonder if she is the girl I saw. I hope she's not the other murder victim."

"Hell, I don't like the sound of that. For what it's worth, I think you might be right. Maybe the good professor isn't involved, but I would stake my career that someone at the college is."

"Other than that piece of bad news, how was your day?" she asked.

"Better now with you beside me."

"Aww, aren't you sweet. I feel the same way. Today was a hard one for me. Finding the body, seeing my sister off, along with Jessie not at the store, and Molly gone too, everything seemed wrong to me." She swiped the tears forming in her eyes. "See what I mean. I never cry, whine maybe but never cry." She took a tissue and wiped her eyes.

"Let's finish off the evening at your place and end the day on a sweeter note."

He parked his car next to hers when they got back to her place.

"Be careful with this case. Someone knows you are asking questions, and they're not happy." She warned him, clasping his arm as she got out of the car.

"I'm sure. And you too. Is it possible someone knows you found the body?" Jaxon took the keys from her hand and unlocked the door to her cottage.

"Gosh, I forgot all about that. Maybe that's what I was sensing at the scene. The guy could have still been there." She shivered.

"Hell. I don't like the sounds of that." He clenched

his fist.

"Let's change the subject. I've had enough for one day." She walked through the door he held open.

"Did I ever tell you how much I like these tiny freckles on your nose?" His finger traced them on the tip of her nose.

"I don't think so. I grew up hating them until Sadie convinced me they were angel kisses." She laughed. "I used to dream of tanning like Destiny and Jessie. Not me." She laughed.

"I get it, but why would you want to mess with peaches-and-cream perfection? I pretty much love everything about you. Your eyes, your hair"—he ran his hand through her soft waves—"and especially, your lips." He placed his finger over her mouth. "You're lovely."

She touched her fluttering stomach. "Thank you." She blushed under his intense gaze.

"Does Katie have any plans for Jessie's old place?" He changed the topic again.

"She told Madi she would hold it open for a month to give her time to reconsider. After that, I'm sure she'll try to rent it to someone."

"Do you think your sister wants to move here?" Jaxon asked.

"Not right now but I wasn't easily persuaded to either, as Reba so graciously reminded me today." Peyton chuckled.

"I think I remember that about you. You were reluctant about a few things including me."

"With the background that I had growing up, you're lucky I considered you at all." She smiled at him.

"See what you would have missed." He pointed at

himself and grinned.

"Point taken." She leaned into his side. "I'm sure Madi will find her place wherever that is. I can simply hope she will land here." She handed him the remote.

"Thanks." He took off his jacket and loosened his tie. "I may as well be comfortable." He turned on the TV.

They settled on a movie while they snuggled on the couch, each lost in their own thoughts. Peyton loved moments like this. Jaxon was content to hold her. If she had to describe the feeling to her sister, it would be safe and cherished. Something she wanted her sister to experience at some point. She had more to overcome and work through than Peyton did.

When she went away to college, Madi had to endure the abuse alone. As sorry as she felt, she couldn't go back and undo the past. The best they could both do was to move forward.

Easier said than done when past memories reared their ugly heads time and time again—working their way into every relationship, seeking to destroy any trust they had built. She glanced at Jaxon. She had high hopes that she finally was on her way—thanks to Jaxon.

When the movie was over, Jaxon stood. "I should get going. I have a busy day tomorrow. I'll let you know if I get the okay for you to go with me on the interviews. I'll try to fit it into your time schedule." He pulled her into his arms. "Sweet dreams." He kissed her good night.

A kiss she could feel all the way to her toes. "Same to you." She walked with him to the door and set the deadbolt when he left. Leaning against the door, she sighed. Jaxon was a keeper no doubt about it. She hoped his patience didn't wear thin while he waited on her. She could be hot and sometimes cold. Even she was frustrated with herself. How could he not be?

****

Peyton's premonition of a missing girl along with finding the body at the college earlier had him thinking about her. Could Peyton's life be in danger? He needed to show her the picture the father gave to them. Was she the same girl that Peyton saw? He could almost bank on her being the same girl. Peyton, like her cousin Jessie, was accurate to a fault when it came to premonitions or whatever they were. Jaxon couldn't understand the how's or why's. He simply knew that they were spot-on.

She surprised him often, and he had found himself off-center more than once in her presence. He liked the mystery surrounding her. She wasn't predictable. Only time would tell if they continued to suit. Convinced they would, he was ready to go all in, but she still seemed jumpy whenever he talked about a long-term commitment. In his mind he was up to the task to convince her, but he still often second-guessed himself whenever he sensed her pulling away. He frowned. Not one to run away from a good challenge, he wasn't about to start now. *Sweetheart, consider yourself duly warned. I'm going to win you over.*

When Jaxon arrived home, he sent the photo of the girl in a text to Peyton and waited for her response. He sat in his favorite chair. The soft leather recliner that Peyton picked out and made him purchase. Damn, but she had good taste. He glanced around the room at the transformation her skills had wrought in his living room. It was no longer a place to crash in but one he could enjoy. She seemed to like the results too. She helped with the color choices on the wall and the furnishings along with the accent pieces. The rest of the place could use her touch as well. He hoped her investment in his place would make her see herself there someday soon.

He picked up the remote and answered his phone at the same time. "I take it you got my text with the photo."

"I did, and she looks like she might be the same girl. I can't say for sure. I didn't see her clearly. Her mouth was taped shut, and her hands were tied to the chair. The fear on her face was what I registered most. If she isn't the one, then we might have two."

Jaxon frowned. "Damn," he said. "I'm still waiting for an ID on the murder victim, which makes me wonder what is going on at that college besides higher learning. If there was a rose or a talisman, it wasn't mentioned in the file on this one. But I will check to see if there are other murders in the area that fit the criteria."

"Good idea. If Dylan approves, I will send you the photo of the talisman. Especially if you find other victims with the same calling card. I doubt they will release that knowledge to the public. Do you think we might need to call Frank and have him bring Carlene to attempt to find the missing girl?" she asked.

"Frank is a good call. I'll put a request in with Maxwell, and if he's on board, we'll call Frank together. Hopefully we'll save the girl you saw before she becomes another victim."

"She already is. She'll never be able to trust a man again. You don't ever forget, I know. It has taken me years to get to the place where I am, and I still revert back into my cocoon for safety when I feel threatened," she said. "Trust is hard for me. Girls have always seemed to pay a heavy price. I can see why my cousin is such an activist. I'm tired of seeing young girls and women as the victims of someone's perverted plans."

"I understand. That's why the authorities always have victim advocates. But we also know it's only a bandage on a wound that may take many years to recover from. They could use your and Jessie's perspective."

"Speaking of my cousin, she will be calling me soon. I need to go. Let me know about the interviews with students, and I will try to go if I can. See you soon."

"I'll hold you to those words. Just so you know, I'm sitting in the chair you picked out, and I'm sure glad you convinced me to buy it. I like all your special touches in my living room, and I want you to consider doing a few more rooms for me. As you know, I have no talent in that department. Tell Jessie hi from me."

"I'll tell Jessie, and as for helping you decorate more rooms, I would love to. Decorating is right up there with teaching my kids. I love doing it. We'll go shopping." Peyton hung up.

****

Peyton stretched out on her bed to wait for the call that was sure to come. After a short time, she reached for her ringing phone.

"Hey, cousin. I'm currently in the bathroom trying to get a moment alone. It was the only way I could escape Matt long enough to call you. He hardly lets me out of his sight." Jessie laughed. "Anyway, I'm sending you a long email that I wrote while he was still sleeping this morning. Now he's ready for breakfast and calling my name."

"You'd better go. I can't be responsible for you hiding in a bathroom from your hungry new husband. Before you ask, the store is great but strange without you. And yes, there may be a bit of trouble brewing. I will email you details to read when Matt is sleeping or watching TV."

"Sounds good. Tell me what you think after you read what I sent."

"You know I will," Peyton said.

"Love you."

"Love you right back. Enjoy every minute with your new husband." Peyton clicked off the phone and opened her laptop to read the note from Jessie.

Chapter 5

Peyton stretched out on her bed and smiled at the quips and details that Jessie used in her description of places she had seen.

After Dublin, and Kilkenny. I wanted Matt to see the Cliffs of Moher in County Clare, so we made our way to Galway where we spent the day exploring. We did a walking trip with a local guide. We immersed ourselves in the culture, music, and local traditions. Cous, there were so many beautiful buildings, small canals, and lively streets filled with pubs and shops. Matt especially liked Quay Street in the heart of Galaway. The street was filled with pubs and all the traditional Irish music you ever wanted to hear. You know how I enjoying shopping, and I let Matt have a few pub stops along the way as he trailed in my wake from store to store.

Peyton knew how her cousin loved to shop. Almost as much as she did. She could see the look on Matt's face as he trailed behind Jessie.

Later in the evening we visited The King's Head Pub for dinner. Remind me later to tell you about the grim history behind its name. Oh, what the heck, I'll tell you now. After King Charles I of England was sentenced to death in 1649 following the civil war, London's executioner refused to decapitate him. A call went out for volunteers from England, Ireland, and Scotland. Isn't that wild? The building the pub is in is over eight hundred years old. Everywhere you go, you trip over history. I love it.

Peyton loved that about Ireland too. It would be fun to go there again sometime. She continued to read.

Today we decided to take a road trip through the county to see the Cliffs of Moher and Burren National Park Ireland. A region of limestone hills known as Lunar Lands and caves on the west coast. Peyton, there was so much to see dating back thousands of years. There is evidence of humans living in the area for over seven thousand years. How cool is that? There were tombs, ancient cooking sites, and stone forts. I swear the place seemed alive with the spirits that rested there. I know you understand what I'm talking about.

Peyton chuckled. Boy and how did she understand.

We also visited a few sites that maintained old records. Tomorrow we are headed to Donegal. I know I whetted your appetite about old records, and you should be.

"Should be what?" Peyton wondered.

Her cousin could get lost in the details. Peyton waded through all the things locals told Jessie about Donegal before she got to the meat of her email.

To make a long story short, we sifted through records to find relatives to great-grandmother Kathryn, and lo and behold, we found another relative who had the gift in our family line. Aine pronounced like Anne O'Flaherty. Up until the seventeenth century, Galaway was inhabited by a few powerful Gaelic families. Peyton, the description of her sounds like you. You have to read the scrolls to see if you can find her name. I believe you'll learn more about yourself if you do. I will send you more if I learn more. Nighty night, cous.

Peyton sent Jessie a quick message wishing her a good day. She closed her computer and shut off her light. The scrolls would still be there in the morning. Stretching out her legs, Peyton snuggled under the covers. She closed her eyes, but sleep seemed far away while her thoughts raced on. There was no way her mind would shut down long enough to rest. Not with an invitation waiting for her to discover more about herself.

She pushed up into a sitting position and reached for the computer on the small table beside the bed. With the press of a button, the computer came to life, its screen light chased the darkness into odd dancing shadows on the walls at the edge of the room. There those eerie little shadows moved until she clapped on the lamp. She opened up the file that contained photos of the scrolls. "Okay, Aine O'Flaherty, here I come. Tell me all your secrets and what I need to know," she mused.

Peyton worked meticulously, reading page after page in the file until she came to Aine's name and notes. Many of them were written in Gaelic, or at least that's what she thought the foreign words were. *Looks like I have a bit research to figure out how we are alike if at all.* Peyton shook her head but continued to follow through the lines extracting what she could understand.

She started to put the pieces of her family line together with details she had learned in previous cases. The Cassidys, Campbells, and Donovons were all connected in their family tree. Scanning the notes she took from Cara's Journal of her family's trip from Ireland in the eighteen hundreds, Peyton was reminded that Cara's mother was a Campbell. One of her sons, Ian, married Maggie Connor who gave birth to Andrew Campbell who married Katie Donovon. Not the Katie they all knew, of course. Katie gave birth to Kathyrn Campbell or better known as their great-great-grandmother. The very same person who Peyton had traveled back in time to live a few days in her life. What an adventure that had been. Pulled through the pages of book back to nineteen-eighteen to the years of World War One and the Spanish Flu. She got to see the time up close and personal living in her grandmother's life. Peyton still marveled at the whole experience that happened to her. How it happened, she would never be able to explain except she was a traveler of some sort. Something she had a lot to learn about.

Cara's grandmother, Alanna, was gifted with great mystical abilities, which seemed to pass down through some of the women in her family line. Some of the gift was broken at that time when a powerful sorceress put a curse on the village where Alanna's family lived. Those who were cruel and refused to change were cursed and lived out their lives under the burden of that curse. But not Alanna, whose gift grew over time.

Now all she had to do was figure out where Aine O'Flaherty fit into her family, or better yet how she fit into hers since Aine lived long before Cara wrote her journal. How did Aine come to learn about her gift? Did she know Johanna, or did she come after her? This was a mystery Peyton wanted to figure out. Doing this kind of research was right up her alley. She loved the process. Once a thought caught hold of her, she would be off and running. She'd followed more than a few rabbit trails over the years too. Research, yes, but not tonight. She needed rest, or the kids would eat her alive tomorrow. One again she shut of her computer and light and determined to shut her mind down long enough to go to sleep.

How and when had Aine got to the area of County Clare? At least that's where Jessie discovered the record of her. Maybe she never lived there at all. Who was she, and how was Peyton like her? All questions for another day. Maybe she would find the answers, and maybe she wouldn't, but she certainly was going to try. Peyton stretched her legs out, plumped her pillow under her head, and snuggled beneath the warmth of the blankets. Another adventure was about to begin. No longer hesitant, she was up for the challenge.

Chapter 6

Peyton rushed out the door. If she didn't hurry, she'd be late. Thankfully, there was no frost on the window to scrape—she couldn't afford the delay this morning. Her late night, followed by tossing and turning, meant she slept later than she should have. With the press of her keyless button, her engine purred to life. She would always be grateful for Jaxon's help picking out this little beauty. Her car was perfect. Although, she wasn't looking forward to clearing any snow off its exterior this winter before she could drive. The garage at Jaxon's house looked better the closer the cold weather came. Her cousin bought her a frost protector to cover her windshield. Now all she had to do was remember to put the darn thing on at night.

Peyton arrived at the school a few minutes before the first bell rang. She opened her classroom just as Kimmy, one of her students, was wheeled in by her mother.

"My daughter was excited to get here this morning. She always loves art and music days."

"I think most of the students do. They seem to especially like the rhythmic instruments. The boys love to bang the cymbals. The noisier the better." Jessie chuckled.

"I'll leave her in your capable hands." She kissed her daughter goodbye. "Mama will be back soon."

As soon as Kimmy's mother left, more of her students arrived, and Peyton was kept busy until her morning was done. The kids seemed louder and more excited today than normal. Some days were like that. At least, she didn't need to sub for the afternoon art class. The teacher was back. She would be able to give Audrey a breather for an hour or two at Jessie's store. She wouldn't mind a bit of a pause herself.

Once in her car she left the school and drove to the back of the store where she parked. Her phone was buzzing with an incoming call, but she didn't feel like answering. She let it go to voicemail.

"Are you ready for a break?" Peyton asked Audrey.

"I could put my feet up for a few minutes. And if my stomach grumbles are any indication, I could eat my lunch too." She placed her hand over her noisy middle.

"Be my guest. I'm here to relieve you for an hour or two. Has it been busy?"

"Not too bad. Busy enough to keep you from getting bored and make the day move faster, which is what I like." Audrey grabbed her bagged lunch from behind the counter. "Before I forget to tell you, a man has called here a couple of times looking for you. At least I think it was a man."

"What do you mean?"

"The voice sounded a bit distorted, but it might have been because of some background noise. Anyways he seemed put out that you weren't here to take his call. I didn't offer him a time or any other information on when to expect you." Audrey sat in one of the comfy chairs by the small tables and opened her bag.

"That's strange. Enjoy your lunch. Do you want me to get you an iced tea? I'm going to go to Joe's and order lunch." Peyton took her wallet out of her purse.

"Yes, please." Audrey took a bite of her sandwich.

Peyton walked into Joe's, which still seemed strange seeing others work behind the counter where Molly usually stood. She placed her order and took the two iced teas with the promise of them bringing her lunch to her as soon as it was done.

From the moment she walked back in the store, the day's pace picked up. At one point it took both her and Audrey working in tandem to take care of all the customers in the store. She never did get a chance to eat her lunch. At least she knew what she would be having for dinner. Audrey manned the phone when it rang and never let the man who called again twice talk her.

Both times Peyton heard Audrey say, "I'm sorry, but she's with a customer and is too busy to come to the phone at the moment. No. I can't tell you when she'll be available."

"Thank you, Audrey. I'm not in the mood to deal with a crackpot right now."

"I'm happy to be of service. Truthfully, there is something creepy about the voice, and after what happened to you and Jessie in this store before the wedding, I don't want to take any chances. I don't know how or why this crazy stuff keeps happening to the two of the nicest people I know." Audrey took the phone of the hook for a moment. "I don't want to aid someone else in another plot against you or this store."

"I appreciate your thoughtfulness. Someday when we understand the reason ourselves, we'll tell you what we know, I promise, but I doubt you'd believe me even if we could explain it."

"I've worked in this store long enough to know

some unusual things happen here and across the street." She pointed at the church. "I can still remember when that guy held me by knifepoint. I could have quit then, but what can I say? I like you both and this store. Working a few hours at the church each day, I know for a fact the atmosphere is pretty odd over there too."

"I forget that you still work at the church. You'll have to tell me about the whole knife story. I bet you were shaken."

"It scared the liver out of me." Audrey chuckled. "A phrase my mom used to say to me. I'm still not sure how that's possible, but it stuck with me. Jessie worried about me the whole time."

Peyton heard the bell ring and saw several customers come in from Joe's at the same time. "Looks like you'll have to tell me later, we're about to get busy again."

Frankly she was happy to stay busy. Busy meant she wasn't thinking about the murder victim or the girl she saw tied to the chair. She continued to let Audrey answer the phone. She didn't want to mess with the nonsense of some crackpot.

When five o'clock rolled around, she was happy to call it a day. Audrey locked up the front of the store, and she went out the back and locked the door. She did a quick look at her phone before she put her car in drive to check her text messages and listen to her voice mails. She wished she had ignored the second message altogether.

"You can run, but you can't hide from me. I saw you when you found the present I left. I got your number and will be calling you often. Follow my instructions in our game, and you just might stay alive. Don't bother trying

to call me. I'll stay in touch."

Peyton listened to the message over again, hoping something about the man's voice would seem familiar. Like Audrey said earlier, he sounded creepy but not the least bit familiar to her. Jaxon would need to hear this. He was worried someone might have been waiting to see who discovered the body. *He must have gotten access to my phone number when I called the police.* Jaxon had told her about new devices that could trace a number on an open line. At the time his idea seemed far-fetched, but the reality was a bit scary. She slapped her hand to her head. *People worry about chips being inserted through vaccines, and yet we carry the easiest tracking devices right in our pockets and purses.* It would almost be comical if it weren't so scary. *Everyone carries mobile phones these days. Besides advertising our every movement on social media, these little guys can help others know our locations day or night. I guess that's what they mean by it's a small world and getting smaller all the time.*

After she sent a text to Jaxon to call her later, she turned off her phone for a while. Which, when she thought about it, almost seemed silly but somehow made her feel a tad safer. Jaxon would probably tell her no way, but for now she wanted to believe she had come up with a solid plan. She would turn it back on later. She pulled out of her parking space and drove toward home. When she opened the door to her cottage, a sense of peace filled her. She kicked off her shoes and set the alarm after locking the door. Home was her happy place.

She changed into some comfy clothes and turned on the teakettle and her computer along with her phone.

While she waited for Jaxon's response, she decided to see what she could find out about Aine O'Flaherty.

Chapter 7

"Hey, I read your text and thought I'd swing by your place on my way home. Are you in the mood for pizza? I'll order one if you are. We should both arrive in thirty or forty minutes."

"Sounds good. I wouldn't mind pizza and your company. I have something you might want to hear anyway. I'll see you when you get here," she told him. "Tonight, what you see is what you get."

"I'm not sure how to take that, but I'm sure you'll look great to me." She would look beautiful no matter what she wore.

"Let's simply say I'm comfortable."

"Works for me. See you soon." He disconnected the call. From the first moment her beautiful hazel green eyes locked on his, he was lost. Not even telling him she saw Elliot Dawson Jr.'s ghost could stop him from trailing after her like a lovesick puppy. Okay, not totally true, he fought the attraction, writing her off as a kook until he couldn't anymore. She was gorgeous, but more than that her premonitions were too accurate to ignore, and she was sweet with a super strong high kick. Damn, they left him feeling vulnerable but didn't deter him from making his way to her house whenever he got the chance. Every man has a weakness, and Peyton was his. He was hopeless.

He turned onto the lane leading back to the inn

followed by the guy delivering the pizza. After tipping the young man, Jaxon carried the pizza to her door.

"I've come bearing dinner, sweet lady," he said as soon as she answered the door. He followed her into the kitchen and placed the pizza on the table. When she opened the cupboard to reach for the glasses, he wrapped his arms around her waist and turned her around in his arms. "Dance with me." He grinned.

"There's no music." She laughed, gazing into his eyes.

"We'll make our own music." He started to hum while he twirled her around the kitchen.

"What's gotten into you? You're usually reserved." She pulled out of his arms.

"It's the job. I've come to realize some things are more important than work and life is too short not to grab all you can when the moment presents itself. And you reaching into the cupboard presented me with a moment, as well as a perfect picture."

"Thank you, I think." She chuckled. "Do you want to know what I thought the first time I saw you? I mean besides your unpleasant behavior. You turned those honey brown eyes of yours on me. They seemed to look straight through me, and my first coherent thought was that your dark, thick, super long eyelashes were wasted on you. Those beauties would be the envy of every woman who ever saw them."

"Really, that's what came to your mind. Not even a hint of my masculine good looks." He laughed.

"Did I mention your eyes were memorable? I did remember the color after all." She filled two glasses with iced tea and opened the pizza box. "Let's eat."

"As a matter of confession, you need to know I

purposely baited you as often as I could. I loved the challenge, and your reactions were priceless." He took a bite of his pizza. "I admit I was taken back when you told me you saw Dawson's ghost. I wasn't expecting that. I'm nothing if not logical, and that blew my logic to smithereens."

"We did have an interesting beginning." She sipped her tea.

"I would add that the past year hasn't been bad either." He reached for another slice of pizza.

"With all that's happened to me in the short time we've known each other, it must make you wonder what our future might look like together."

"Amazing and unconventional comes to mind." He took a drink of his tea. "I forgot about dessert."

"I didn't. I picked up brownies at Joe's for lunch along with my entrée and never got a chance to eat either. You are in luck. Let's go into the living room, and I'll bring you in a coffee to go with the brownies. Does decaf at this time of night work for you?"

"Perfect. Do you mind if I turn on the TV?" Jaxon asked.

"Be my guest," she replied.

****

While she made the coffee, Peyton went through the conversation in her head that she wanted to have with Jaxon. He needed to hear about the calls at the bookstore and the message left on her voicemail, but he looked so relaxed right now she hated to disturb his peace. They both could use some downtime. She carried the coffee and sweets in on a tray.

"Thank you." He nodded at her, reaching for a brownie. "Joe's does have some great treats." He sipped his coffee.

She sat beside him. “Before you leave tonight, I have something I want you to listen to.”

“Okay. That sounds a bit ominous to me.” He glanced at her. “Do you want to talk now?” He muted the sound on the TV.

“I don’t want to interrupt what you’re doing. We can wait until later.”

“I’d rather not. What’s on your mind?” He draped his arm over her shoulders. “I’m never too busy to talk to you.”

She snuggled into his side. “Today Audrey fielded several phone calls from some creepy guy at the shop.”

“What?” Jaxon turned to look at her.

“She said he sounded strange and only wanted to talk to me. She kept telling him I was busy with a customer. He also called my phone, and when I didn’t answer, he left me a message.”

Peyton reached for her phone.

“The guy must have been waiting for someone to find the body. Did you use your phone?” Jaxon lifted a strand of hair out of her face.

She pursed her lips. “Of course, I called the police. I did thc right thing.”

“Yes, you did. But he must have used a stalking devise. The darn thing lets anyone hack into your phone and spy on you while you’re on the phone. I mentioned that it could be a potential problem, yesterday. Anything we could use to prevent him tracing your phone won’t work because he already has your number. We might need to change that at some point in the future. At least, for now we can track what’s on his mind. Let me hear his message.” Jaxon frowned while he listened to the voicemail. “Hell, what kind of sick game is this guy playing?”

“I have no idea. I can’t imagine what kind of instructions he will be giving me. I don’t want to be a part of his game at all.”

“I’m sure you don’t want to be, but like it or not, you have no choice—he has pulled you in. Now all we have to do is figure out what he’s up to. My guess is, he’s the murderer and wants your recognition in some sick way. He’ll reveal that soon enough. I doubt we’ll get him by trying to trace this number. In all probability, he used a burner phone. Which means he’ll use a throwaway and each time he calls, the number will be different. Don’t answer any calls from a number you don’t recognize.”

“I don’t anyway. There are too many scams out there.” She placed her phone on the table beside her. “I don’t want to hear his voice again, or I won’t sleep.”

“Hey, babe, be sure to tell me each time you get a message. Don’t act on anything he tells you to do unless I’m with you.” Jaxon took a bite of brownie followed by a sip of coffee.

“No need to worry. I won’t rush into anything. Did you find out who the murder victim at the college was?” Peyton asked.

“Sarah Crammer was her name. She was in her freshman year. Her roommate reported her missing, and so did her parents when she hadn’t checked in with her family. She was strangled, and there were signs of torture. The agency has been working with the locals to solve her murder.”

A sick sensation hit the pit or her stomach. “Was she violated? You know what I mean.”

“It’s too early to say yet, and the few details I know,

I'm not at liberty to share now. It looks like we may have a serial killer or some kind of initiation rites on the campus."

"That's sick. I guess that father looking for his missing daughter has every reason to be worried." Peyton reached for a tissue.

"You're right, and we'll do all we can to find his daughter."

"We have to." She stifled the sob rising in her throat.

Their talk turned to a conversation about their work as they finished their brownies and coffee. Her last bite went down more like dirt than the yummy treat that it was. She couldn't get the image of the girl tied to the chair out of her mind.

Jaxon pulled her tightly against him. He had to know what she was dealing with. This was the part of their relationship that Peyton liked the most. The quiet moments stolen without the craziness that could surround them. He always managed to find a way to console her and give her a sense of security. She leaned her head against his shoulder and let the sensation wash over her.

An hour later Jaxon stood. "I should go. Tom said I could take you with me to the college for interviews with some of the professor's students. I've scheduled the interviews for Friday after your school hours, if you can arrange the time with Audrey to cover the store. I want to talk to the missing girl's roommate and now the murdered girl's also. I need you to watch them and evaluate what you see while I question each of the students. Of course, you can ask any questions that come to your mind too. You don't have to be a silent partner." He reached for her hand.

"I'll talk with Audrey tomorrow. I'm sure we can work something out." She walked him to the door.

"Be careful." He kissed her. "I'm concerned our suspect not only has your number but already knows where you live. Be sure to lock up nice and tight and turn on your alarm. If you get any more messages, tell me right away."

"I will." She walked into his open arms. She anticipated his kiss that she knew would soon come.

"I forgot to mention Evan and Destiny would like to go to dinner with us soon. Think about a time that might work for you." He gazed into his eyes.

"I will. I haven't seen Destiny since the wedding. If it hadn't been for her setting up that crazy trip to Arizona in the middle of the summer, I wouldn't have met you. Even though she didn't show up and Arizona was hotter than blazes, you were the one good thing that came out of that experience." She reached up and touched her lips to his.

His response was one for the record books. She fanned her face playfully when she closed the door and locked it behind him. Yes, indeed that was the reaction she was hoping for.

Chapter 8

Jaxon walked to his parked car and sat there for a while. He didn't like the idea of a potential murderer knowing Peyton's phone number. It was an easy path from a phone to her name and information on the web. Anyone could become a target these days. He drove away only after he was sure there was no one in the vicinity of her house that shouldn't be in the area.

Peyton had gone through enough the past couple of days. He didn't want to add to her concern at the moment until he had more details. There was an undercover operation going on at the college. This had been ongoing for many months. The agency had traced dark web activity to an IP address operating in one of the dorms on campus. More than one actually, meaning several people on campus could be involved. A sting operation would soon be in the works.

The web site went by the name Anything Goes, or at least the department gave it that name to avoid repeating the disgusting real name. And according to information acquired to this point, the site users literally lived up to the description of the site. An underground marketplace of sorts to purchase drugs like heroin, fentanyl, and cocaine, which was bad enough, but also pushed violence against women or anyone who got in their way. He had seen the photos and the garbage that was posted by users on the site. Jaxon hoped the underground marketplace users weren't involved in the recent crimes on campus. But with the bodies found recently of two college coeds, it seemed someone was taking the messages seriously.

Undercover agents were investigating an anonymous tip of hits called assassination ops and silent revenge assignments initiated by the site operator. Jaxon understood the crazy stuff that could take place on campuses—he was a guy after all. There was always tough talk and rumors swirling around campus, but this was taking craziness to a whole new level. Trouble seemed to be amped up more than when he was in college. He wasn't that old, and he found the idea sad that kids today couldn't have the carefree days he had growing up. This wasn't a political movement. The group seemed to be all about intimidation, and doing anything they wanted to do from drugs to abuse in many forms.

They were close to finding the source of the site. They had proof of more than six young people who died from drug poisoning after purchasing drugs off the marketplace. Requests for date rape drugs were in high demand on the site too. There's a reason they call it the dark web.

Jaxon pulled his car into the garage.

Once inside his home, he sat in his favorite chair. The one that Peyton had picked out, and she had been right. The chair looked perfect in the living room. He pushed the remote button, and his feet were lifted to their happy place. He reached for the TV remote and turned it on, muting the sound.

Was he being fair keeping all this info from Peyton? She needed to understand how dangerous this assignment could become. There were millions of dollars involved as well as murder, and she needed to know. He'd see what his boss would let him reveal to her. He texted Maxwell and waited for his reply.

"Let's get it done, man," he mused when he got the okay. He wouldn't blame her if she backed out, but he hoped she wouldn't. He could use her amazing abilities to help solve this one.

He grabbed his phone from the table.

"Did you forget something?" Peyton asked.

"I came to a critical decision on my way home, and after talking to Tom, I have information that I believe you need to have to evaluate your involvement on Friday." Jaxon went over the information regarding the investigation. "You must keep this under wraps because the undercover operation is ongoing, and leaks could put lives at risk. Maxwell told me I could share vital info with you because he knows you're an asset. I told you about Sarah Crammer, but we have a second murdered coed the agency is working to ID."

"Well, that changes the situation a bit. I knew there was a dark side to the internet. We saw how potent and far reaching the impact had become in the past couple of cases, but this hits close to home. As much as I appreciate the warning, I seem to find myself in the middle of the case whether I want to be or not. I believe a smart man I know told me that recently."

"You think I'm smart?" He flipped through the stations as he talked. "How do you want to handle this new info? Do you still want to come with me on Friday?"

"I'm in, unless of course I wake up tomorrow feeling differently. I can't image I'll do that, since I promised the girl I saw I would find her."

"I can't say that I'm surprised. You're not one to give up a fight. Do you think she knows you will follow through?"

"As strange as this may sound, yes, I do," she told him.

"I thought you'd say that. Promise me you'll be careful. If you feel threatened or afraid and you need a protection detail, you'll have them."

"I will. Life can be risky at best." She paused. "But there's no way I could walk away from a cry for help."

"I don't want to pressure you, but I hope you know the respect I have for you."

"I do."

"Good to hear. I hope your feelings for me are as deep as mine are for you." He crossed his fingers.

"I know sometimes I can seem distant, but you must know how I feel about you. You're the first man I even considered sharing my life with. I've let you into my inner circle, and I plan on you staying there. You already know I have trust issues, and baggage. I'm learning to let the hurts of my past go and move on. I know I can't ask you to be patient forever, but I hope you don't give up on me."

"Sweetheart, I get it. I'm not giving up, and I'm willing to wait until the right moment. I guess I need reassurance that I have a chance."

"I hope you know that you alone have my heart. I'll try to make you aware of it more often. And as for a chance, the answer is a big yes."

"As strange as this may sound, all that is happening around us reminds me how short life can be. My heart is in your hands. Sorry, but I've been a bit raw since the agent on one of Matt's cases was killed. Add the revenge enacted on Matt and Jessie before their wedding, and I'm thinking more about the danger of my job. Awareness of someone tracking you doesn't help either."

"I get it. I know what being vulnerable is all about."

"At least I know we're on the same wavelength."

"Right and from the sounds of it, we are wrestling with similar issues. We should talk more," Peyton said. "Next time we're together, remind me to tell you about how Matt and Jessie finally got engaged. They had a strange courtship too. Love you, Jaxon."

Jaxon talked with her for a few more minutes. "I love you. Sweet dreams, babe." He blew her a noisy kiss and disconnected the call.

He hadn't wanted to start that conversation with everything else going on in her life. But he learned she needed the reassurance too. Life presses in hard and time slips away before you know it's gone. They had spent more time away from each other than together in recent weeks. A situation that wasn't working for either of them, and left them both unsure of where their relationship was heading. Hot then cold but tepid at best would be the way to describe their connection of late. Jaxon was ready to move forward.

****

Peyton sat on her bed with her computer open. Jaxon always seemed to know her mood and the right thing to say. She had no doubts about him but only herself. She had a lot of baggage, not to mention the odd things that were a part of her life since meeting him. Still, no one since leaving home had captured her heart like he had. She wanted to try because of him.

"Let's see if we can learn more about ourselves, shall we?" Peyton opened the file she was looking for.

"Aine, tell me your secrets if they'll help me discover myself."

A message popped up on her screen that she had a message from Jessie. Without hesitation she moved over to the email and began to read.

Matt slipped out to get us coffee, so I have a chance to send this to you before he gets back. Most of this I wrote last night after he had gone to sleep. I must say Matt is such fun to travel with. He's gotten into the spirit of Ireland and now is digging for information of our ancestors in church records and beyond. He's such a sweetheart, and I love being married to him.

Okay, now for my important findings. Aine had a sister named Brigid. They had a harsh childhood. I don't know how as of yet, but they lived in poverty until Aine's marriage. Brigid was a healer with herbs and potions like others in our family line. I found that interesting since your sister works in a hospital. I hope we can discover a portrait or some description of how they looked. Matt is leading the charge in this area. I think it suits the investigator side of him. If their names were chosen for their personalities, then I would say you come from good stock.

The O'Flahertys along with other Irish families came to our country during the Great Potato Famine. Many early passenger lists revealed the name of Flaherty with the O removed. I wish I could find out more about Aine and Brigid. I promise to keep looking. I'm sure we could find more information about all of our ancestry if we searched through genealogy records online, but it wouldn't be nearly as much fun as we are having. Love you, cousin.

Peyton wrote a quick note back to thank her for the

information. Of course, she could and would do research online, and maybe Jeremy would help her too, seeing as he got pretty chummy with Madison at the wedding. She knew Jeremy from New York although she was never as close to him as her cousin was. Peyton wasn't into investigating anything while she lived there. Except for looking for a larger apartment that didn't cost an arm and a leg.

"Aine, I want to learn your story." Peyton closed her computer and stretched on the bed. "Are we at all alike? Did I get your gift? How can I possibly find out?" she whispered into the dark room right before she closed her eyes to sleep.

Chapter 9

Peyton's vibrating phone awakened her bright and early. "Hello," she said, sounding half-awake even to her ears.

"Sorry to wake you, cousin. I have a few minutes while Matt is in the shower. We are having a night out. Matt's getting into the spirit of things over here. After listening to a guide today telling one of their awesome stories, he only rolled his eyes halfway at the talk of the wee people." Jessie laughed. "This is a major challenge to my hunky cop's sense of logic. Still, he listened and followed me into another place to research records. All I have time to say is we have a strange but equally amazing ancestral line."

"I can only picture him traipsing after you on one of your research missions." Peyton chuckled.

"The funny part is today he was leading the way. I believe it's because he's trying to figure me out. After being raised with brothers, I think he may be a little stumped by me and the emotions that come with me and my ever-growing hair in the humidity. Oh well, we're having fun. I'll be sending you more information, which should help get your juices flowing. How's my store?"

"I knew you were going to ask that. All is well and business is good."

"How are things going in town?" Jessie asked. "Should we be worried?"

"Nothing to be concerned about." Peyton swung her legs over the side of the bed.

"In other words, you won't tell me."

"Don't worry, everyone here is doing their jobs, and things will be okay. You need to enjoy your honeymoon. Soon enough you'll be back in the grind. Have fun."

"You're right, of course. Matt's singing and happy. Why mess with a good thing!"

"I can hear him." Peyton laughed. "Let him leave his job behind for a few weeks. Love you, cousin."

Wide awake now, Peyton got into her morning routine, including a shower. She loved stepping into the warm water first thing in the morning. There was something almost magical about letting the warm droplets rain down on her. Tired going in and relaxed and invigorated when she walked out. The perfect way to get her morning started, followed by coffee, and she was ready for what the day held. At least she hoped she was.

Peyton drove to school where she would spend her morning with her special needs students. Today was fingerpaint day, which was always a messy but fun time for the kids. They loved to be creative in their own special way. Lot more work for her but it was worth every spilt mess of bright colored paint splashed in many directions to see the happy smiles on their faces.

At least her morning was bound to fly by, and she'd be at the bookstore helping Audrey not long after the last of her students left for home. She couldn't wait to read what Jessie had learned today. Although she had no idea how that knowledge would help her now.

****

Jaxon found himself in the middle of meetings at work. He didn't quite detest meeting with the other agents because there was some valuable information to be gained. But he rarely enjoyed sitting through hours of lectures or repeated questions. It never took long for the subject matter to get lost among the conversations and questions until he couldn't remember the reason for being there to begin with. He counted himself lucky when Clarie the office secretary came in and told him he had an important call he needed to take. Happy for the reprieve he followed her out of the conference room and picked up the phone at his desk.

"Hello, this is Agent Kincaid. How can I help you?" He pulled out his desk chair and sat down.

"I heard you are looking for information about the murders at the college. If I know, others do too, and you'll have a target on your back."

"Who am I talking to?" Jaxon asked.

"I'm putting my life at risk to call you. If anyone finds out, I'm dead. I can tell you there's more going on at this campus than higher learning. Be careful. Don't try to contact me. I'll call you if I have anything more."

Jaxon heard the click on the other end of the phone. Damn, he wanted to keep the guy talking. He was sure there was more information to pulled out of him with the right questions. The phone call made it more important than ever for Peyton and him to interview students. If what the guy insinuated was true, there was something criminal taking place on campus. Hidden from view but operational, nonetheless. The caller's life was in danger because of that knowledge. And he said murders, not murder, damn.

Jaxon remembered in college, one of his professors told them that major crimes were going on under the radar committed by kids sitting in front of their computers in basements, garages, and college dorms around the nation. Some computer nerd found a way to promote conspiracies and get other loners to listen. It seems that the teacher was ahead of his time, even though he didn't have a clue about how to fight against online crimes. His response was not to visit those sites or to turn off their computers. Impossible with the way computers and online contacts have connected the world in a way like nothing else has ever done.

In the years since college and the police academy, the advancement in technology and people with computer skills have made great strides. The agency now has a division devoted to tracking, monitoring, and following online criminals twenty-four -seven. One of the meetings this morning gave them valuable information on activity at the college.

An informant's call not long after Peyton made him believe the murders, abduction, and underground marketplace were all connected reminded him how accurate she could be. He picked up his phone and checked with Tom Maxwell's secretary to see if the department head had time for a meeting. He couldn't believe he was requesting another one. Tom was available for the next few minutes. He rushed down the hall to talk to his boss.

Jaxon knocked on his open door and was motioned in. "I needed to bring you up to speed on what's going on." He told Tom about Peyton's vision, which was spot-on, and the calls she received along with the message left on her phone. He also told him about the call he had just received. "I wanted you to be aware that things are heating up and see how you want me to proceed. Should we inform the agents working undercover?"

"I wondered why you left the meeting with Claire. I know how much you all love meetings. I'll take care of notifying them when we meet," Tom said. "Now, what are we going to do about the immediate threat?"

Tom made suggestions while Jaxon took notes. "We are dealing with more than the simple pranks of college students. I've seen the web site. It's disgusting, and no one involved seems to think it's wrong. I'm rarely surprised by anything criminal anymore, but I have to admit this has shocked me. I believe the call I received was from someone who wants to help but is afraid for his life. He did say he would contact me if he had more."

"This might be the first break we've got in this case. When do you do your student interviews?" Tom asked.

"Tomorrow afternoon," Jaxon answered.

"Is Peyton still going with you?"

"Yes."

"I'm going out on a limb allowing her to be a part. I know how the Reynolds work, I trust those girls, and I'm willing to stake my career on this. Don't let me down."

"We won't, sir."

"I know you won't. I'm Tom to you, unless newbies are present. Keep me in the loop."

"You can count on it." Jaxon left Tom's office. He needed to work out a list of questions to ask the students. He wanted Peyton to observe and let him know what she sensed.

****

Peyton scrubbed the paint off the desks as soon as her last student was wheeled out of the room by her mother. Happy chaos was worth every minute because it gave her mind a break from a dead body, and all that came with finding her. Her kids with all the obstacles they had to overcome in life reminded her how to find joy in living. Small things like finger paints and banging the instruments made them smile and giggle with joy. She found herself smiling and laughing along with them. They also taught every person's life had meaning. No matter what their ability or accomplishments were. These kids taught her more about love, acceptance, and joy than she could ever teach them.

As soon as Peyton restored order in her classroom, she shut off the light, closed the door, and walked down the hall toward the office. She stopped long enough to clear her box and speak to the office staff. She always enjoyed chatting with the women behind the desk before leaving for the day. They made working at the school a pleasure.

Once in her car, Peyton scrolled through her phone and saw a voicemail from an unknown number. There was no way she would listen to it now, but she texted Jaxon to let him know that she had received another message.

She was determined not to let anything destroy her good mood. She had to work with customers all afternoon and didn't want to be a Debbie downer. Audrey waved at her when she walked into the bookstore.

"You're right on time for me to go get some lunch. Are you ready to take over for a few minutes?" Audrey grabbed her wallet and headed toward Joe's.

"Go ahead. I'm ready to get to work." Peyton placed her purse behind the counter.

She hummed while she straightened the bookmark basket and went to help a customer who walked through the door.

Chapter 10

Peyton was about to get her lunch after Audrey came back after taking a break. Reba walked in and waved at her. Reba's arrival meant her day was about to take an interesting turn for sure. "Would you like something to eat?" Peyton asked Reba. "I was just about to go get some lunch."

"I'll go with you, and we can chat. As I'm sure you know by now, I have an important reason for stopping by to see you." She leaned close to Peyton. "I'm happy to see our friend keeping watch over the store. He's a comfort to this old lady." Reba stuck her arm through Peyton's as they walked through the open doors into the coffee shop.

After they placed their order, Peyton found an open table where she watched the store in case Audrey needed her. She pulled out a chair for Reba.

Reba sat down, taking her time to adjust her legs just so. She pulled her dress down to cover her knees, which made Peyton smile. She might be eccentric, but she was nothing if not proper. That's part of what endeared her to both Jessie's and her.

As soon as their food arrived, Reba said, "I'm sure you're wondering why I'm here."

"You know I am." Peyton took a bite of her salad. "I enjoy your company, but you rarely come in to see us without a distinct reason."

"Not true, dear, I do come once in a while only to see you girls. You're both like daughters to me. Having said that, this is not one of those times." She patted her lips with her napkin.

"Okay, let's hear it." Peyton rested her elbows on the table and studied Reba's face.

"Don't slouch, my dear. It doesn't do anything for your beautiful figure." She tugged on Peyton's arm. "Sit up straight."

"I don't mind." She straightened in the chair. "I sit like this all the time, but I know you're stalling for time. Out with it, sweet friend."

"I don't like when you look at me so intently. It's as if you're trying to read my mind." Reba frowned.

"Not at all, but now you know how Jessie and I sometimes feel when you come to deliver one of your cryptic messages. You mean no harm and neither do I. I'm trying to figure you out. How can such a prim and proper lady be, well, you?" Peyton gestured with her hand.

"I could say the same about you girls, leaving off the prim and proper tag." Reba chuckled. "We are definitely from a different era." She took a bite of her salad. "Let's get down to business, shall we? You'll need to get back to work soon."

"I'm ready when you are." Peyton sat back in her chair and sipped her tea.

"You girls come from a long line of amazing women. Each time we chat, I can see enormous growth in both of you. This case will be no different. You will learn from your past but find new ways to express your unique gift in the present. You will process a crime scene through a lens of colors, which will take you learning their meaning. I can't wait to see how you navigate these new uncharted waters. You've time traveled, had visions, and premonitions, which is only the beginning. Aine has passed down a few surprises too. And the next few weeks will be quite enlightening in more than a few ways for you and Jaxon."

"I can hope you mean that in a good way. I wouldn't want to chase Jaxon off just when our relationship is starting to heat up." Peyton pursed her lips.

"Time will tell." Reba boxed up her leftovers when the help dropped a box at their table.

"Anything else? If not, I should go help Audrey. She's getting busy over there." Peyton stood and then leaned down near Reba's ear. "I hope you know I appreciate you even if at times I don't understand you. I see you as my mentor like my cousin does. You and your messages are always welcome to come and visit anytime."

"I know." Reba smiled at her. "I love watching you girls in action. Almost makes me wish I was young again." She stood and reached for her box. "I'll go with you. I want to pick up a couple of books."

They walked through the open door back into the bookstore. Reba went to the shelf that housed her favorite author's books. A spot where Peyton had stood with her many times in the past year. Now she went in the opposite direction to wait on a customer at the book display table.

The rest of the afternoon flew by. Once Audrey checked Reba out, she remained at her favorite spot, reading her new book. Peyton couldn't help but wonder if she was keeping tabs on her and the store. Why? She had no idea how to answer that in her head, but Reba was still there when it was closing time.

"My, I didn't know it was this late. Lawerence will be wondering what happened to me. When I get into a new book, I tend to get lost. See you, ladies," Reba said as she stuffed her book into her bag and raced toward the door. "Have a lovely evening."

Hmm. Maybe she was simply reading. Peyton needed to quit jumping to conclusions.

"I'll lock up the back, Audrey. See you tomorrow." Peyton locked the back door and walked out to her car. At some point she would need to listen to her phone messages but not unless Jaxon was with her.

****

Jaxon had left two messages for Peyton, which had gone unanswered. He needed to make sure she was okay. He pulled into the parking space next to hers and waited for her to get home. He leaned his head back against the headrest. It had been a long day. Rubbing his temples, he turned when he heard a car approaching. Jaxon still loved the looks of the car he helped pick out, and the woman behind the wheel was still as stunning as ever. The more he got to know Peyton, the more he loved who she was. He stepped out of his car and went to open her car door.

"Thank you. What brings you here?" Peyton asked.

"After leaving you a couple of messages and texts and not hearing back from you, I wanted to make sure you were good."

"As you can see, I'm fine."

"You look very fine from where I stand." His eyes traveled over her slowly. "Very fine, indeed." He pulled her into his arms. "Why didn't you answer me?"

"I didn't check my messages once I saw I got a message from you know who. I didn't want to deal with it today."

"Makes perfect sense to me. The only question I need answered now is where am I taking you for dinner? We need to talk."

"Lead the way, I'm with you. Your car or mine?" she asked.

"I wouldn't mind driving yours again. My company car isn't as nice as yours."

"Mine it is." She walked to the passenger side and slid in when he opened the door. She dropped the keys into his hand after he closed his door and latched his seat belt. "I like my car not as fancy as yours but perfect for me." She glanced at him. "Cheaper too, I'm sure."

Jaxon backed the car out and drove toward the main road into town. "I know a little place outside of town. Do you mind if we go there?" he asked.

"I am in your hands. Lead the way." She glanced at Idle Time Books as they drove past the store on Main Street.

"I take it your resident ghost is still standing guard." He moved into the turn lane. "It's only a few miles up the highway." He merged into traffic.

"He was there when I left. Although, I often wonder what he does after we're gone in the evenings."

"It might be fun to put cameras in the store to find out." He laughed. "If nothing else it would make for a great episode on one those ghost hunters' shows if you captured him."

"Heavens no, can you image all the crazies who would show up at the store wanting to see if they could detect or see our ghost? I would never do that to him. He may be grumpy, but he's stalwart and vigilant."

"You're right, of course." He turned into the

restaurant's parking lot. "I hope you're up for some great Mexican food."

"Always." She took his hand when he opened her door and extended his.

After they ordered dinner, Jaxon told her about his unusual call at work. "I honestly thought the guy wanted to share more but was afraid to. Something is going on, and it's more than a few murders, which is bad enough."

"I often wondered what I would do if I had to face a threat to my life. Would I do what was right? My grandmother lived in the sixties and during all the protests. She actually marched for civil rights against her parents' wishes. She had to make choices in her generation. It seems this might be mine. We are living in a strange time. Besides the fact everyone seems to be on the edge, I have someone calling me every day telling me I have to do what he says or else. I have to admit the 'or else' bothers me a bit." Peyton thanked the waitress who placed her dinner in front of her and left. "I mean people are bullying others online. People feel free to say what they want to anyone whether they know them or not. If you say something someone doesn't like, you have a target on your back. Or like me you get calls for discovering a body and doing the right thing."

"It can make you wonder for sure." He took a bite of his cheese enchilada. "One thing I do know is this is some great food."

"I agree with you. This green chili is excellent. Thankfully, they had a mild version. I'm not into too much heat. I like to taste my food not burn my taste buds." Peyton took another bite of her smothered burrito. "I have a great idea. Let's enjoy our dinner and forget the other at least until our ride home."

Chapter 11

Peyton was grateful that, once they changed the subject, they never went back to talk about the elephant in the room as she liked to think about the case. She understood tomorrow on the way for the interviews with the students Jaxon would have more to say, but after listening to the man's messages he left on her phone, she had enough threats for one day.

What she wanted to know was what could she do about the calls? There was no way that she wanted to answer them several times a day. The guy really needed to get a life. He had way too much time on his hands.

She opened her computer and went through an email from Jeremy who said he would be happy to do research on Aine O'Flaherty for her and send her any info he found. He also asked for Madison's phone number. He wanted to take her out for coffee or something. Peyton smiled. She liked the idea of Jeremy and Madison. At least, she didn't object.

Next was her daily email from Jessie. She wrote details of their sightseeing for the day. There wasn't much to grab onto until the end. Jessie wrote about a dream she had of the Cove, and she would call later because Peyton was in the dream. *I don't want to write you about the details. We need to talk about them.*

Peyton wasn't sure she wanted to hear about any dreams at the moment. She closed her computer and got ready for bed. Enough was enough. She climbed beneath her soft blankets, and before she could silence her phone, the darn thing rang.

"Hey, cousin, I bet you hoped I wouldn't call you, am I right?" Jessie laughed.

"You know me so well. I didn't get my phone off in time, or I would have slept through without hearing, but you would have called again tomorrow anyway. I would've been putting off the inevitable."

"I figured as much. But you know me and my dreams. They come when they come, and there's not a whole lot I can do about them. And you need to understand the importance, or you wouldn't have been a part of it."

"I know, but I've had about all I can handle for one day. Between phone calls from a strange man, and Reba's message at lunch. I want to put it all away for tonight."

"Wait a minute there, cousin, do tell all. I want to understand what you just said."

Peyton told her about finding the body on her run and the man who contacted her afterward. She smiled when Jessie gasped. She went on to tell Jessie about her conversation with Reba.

"Why didn't you tell me about finding a murder victim?" Jessie asked.

"You're on your honeymoon for heaven sakes. You don't need to be worried about a murder here. Dylan and Jaxon are on the case. And what are you doing talking to me when you should be with him?"

"Don't worry about Matt. I'm taking good care of him." Jessie chuckled. "At least, I understand my dream. I saw you in my dream. You were standing in a field with a baseball glove, and at first someone in the shadows who I couldn't see tossed a ball your way softly. Of course, it was an easy catch. But then the balls came harder and faster until you seemed to wilt under the onslaught. At the moment that I thought you would surely fail, two strong arms surrounded you and your energy returned and a renewed sense of purpose. I don't know who the arms belong to or where the strength came from within you, but I believe Jaxon is part of the equation, and I'm sure you'll be okay. Don't give up. I agree with Reba. You will learn new ways to use the gift you've been given. I can't wait to hear what you do with this one. I need to go. Matt is stirring and calling my name. Love you, cous."

"I love you too. Have a fun day with your husband." Peyton shut off the light and rolled over on her side.

Her mind went over the events of her day. From Reba's message to Jessie's dream, Peyton didn't see an easy way to walk away from this case no matter how much she wanted to. From the darkness of her room, she could see the fairy night-light glowing from the bathroom. The light her grandmother had given her when she was young. That shining little fairy had seen her through some dark lonely nights growing up. Peyton had high hopes that the comfort that the fairy's light brought to her as a little girl along with the magic that Grams told Peyton she had wouldn't fail her now just because she was older. She had guarded the precious gift from her grandmother through all the turmoil at home, through her years at college and living in the city. Maybe her magic would guard her now.

****

Jaxon hadn't liked the last message the man had left

on Peyton's phone. He seemed angrier, and that didn't bode well for Peyton. He wanted her to dance to the tune he was playing, and Jaxon wished he understood why. What was the guy up to besides trying to figure out what she knew? The man kept saying if she played along with everything he told her to do, her life would be saved. Their suspect didn't like the idea she wasn't answering his calls. Jaxon didn't want her to, but he was also concerned that ignoring him could set the guy off.

Maybe taking her with him to the college might not be a good idea. He doubted she would agree with him. Once she jumped into a case, she rushed in where angels feared to tread. His gal was something else. Although, he had detected a bit of reticence when they talked at dinner. She might be getting tired of facing off against some of these criminals and not being paid for the trouble. Hell, she was an editor and a special needs teacher and had no training in law enforcement. What she and her cousin Jessie did to help them with cases was invaluable. Their strange and uncanny ability made the PD and agents who they worked with look good more than once. Jaxon put his feet up and turned on the TV.

****

Peyton watched out the shop window, waiting for Jaxon's arrival. Her morning at school had been a relatively sane day. The kids were quite good, but it was her stupid phone vibrating against the desk every hour on the hour that was the problem. No caller ID told her that it must be her nasty friend calling, and she finally shut the darn thing off altogether. Giving her uninterrupted minutes of calm during story hour and when parents arrived to pick up kids. She needed some input on what to do about the calls. The man was becoming a big nuisance.

"You're quiet," Audrey said. "Is everything okay?"

"Yeah. I was thinking about my morning. Those kids can be such a ray of sunshine in any day. When they're being good and not stinkers, of course." Peyton chuckled.

"I bet every teacher must feel that way." Audrey placed one of the new orders on the shelf. "It must take a lot of patience working in a room full of kids. No ordinary person would be comfortable with those little people with all their energy ready to break loose at any moment waiting for you to make a mistake."

"I have to be on my game for sure. They can take advantage if I'm not."

"I like working here with you both and at the church. Both jobs are at times strange, as you know, but I still manage to think of them as safe environments to work in. I'm content doing what I do."

"Safe? Didn't you tell me you were threatened at knifepoint here once? And if I remember, you were shaken a few times by a couple of thugs coming in the store after us. You've held up pretty well, Audrey, all things considered."

"You girls have added excitement to my life. Sometimes maybe a tad too much, but I still like working here. I guess everyone should learn to be brave once in a while and reach outside their comfort zone. You two have done that for me. I've often said we like to remember the good and forget the unpleasant in life."

"True and it's a good thing." Peyton smiled. "I'll try to get back before closing." Peyton told her when Jaxon pulled up in front of the store.

"Don't you worry none. I've closed up plenty of

times. Just be sure to fill me in on some of the details you are free to share tomorrow."

"I will." Peyton waved as she walked out of the door. She slid into the front seat of Jaxon's car and latched her seat belt. "I see you brought your sedan and not your sports car."

"I only bring her out for special occasions, which is definitely not agency work." Jaxon smiled. "I don't want to flaunt the fact that I inherited money."

"Speaking of money, have you talked to Mrs. Dawson?" She saw him nod his head. "How is she doing?"

"She is doing as well as anyone can who loses their only son and then her husband. Thankfully, she has her sisters and friends." He pointed at the yellow legal pad on the center console. "Take a few minutes to look over the few questions I jotted down to ask. I would like your feedback and any observation you have when I ask the kids."

She read over the questions and wrote a few notes of her own on the page. "I've only been out of college a few years, and what these people can do on the computer is astounding. I've been reading about a few of the whiz kids who are really criminals in what they do. They can hack into systems no matter how good the firewalls are. It's actually quite scary. Jeremy is like that, but he works with the law."

"You're telling me. The bureau has a cyber unit that operates around the clock for just that purpose." Jaxon pulled into a parking space at the hall he was told to go to. Students were already present to be interviewed. "I forget how many times Jeremy has helped you and your cousin with research. He knows his way around the computer and a few firewalls himself."

Peyton observed the interviews and took notes. One particular girl seemed hardly capable of holding her emotions together. While Jaxon talked to one of the boys, she sat down beside the girl.

"Are you okay?"

"Not really. My roommate is missing, and I was too busy to listen to her when she tried to tell me she thought someone was stalking her." The girl wiped tears running down her cheeks.

"Did she tell you why she thought someone was stalking her?" Peyton introduced herself to the girl and found out her name was Kelsey Fox.

"I remember her mentioning something about research on drug use on campus for an article she was writing for the *Campus Record*."

"Is that the college paper?" Peyton asked.

"Yes. She loved writing for the paper." Kelsey took the tissue Peyton handed her.

"Look, Kelsey, if you can remember any small detail, that might be helpful. Please call me." Peyton wrote her number on a slip of paper and handed it to her. "We want to find your roommate. Tell me about her and please include her name and description."

Kelsey took a deep breath, dabbing at her eyes. "Emily Hart is my friend. She's one of the nicest people you would ever meet. She's a third-year journalist student and loved writing her hard-hitting articles for the school paper. She took the job seriously. We often talked about the stories she was researching." Kelsey wiped the tears running down her cheeks.

"Did she have any enemies that you're aware of?"

"No, never among our crowd. She's super popular

and friendly to everyone. Although, she was worried that her boyfriend Greg was becoming distant. But I told her that Greg would have to be stupid to leave her. It always gets nuts around here before holidays with pending finals." She pulled up a picture of the pretty girl on her phone. "This is Gregory Taylor her main squeeze." She showed Peyton his photo.

"Could you please text me a copy of those pictures?"

"Did you get the text?"

"Yes. Thank you."

"What do you think happened to her? I'm worried. I thought maybe she had gone home for the weekend or something, but now it's been almost five days. She's not answering any of my calls, which is not like her. No one I've talked to so far except her father seems concerned at all."

"We are going to do our best to find your friend," Peyton told her. "Did Emily seem anxious or tell you she was concerned about anything?"

"The last time we were hanging out, she told me she had a strange feeling someone was following her. Come to think about it, she seemed to be jumpy the whole evening. But then when we got back to the dorm, she laughed it off as an overactive imagination."

"If you can think of anything else you talked about in the days before she disappeared, don't hesitate to call me."

"You don't suppose she could be hiding somewhere because she's scared?" Kelsey sounded hopeful. "The story she was working on was causing a quite a stir and aroused some angry debates among students. She did an introductory story last month, teasing readers about what she was discovering."

"She could be in hiding. Let me know if she comes back, would you?" Peyton tried to sound convincing. More than likely someone wanted to stop her from finishing her story.

"I sure will." Kelsey stuck her phone into her pocket. "She's pretty, you know, and guys always followed her around. But it never bothered her before, and that's why this time seemed different. The more I think about her response that night, I get scared."

Peyton jotted down a few notes as she waited for Jaxon to finish talking with a group of young men. There was a grayish color that swirled around them as they talked. She had to take a second look, and the gray still surrounded them. What did it mean?

She opened the text from Kelsey and studied the picture of the young woman again. Was she the one she saw tied to the chair? Peyton felt sure she was the same girl. What was happening on this campus? She would stay the course. Her promise to Emily, Kelsey, and to the young girl whose body she had found made it impossible to walk away. At the end of the day, she had to live with the decisions she made. She waited and kept looking at the smiling girl's picture on her phone.

****

"Earth to Peyton." Jaxon touched her shoulder when he sat down beside her. "You seem distracted. I trust that your conversation with the young woman I saw you with was productive."

"Likewise, for you, I hope. I learned a few interesting details. I think we should leave the campus before we talk, though. Something scary is going on here." Peyton stood and gathered her notes.

Jaxon pulled out of the parking spot. "You're right.

Those boys might be part of the problem. It's not what they said as much as their actions and what they didn't say."

"What do you mean?" she asked.

"This may come as shock to you." He chuckled. "Young men this age can be braggarts. I got them talking and learned a lot. I heard about a secret society meeting on campus. Most snickered, trying hard not to give any information. But I found it easy to fill in the blanks, and they said more than they realized."

"Secret society, like a men's only group or what?" she asked.

"A toxic male society and much more I believe. Something that's been on the agency's radar for a while. Not only on this campus but a rising movement on the internet. I need to learn all I can about the movement because I think we are dealing with the same philosophy here."

"That would account for the grayish color I saw swirling around those young men as you talked. It's strange how you think criminal activity can't happen close to home. Blue Cove has blown that misnomer out of the water for me and makes me wonder about other towns in the area. When I lived in the city, crime was out front. That's why I took a self-defense class." Peyton preceded to tell him about what she learned from Kelsey about her missing roommate. "She sent me a picture, which I will send along to you. She could be the girl I saw. No matter what, she's somebody's daughter, friend, and maybe girlfriend. How can we not try to find Emily Hart?"

"I take it you're in on this one, but I want you to know you have to be extremely careful. This isn't a simple case of a missing girl. There are a lot of moving parts to this case, and you already have a murderer's attention."

"I hear you and I understand. He's calling me all the time and leaving his creepy little messages at least once or twice a day. I'll be careful."

****

From a distance the small vehicle turned out of the parking lot and followed the man's car as he drove onto the highway entrance. He seethed with anger at the man behind the wheel. The strength of the rage came as a surprise to him. She belonged to him—he had discovered her first and even spent time learning more about her. He frowned while tapping his fingers on the steering wheel. Peyton was his, or at least he liked to think of her that way. With every phone call and message to her, he inserted himself into her psyche. He couldn't wait to let her know that he'd seen her talk to the girl at the college. Quite possibly Ms. Reynolds had inadvertently drawn his attention to his next victim or maybe not. Using the girl as a possible victim might be a nice way to control Peyton, and it might be fun to string her along with the thought she could be responsible for another girl's death. What he knew of Peyton meant she bore watching. She was a sneaky one. There was something about her that bothered him. He wanted her close enough to impress her but not close enough to discover him.

Spewed expletives echoed inside the car. Those stupid boys with all their talk didn't have a clue what was really going on. They played silly games compared to him and others. He wondered how long it might take them to uncover even a small portion of what went on in the circles he moved in. A game, but a deadly one. There was really a dark side to people. Some were quite diabolical—actually. He smirked. Not him of course, there truly was a method to his madness. He was doing the world a favor in some odd way. One day his genius would come to be appreciated. Most of those lowlifes would never understand how meticulous and careful he was. His victims did. He worked hard to win them over as a father before he put them to sleep. It was a kindness that he did for them. Those dumb boys sought only a moment's satisfaction while he built an enduring legacy. He continued on the highway when the car he followed took the Blue Cove exit. He needed to work on his next message to her.

Chapter 12

"Hey, babe, thanks for going with me today. I'll be interested in hearing any more of your observations after you have time to think about them. I owe you." Jaxon drove toward town. "Are you hungry? Dinner is the least I can do after the day I put you through."

"I could eat something." She smiled at him. "I'm all in."

"What sounds good?" Jaxon asked.

"Surprise me." Peyton glanced out the passenger window.

"I can do that." Jaxon slowed down to make a turn.

"By the way, I think we were being followed from the college, and the car went on when you took the exit into town."

"You're observant. I saw our friend and got the first few numbers on the plates. But I'm betting we'll find out it's a rental. Unless the guy is stupid enough to hand us a gift and our first break in the case. Call me skeptical." He pulled into the parking lot at Angelo's. "Does Italian work for you?"

"Works for me." She unlatched her seat belt. "Thank you," she told him when he opened the door for her.

Inside the restaurant, Jaxon pulled out the chair for her. "We've had a long afternoon. I suggest we don't talk about the case tonight at all."

"I can live with that."

After they ordered, she told him about Jessie's emails and phone calls. "She sounds happy and relaxed. Exactly what they both needed, a break."

"What did you like about your trip to Ireland?" he asked.

"The people and the music. There's a sense of magic in the land. I loved all their legends. There were some guides that could really spin a yarn as Grandma Sadie said more than once."

Through dinner, they talked about family and growing up. And as the evening wore on, Peyton realized what a wonderful family and childhood Jaxon had. How fun they all sounded. She felt safe with him and opened up a little more about her parents. He took everything about her family oddities in stride and didn't seem overly worried that she had this strange part of her life passed down from her ancestors. Of course, he asked questions, but it seemed to her those questions weren't about her sanity but how she was dealing with each new experience and what she was learning.

After dinner they walked out of the restaurant holding hands. "Thank you," Jaxon said as he opened the car door for her.

"For what?" She slid into the passenger seat and latched her seat belt.

"An enjoyable evening and reminders of all the reasons I love my family and am happy to be living close to them again," he answered her.

"Your family is great. I've loved getting to meet and spend time with them. Especially, your darling Down syndrome niece Emma. She is such a delightful happy baby. I love how your family supports your brother and his wife. The love that surrounds Emma is a joy to watch.

She will flourish. She'll surprise you with all that she can accomplish."

"And she loves you. Emmie can wrap me around her little finger. There isn't much I wouldn't do for her." He smiled at her. "I hope someday they will be your family too."

"We'll see." She smiled at him. "Your family dinners are noisy and wonderous affairs. The first time I was unsure how to handle them all."

"They can take a bit of getting used to, but they're great, and they all thought you were too."

"I'm happy to hear they like me."

The ride back to her cottage was nice, and his kiss goodbye at the door was nothing if not dreamy. Her evening had been enlightening in so many ways. She was close to making a monumental decision. When it came to Jaxon, she knew she loved him but cautiously kept a way out of the relationship just in case.

"I mean would it have killed you, Peyton, to say I hope they'll be my family someday too? No, not you. You couldn't even give him a small lifeline," she uttered to herself. Her lips weren't sealed, so she said, "We'll see." She got ready for bed and stretched out beneath the cozy blankets. After she shut off the light, she glanced to make sure her fairy light was lighting the bathroom as she did each night.

"Peyton, sometimes I don't understand you," she whispered. "Jaxon is a keeper."

All evening, he praised her as if she was an asset and not a liability, which was nice for her ego, she had to admit. She still had trouble believing anyone could see value in her. Therapy helped and so had going away to college and later finding success in her work life. But no matter how much she had grown, she still felt the need to prove herself by working hard, going the extra mile when asked, and volunteering as often as someone needed help. Learning to say no was a biggie, and an even greater challenge was learning to trust her instincts and relationships. She usually sabotaged them before they had grown cold.

What was it about Jaxon that got through her defenses time and time again? Oh, he was handsome to be sure, but it wasn't his looks although they helped. No, it was his low-keyed, steady personality and his gentle way with her. The way he loved his family and played with Emma his niece. He lovingly called her Emmie and lit up whenever he spoke of her as he had tonight.

Jaxon gave her the time she needed to adjust to a situation and never belittled her. Even his safety lectures were easy to swallow. She also liked that he was no pushover—he gave as good as she dished it out to him. And if she were being honest, she liked the way he looked at her like he was a hungry man seeing a table full of food. She smiled at the ridiculous picture.

He seemingly sailed through her on-again, off-again reactions to him, but in reality she knew she could be in danger of losing the best guy who had ever come into her life. Tonight's conversation reminded her of all the dreams she had dreamed over the years. She wanted a loving marriage and a happy family—they were top on the list. As she had listened to him tell some of his favorite childhood memories, she found herself envious. What would it have been like to grow up surrounded by love and fun? Grandpa Max and Sadie provided what stability they could for her and Madison. Limited to when her parents would allow a visit. Maybe Jaxon could teach her how to let go and enjoy the love she knew existed in her heart for him. Trust didn't come easy. She shook her head. She had to stop using trust as an excuse. One day she could kiss him like nobody's business, and other days she was unsure. In her heart there wasn't room for anyone else but him, and she knew it was time to jump in and let her heart and not her brain lead her.

****

Jaxon texted Peyton a good-night message with just the right amount of heat. He was surprised when she texted back something a bit sassy. He smiled. Her message was the perfect end to a nice evening. As his brothers would say, he had it bad. He sure did. During his tumultuous teens, his dad told him more than once the right girl would come along someday and when she did, he would know. He could understand him now. She was the one he waited for to come along and capture his heart and mind. Yep, she was his one and worth the wait.

All he had to figure out was how to convince her of that fact and to keep her safe. She was in the middle of this case, and he didn't have a good feeling about where the investigation was leading. He knew she was capable of taking care of herself, but this case was rapidly revealing some pretty despicable dudes who wouldn't think twice about what they would do to her. His one consolation was those guys had no idea what she could do to them. He chuckled.

Jaxon wanted to know who followed them from the college. One thing being an agent had taught him was to be aware of his surroundings at all times on the job. Thankfully, he had seen the car follow him out of the campus parking lot. Whoever was driving the small vehicle was bound to make contact at some point if he hadn't already. Jaxon reached for the case file and wrote his new notes from today's interviews in a report. Paperwork was the bane of his existence. He glanced at the clock. He wouldn't be getting to sleep anytime soon.

****

Peyton awakened with a start. Her dream had reinforced her memory of the general discontent threatening to swallow the world and Blue Cove along with it. She couldn't forget that fact as she faced the events of the past couple of days. Crimes were often connected in some strange way to one another. In this case a missing girl, a murder victim, and a secret society operating on the same campus seemed too serendipitous to be coincidental. Add the murder victim she found during her run and the irate father Jaxon told her about, and trouble was certainly churning.

The dream began with Peyton searching for something, rummaging through closets and drawers, throwing random items in all directions. Next, she went outside to look through the bushes as she overturned rocks, sifting through the dirt with her hands. At one point she stopped to gaze out to the cove that churned with the same turbulence racing through her. The waves threatened to overtake the ground on which she stood. She understood that part of the dream to mean all that was happening around her was a part of the discontentment of the time. Or as her cousin told her, the spirit of the age in which they lived. The element she didn't understand in the dream was the way it ended with a bright ray of light and the feeling of hope. Hopeful wasn't something she had felt much of in the last few weeks nor did most of the dream imbue. Maybe what she was searching for in her dream was a glimmer of hope.

Over the past year, she had heard Reba and Jessie say several times the only way to fight hate is with love. Not so easy to remember when you are faced with the sad cold hard facts about what humans can do to one another.

Peyton glanced at the clock and jumped out of bed. If she didn't get a move on, she would be late opening the store. She told Audrey she would work today and gave her the day off. She wasn't used to working on Saturday, but Jaxon would be too.

Peyton made it just in time to open the door into Joe's and for a lady waiting at the front door for her to unlock it.

"Good morning," the petite blonde woman said. "I have a list of books I want to find."

"If I can help you, let me know," Peyton told her.

"The thing I love most about a bookstore is browsing and taking my time. I told my husband when I left the house this morning not to expect me anytime soon. He can handle the kids for a few hours. This is my time for me." She laughed. "Coffee, books, and quiet, what's not to like about that?"

"Sounds perfect to me."

"Do you own this store? It's a wonderful space." She took off her jacket and draped it over the back of the chair.

"No, my cousin does. She's on her honeymoon, and I'm helping out while she is gone."

"Well, I love it. There's a certain something about the atmosphere in here. Dare I say there's something a bit otherworldly about it." The woman reached for her wallet and headed toward Joe's. "My name is Carolyn Cassidy by the way. My friends call me Cara. I'm sure you and I will be great friends, Peyton."

Peyton couldn't remember telling the woman her name. How could she know? She instantly was on guard, but their resident ghost didn't seem too concerned when she glanced at him. Cara was a familiar name to her.

Earlier this year while rummaging through the inn's attic, she found the diary and writings of Cara Cassidy whose family emigrated to America from Ireland during the potato famine. That's the time she began to have an interest in understanding her Irish ancestors. Which eventually took her along with her cousin Jessie and grandma Sadie to Ireland this past summer. In her heart of hearts Peyton was sure she was about to learn something important from this woman whoever she was. Peyton turned on her computer and waited for Carolyn to come back. This might turn out to be an interesting Saturday.

Chapter 13

"Did I leave you with questions?" she asked when she walked back in the door. "If I didn't, I'm not doing a good job. Cara was one of my ancestors and yours too. I know you read her journal."

"Yes, I did." Peyton sat beside the woman and closed her mouth. She was sure it was hanging open in a stupefied way. "I found the book in my search through the treasures in the attic at the inn near where I live. How did you know my name? I don't remember telling you."

She waved with her hand. "That's not important."

"If you don't mind me saying, it is to me. I'm interested in how all this works, and something tells me you have an unusual way of knowing who I am, and I would like to be on equal footing."

"We are not so different, you know. From different worlds or dimensions, but with ancestors that we know well. But that is not why I'm here. I'm here to be your friend. I'm one of the Cassidy descendants. And before you ask, I have the gift of sight that runs in my family line among the women."

"When you say different worlds, do you mean you're not from here?"

She laughed. "No, I live in the area. I used that because I want to remind you of something very important. When you deal with the dark side of life as we often do, and when you have premonitions and dreams, you tend to forget that, for all the bad in the world, there is still a lot of good. There are people doing their small part to make their place in the world better. Believe me, I'm not a Goody Two-Shoes. I've seen a lot of evil, but I refuse to let that define me. Do you know what I saw while in New York?"

"Another mugging," Peyton said sarcastically.

Carolyn shook her head. "While I waited on the subway platform, someone began to play a Beatles song, and before you knew what was happening, people were dancing, clapping, and singing along. It was like everyone was waiting for a reason to join together. The loud voices tell us we should not trust each other and fear each other, but in our hearts most of us know we are not so different after all. Don't get me wrong, I'm not naïve. I walk in similar shoes as you and understand the anger and the angst among us. All I'm saying is given the right person, words, or moment and it could all change for the good."

"I get what you're saying, but why do I need to be reminded?" Peyton frowned.

"Because you, dear friend, have had way too much hurt in your life, and though you will remain who you are with the gifts given to you, you're free from a past that doesn't define you. Don't let it. You're worthy of love."

Peyton reached for a tissue. "Thank you, Carolyn." She wiped the tears running down her cheeks. "I think you might be right. We are bound to be good friends."

"I've heard of you and your cousin. Your exploits to help others is a bit of a legend beyond the door among those whom you've helped." She smiled. "You have people to help, and I have books to look for. Believe me,

I'll come back when your cousin returns to meet her too. Now, I have some quiet time for myself, and I don't want to waste a minute."

"Enjoy, I'm here if you need me." Peyton watched Carolyn most of the morning as she picked out one book after another, adding them to a small stack she created. For the most part Peyton thought of herself as optimistic, but the last few days had been tough, and anyone in her shoes would've reacted the same. Still, what Carolyn said to her reminded her of the light at the end of her dream. She needed to look for the good and beauty amidst the dark and ugly. Finding the good around might not always be easy, but she would find a way. As she was ringing up Carolyn Cassidy's purchases, Reba walked in. Of course, she would. Peyton smiled to herself.

"Reba, what are you doing here on a Saturday?"

"I asked Lawrence to drop me off while he went to the hardware store. One of my least favorite things to do and then he will take me to lunch."

"My friend, this lovely lady is Carolyn Cassidy." Peyton introduced them.

"She is one of us, isn't she?" Carolyn reached for Reba's hand. "I can see it in your face. There's a strong ancient presence around you," she told Reba.

"Yes, and with you also. You've been on a mission today, haven't you? And now I know why I was supposed to come here. You must be another one in the family line of Cara Cassidy."

"I am." Carolyn reached for the bag of books on the counter. "If you have a few minutes, I think we should talk."

Peyton couldn't join them because the store had a few customers. Boy, she wished she could hear what they were talking about. She could remember hearing in a Sunday school class one time about divine appointments. She had no idea at the time what it meant, but the two of them sitting there talking like old friends made her believe this was no coincidence. While they chatted, she had two phone calls on her personal phone which she didn't answer, followed by two voicemails. Peyton refused to let the man's voice ruin a positive few hours for her.

When the two women finished their conversation, Peyton walked toward them to say her goodbyes. "Did you have a nice visit?" she asked.

"Enlightening, dear girl. It's nice to know that we aren't an oddity and there are more people like us around."

"I couldn't have said it any better, Reba. Remember what I told you, Peyton. Your past doesn't define you." She picked up her bag from the table. "Friends, I've enjoyed this day more than you'll ever know. The times may not get any easier, but we can always find something to be grateful for." She waved as she walked toward the door. "I'll be back again as soon as I can convince my husband that I should when he sees the stack of books I bought."

"Carolyn is an interesting woman. I like her. Her message to you was timely. Your recent past doesn't define you as much as your ancient past." She squeezed Peyton's hand. "I'm right, aren't I?"

"Yes, ma'am." She walked Reba to the door.

"Remember what I told you. I believe this is your time to discover the depth of your gift and fly solo."

"How can I forget?" Peyton kissed Reba's cheek and held the door open for her. "Have a nice day, my friend."

Peyton understood what Reba meant, but she was also sure as long as Jaxon was by her side, she wouldn't be completely alone. She walked back to the counter and reached for her phone in her purse behind the counter. Her phone screen photo stopped her in her tracks when it lit up. She sighed as she got lost in the image. Jaxon was such a handsome man. The attributes she had noticed about him the first time they met were still what she noticed five months later. She could get lost in his honey brown eyes, perfectly framed with the long, dark lashes that made her envious every time she looked at him. No amount of mascara could produce the same effect on her. Why a man needed such long lashes, she would never understand, but they made him even more dreamy. And the way his sandy blond hair often fell across his forehead made him very sexy to her way of thinking. All in all, he was one good-looking man.

She needed to quit dragging her feet, learn to flirt a bit more, and open her heart to the wonderful gift of the man that life had handed her. Before she could get to the messages on her phone, the bell above the door rang, calling her back from her daydreaming to work.

****

His frustration level had reached a fevered pitch. Who did she think she was not taking his calls? He might need to show her his abilities. No woman could defy him and last for long. He paced around the tiny room, knocking over chairs and punching a wall along the way. He could snap her neck with little effort.

"Patience, man," he muttered. "She'll understand how serious this is soon enough. You have your ways of getting her attention beyond a phone message." Slipping on a pair of gloves, he grabbed some paper off his cluttered desk, an old magazine from the stack in the corner on the floor, and a pair of scissors from the pencil caddy. There were many ways to create a message to get her attention. With a solid plan in his mind, he went to find a glue stick and sat down to his art project. "Just like in school." He snickered as he cut out the first word he would glue to the paper. He quickly shuffled his project when he heard the knock at his door and the handle turn. "I'll be with you in a minute." He frowned and opened his locked door while plastering a smile on his face that he didn't feel. He made small talk with the person who interrupted his momentum and stepped outside, closing the door behind him. He couldn't risk anyone seeing his treasure.

****

Jaxon had his first break of the day, after a morning filled with meetings. They were necessary to catch up on open cases but not his favorite part of investigative work. How many hours had he spent in meetings from his first day on the job in Phoenix to working for the agency all total, he mused. It had to be quite a few.

He learned some new facts regarding the murder victim found on campus, and the one that Peyton had discovered near her place. Both were young women, but the similarities stopped there, which could mean there were two suspects that they were looking for. The other concern was the secret society and the role the online group might be playing in extorting professors and promoting crimes against women. More information was needed, but they had a young agent working underground in the group. It might take time to earn the trust of the leaders to understand how the group operated.

They were considered secret because people hadn't been able to discover much about them other than the exterior workings of the group Anything Goes. The availability of drugs to the students who had the money to buy them was what most people knew about. But as he learned this morning, they were a closed book when it came to the darker side of the group. People were afraid to talk for fear of being outed.

His job after lunch was to gather information on the missing girl, Emily Hart. Her father's house was near Blue Cove, and Jaxon knew where he wanted to go for lunch. He wanted to see his favorite person before he had to tackle an angry and scared father. This was the one part of his job that he didn't enjoy.

Jaxon told the receptionist his plans for the afternoon and left the building. Every time he left the building, he was at peace with his decision to move back here from Arizona. Although, the chillier the weather turned made him wonder if he had lost his mind. The first real cold snap would have him rethinking his decision altogether. Right now, with the fall colors and a few weeks until Thanksgiving with his family, he impressed himself with his choice. Cold or not he wouldn't want to be anywhere else.

As he drove through Hanover, he loved how the trees were alive with color. From flaming red, orange, to gold, every gorgeous color seemed represented in the trees as they lined the middle of Main Street and formed a canopy with each side. Soon enough they would be barren, but for now, they were beautiful. He pulled over to the side and snapped a picture to send to his mom. His mother always liked to hear from him, and he enjoyed surprising her once in a while. Along with showing up unannounced at the house.

He pulled into the flower shop on his way out of Hanover. *Let's make it a big surprise for both of them.* After he ordered flowers to be sent to his mom, he had the florists box a single long-stem red rose mixed with baby's breath and a bouquet of various colorful flowers that reminded him of the dress Peyton wore on their first night out for dinner. When she walked out the door of the hotel, he literally held his breath and couldn't speak until he got ahold of himself. He smiled when he walked out of the shop. How she had rocked his world. The smile never left his face all the way to the bookstore. Buying gifts for her could become a habit with him. He used to see his dad surprise his mom all the time. Is this how courtship felt? He wanted to win her. She was a challenge, but he was up to the task.

He carried the gift box into the store when he arrived, walked up behind Peyton, and whispered in her ear, "Hi, I was thinking of you, babe." He handed her the box.

"You were in my thoughts too." She placed the box on the counter. "Do you want me to open this now?" she asked.

He nodded. "Of course." It was like he was back in high school as he waited for her response. Palms sweating, he wanted her to feel the love that swelled in him when he picked out the arrangement.

"They are beautiful, Jaxon. Thank you." She smiled and rushed into his open arms.

"Do you know what that bouquet reminded me of?" He told her about the dress and how she looked that evening.

"That's beyond sweet that you remembered what I

was wearing." She kissed his cheek.

He glanced around the store and kissed her on the lips. "I want you to know that I love you, and I'm willing to wait as long as you need me to," he whispered in her ear.

"Thank you. I don't want to keep you dangling. There isn't anyone but you. I simply need to get out of my own way. I'll put these in water, and you get yourself some lunch. I have to tell you what happened this morning if you have time."

"Sounds good. I'll be back. Can I get you anything?" Jaxon asked.

"An iced tea would be great."

"You got it." He nodded and walked into Joe's.

Chapter 14

Peyton rushed into the back room and found the vase that Jessie kept there. She filled it with tepid water and arranged the beautiful bouquet in the vase. Placing the red rose in the center of all the glorious colors. She had the perfect place for the arrangement when she got home.

Tears filled her eyes when she read the card he had written to her. *My darling Peyton, these reminded me of the beauty I see in you every time we're together. My love for you continues to grow, and just so you know, I'm not going anywhere. Love, Jaxon.*

She carried the vase to the counter. "You will add a touch of beauty to this space." Peyton smelled their lovely fragrance. She loved flowers, and their rich colors were something Peyton enjoyed. She lived in one of the cottages by the inn after all and walked through the colorful gardens all summer. Bending close to the rose to sniff, she found herself caught in a dark memory. Remembering the fear and the smell sent shivers crawling down her back. When she was young, she often could see a dark color around her father before he blew up in a rage, but when he was happy, it wasn't there. Maybe that was life's way of protecting her and her sister. She knew when she saw the darkness to go hide and stay out of his way. Hand in hand with Madison, they would find different hiding places where he couldn't find them. If and when he found them, she shuddered, the memories were as dark as he was.

All she knew was certain places or people had a sensation of light and darkness around them. Call it atmosphere, energy, or a vibe, the sensation often appeared as a warning to her in some way. She wasn't trying to see anything, and yet when she least expected them, she came face-to-face with the energy whether good or bad.

"Earth to Peyton. Are you there?" Jaxon asked.

"I'm sorry, I didn't hear you come back." She turned toward him. "Woolgathering as Grams would say."

"I hope you have time to join me and let me hear about your morning and maybe what had you thinking and unaware of your surroundings." He placed his lunch on the table in the center of the bookstore.

She told him about the memories the flowers triggered in her mind. "I know seeing that dark color around him spared us a lot of heartache and pain sometimes." She proceeded to tell him about Carolyn Cassidy's visit and what Reba said to her.

"Wow, you live an interesting life. What about now? Do you still see colors around people?" he asked.

"It's more of a sensation of light and darkness. I felt it with Kelsey when she talked to me about her missing roommate Emily. The fear she had was tangible, and I know she cared deeply for her friend's safety. The boys you were talking to though created a different sensation. I had a bad vibe when it came to them."

"Is this something passed to you from your ancestors?" He took a bite of his sandwich.

"It could be. Irish legends don't mention the idea of aura per se, and I'm not even sure if that's what it is. Their legends have many mythical creatures like fairies, leprechauns, and the like. Often their history and mythology lines are blurred. Not unlike any people group. We have our own. I believe it is how we can best define when something is good. Whether you call it a legend, a miracle, or magic we find ways to keep those good stories alive too."

"I can see that."

"Something bad is happening on the campus, and we are only scratching the surface. I know there are ways to dcfine what's happening that blur the lines between the real and unreal. I believe the guy who keeps calling me is part of it in some way too."

"What makes you think so?" he asked.

"Call it intuition if that's an easier word to handle. You know how this stuff works."

"I'm still wrapping my head around your abilities, which seem to have grown over time. All I know is it isn't important whether I understand how you can hear and see what you do, because I trust you and I know how much you care for each of the victims. You may be unconventional, but you get the job done. I'm damn lucky to have you in my life and on my side."

"Always. And thanks for the tea and the gorgeous flowers. They smell wonderful." Peyton stood up to help a customer who walked in from the coffee shop. She bent close to him and whispered in his ear, "I'm glad you're not going anywhere."

"I'll see you after work. I'll bring dinner to your house." He waggled his eyebrows at her. "Unless you'd rather go out. It's Saturday after all."

"My place sounds good to me." She followed the woman to the book display at the front of the store. "May I help you?"

****

Jaxon drove to Mr. Hart's home. He didn't relish this meeting with Emily's father. The man was worried sick along with being angry, and who could blame him? Jaxon could only image what a missing child would do to a parent. If what Peyton saw was correct, and he had no reason to doubt her, Emily was being held against her will, and they needed to find her. He didn't want to give a false hope, but at the same time he didn't want the man to lose hope.

With the help of GPS, he pulled up in front of a tidy mid-century brick home not unlike his own before he remolded the exterior. He took a deep breath and exhaled before he opened the car door. Mr. Hart opened the door as he walked up the porch steps before he could knock.

"You must be Agent Kincaid," the man said as he held the door open for him.

"Yes, sir, I am."

"You can call me Larry." Jaxon followed him into the living room.

"I'm glad someone is finally taking me seriously. I can't believe they arrested me for hitting that weasel. I know he isn't innocent. He was the last one to see my daughter before she disappeared." Larry Hart sat and gestured for him to do the same.

"I can understand your anger, but no matter what you can't assault someone and not be arrested. At least he didn't press charges, or you'd still be there. You have to let the police handle and investigate your complaint."

He huffed. "Like that's ever going to happen. I filed a complaint with the college police and the local police. All I got was the runaround from both departments. One of them had the audacity to tell me, you need to calm down, sir. As if that was possible when my little girl is missing, and God alone knows what's happening to her." He covered his face with his hands.

"The wheels of justice turn slow. Isn't that what they always say? What may seem slow to you doesn't mean nothing is happening. An officer must gather evidence, question people who may have seen her, and follow up on any leads. All the while not to compromise an investigation that will let the suspect go free in a court of law. I know this may be hard for you but let the authorities do their job. The FBI is involved now, and they bring many resources with them that the locals don't have."

"I understand I need to let them do their job, but my mind is imagining the worst. Being idle and doing nothing to find her is impossible for me. Especially after they found another girl's body on campus. I'm telling you something sick is going on at that campus. I would bet my life you'll find something sinister going on."

"Larry, do you mind if I call you by your first name?" Jaxon asked.

"Not at all."

"We are going to do our best to find your daughter. I don't want you to give up. What I need from you is more information about her. A recent photo would be nice and one of her favorite items that she has handled. My friend has a bloodhound that tracks, and I have a request in for him to bring his dog and work the area with our team."

"Too much time has gone by. What good will the dog be able to do at this point?"

"I've seen this dog work abductions before. Let me tell you he does an amazing job. The dog levels the playing field immensely."

"Okay, I'll give you what you need." Larry got up and went into his daughter's room. When he returned, he handed Jaxon a bag. "This was her favorite stuffed animal. She always cuddled the darn thing when she came home."

"Thanks, this will help a lot." Jaxon looked at the photo Larry gave him. "She has a beautiful smile."

"Don't I know. Her vibrant personality lit up this house and my life since her mom passed away. I admit I didn't want her to live on campus, but she promised to come home often, and she did every weekend. She's a good daughter." He frowned. "Her boyfriend took up more of her time lately, and I don't like him. I can't put my finger on why. Maybe I simply don't like the idea of him replacing me in her life."

They talked for a while. Jaxon asked him several questions, and Larry answered each of them, giving the details that he knew.

"One more question before I go. Did Emily ever tell you she was concerned someone was following her?"

"No. I would remember if she had. She did voice that she was working on a story that might shake up a few lives at the school. Oh, and the last time she was home, she seemed more anxious than normal. When I asked her why, she told me she was having trouble in one of her classes." He shook his head. "I should have asked more questions. I should have listened to what she was trying to tell me."

"Don't be too hard on yourself. There's no way you could have seen what was happening. She would have told you if she was worried. Your relationship sounds like a solid one."

"I hope you're right, but I keep second-guessing myself."

Jaxon stood and shook Larry's hand. "If you can think of anything that might be helpful, here is my number. Feel free to call me anytime. I'll try to keep you abreast with how things are going and when Mr. Wagner will do the track with his dog." Jaxon walked with Larry to the door.

"Thank you, for at least listening to me. You can tell others that I will stay away from the professor. I will honor the restraining order and let you all do your job. I would appreciate any updates you give me."

"You'll get them." Jaxon walked out to his car.

The visit went better than expected. Jaxon was waiting on final approval for Frank to bring his dog Carlene, but since there was no cost to the department, he was sure Maxwell would sign off on the request.

Maybe he should have Peyton give Frank a heads-up. He wanted to move fast to start the search for the girl. Before he drove away, he sent a quick text to Peyton to contact Frank. He would check again with Tom on Monday.

He could understand Mr. Hart's consternation. Larry needed to be kept in the loop at what was going on in regard to his daughter. The fact he lost his wife not long ago and now a missing daughter would be tough for anyone to handle. Another piece of proof that life wasn't fair and often didn't make much sense. He'd seen enough of the shady side of humanity over his short career to leave him shaking his head often in disgust.

The drive back to Blue Cove was uneventful, which he didn't mind. The week seemed long and tiring to him, and he could use tomorrow to chill. His favorite football team had an afternoon game. His lounge chair called his name along with the game. Throw in some good food and a beer or two and he had the makings of a great day off. An ongoing bet with his older brother on which team would be going to the Super Bowl this season added a bit of interest week to week. His fantasy football quarterback proved to be quite an asset leading his team, winning Jaxon a couple of pools at work. Only a few bucks here and there but great bragging rights.

Dinner at Peyton's house sounded perfect to him. He knew her week had been a long one and so had his. He pulled into an open place in front of the Chinese restaurant that came highly recommended for takeout by a few of his coworkers.

Chapter 15

Peyton closed the door into Joe's and locked it. Finishing up the routine to close the store, she turned off the main lights, leaving only the night-light on. As she glanced around the store to make sure she had cleared any trash, put all the scattered books and magazines away, she sensed she was being watched. She turned around and caught a slight movement to her left out of the corner of her eye. Another quick check over her shoulder and she came face-to-face with the spirit of the murder victim. "Great," she muttered, "another ghost to join our guardian warrior keeping his vigil on the stairs.

"How are you doing?" She didn't expect an answer but wanted to ask anyway. "You must be as shocked as I was to see you. My cousin often was saddened by the thought of the shock a victim must feel when suddenly ripped from this life." Peyton watched her, and the sad expression on the spirit's face imprinted itself on her psyche. "We will find out who did this to you. I promise. I hope you'll soon rest in peace."

She had no idea if what she said to the spirit got through to her. Could she hear? Peyton had no way to know. But saying the words were important. Words held power to move and change even the one speaking them. Every life was valuable, had meaning, and purpose. Her opportunity to live her life was ripped from her. How must she feel? The profound sadness those who love her must feel seemed overwhelming as they continued to face each other. Peyton reached for the tissues and locked the door behind as she rushed from the store to her car. Would the spirit remain in the store or wander through town? Peyton didn't have any idea how any of this worked. She needed to talk to her cousin who had a lot more experience with these folks than she did. But somehow she figured she would soon get a feel for what her cousin went through.

Peyton glanced in the rearview mirror. So much for the ghost staying at the store or in town. She was riding home with her. Shaking her head, she wasn't sure how she felt about her presence this close. Another first in her life. She had no idea what to do with a ghost looking over her shoulder. Would this become a common occurrence?

The warrior's constant presence while he stood guard in her cousin's store had become a familiar part of their lives. But this one was riding in the backseat of her car. There was never a dull moment in her life. Should she tell Jaxon or not? His response might be interesting. His business-as-usual attitude brought her comfort even if she didn't want to admit the fact. Let's face it, a ghost riding around in her backseat was a tad bit unusual. She chuckled as she glanced in her mirror. As her cousin often said, they lived enchanted lives, and Peyton would add bizarre in there also.

After she parked, before going to her cottage, she went up the back steps of the inn. She opened the kitchen door, and immediately the scent of something yummy teased her nose. Katie's culinary abilities were becoming well known in the area. Peyton walked through the kitchen into the lobby to the front desk to pick up her mail.

Peyton smiled at Katie who looked pretty as a picture standing behind the desk. "Something smells good in that kitchen of yours."

"Hey, Peyton." Katie handed her a stack of mail. "When Jessie gets back from her honeymoon, we all need to get together for dinner here. Speaking of my best friend, have you heard from her since she's been away? I figured if she contacted anyone that you'd be the one. If I'm lucky I'll get a postcard." She chuckled. "Never mind that no one heard from me when I was on my honeymoon. Only my handsome husband." She fluttered her eyelashes.

"Jess called once when Matt was out getting their morning coffee, and she emails most every night with new information she has learned about our ancestors. The honeymooners are having a great time enjoying the pubs and lively music."

"I figured as much. I can't wait to hear details. Wait a minute." Katie reached under the counter. "I have something else for you." She handed Peyton a box. "I'll walk with you to the kitchen. I need to check on my dish in the oven."

"Sounds good." They walked to the kitchen together, chatting as they went. "See you soon." Peyton waved and walked out the door.

The cool air was welcoming after the heat of the inn's kitchen. She shuffled the package to her other hand to get a better grasp… She couldn't imagine what was in the box, because she hadn't ordered anything recently. She glanced around the gardens where mums still bloomed, and more than a few rebellious colorful leaves hung on for life. She couldn't ask for a better place to live. She would miss her cousin living in the cottage next door, but her fingers were crossed that her sister would live there some day. At least for as long as she remained living in the cottage herself. She had dreams of being married to Jaxon someday.

She placed the mail on the kitchen counter along with the box and her keys. She rushed to set the table for whatever Jaxon brought for dinner and filled two glasses with ice. With that finished, a quick brush through her hair was next.

****

Jaxon drove through Blue Cove on his way to the inn. He had no regrets about moving to the area from Arizona. Especially after finding out that Peyton lived there. The last few months since meeting her were a blur but wonderful. He had put in for the transfer before they met, but she made the move worth the headache. He wondered if he would still feel that way after the cold temps settled in for a few months. He grew up in the area, so it shouldn't take long to get used to the cold snowy weather again especially with Peyton by his side. Besides, Christmas wasn't the same with palm trees instead of the white stuff. Which meant a snowblower was in his future. He smiled. He pulled his car in next to Peyton's and grabbed the bag on the seat beside him.

He knocked and swept inside when she opened the screen door. "How was your day?" he asked on his way to the kitchen. "I brought Chinese. I hope you approve." He placed the bag on the table, turned, and took her into his arms. "Now to greet you without my hands full." He kissed and hugged her tight.

"Let's answer your questions." She pulled back to look at his face. "The rest of my day was thought provoking, I do like Chinese food, and hi to you also."

She kissed him back.

"Hmm, I like the way you answer questions." He kissed her again. "A guy could get used to a greeting like this," he whispered in her ear. "Let's eat while the food is warm, and you can tell me about your day. I know you well enough to know that means unusual." He grinned and pulled out her chair for her. "I'm all yours, and the night is young."

"I want to hear about your interview with Emily Hart's father too." She spooned up some rice and sesame chicken onto her plate along with a fried egg roll.

"The guys at work recommended this place. I hope they know what they're talking about."

"Well, this egg roll is yummy. That's a good start." She took a bite of the chicken and rice. "They didn't steer you wrong."

"Good to know. We can keep this one on the list." He reached for another egg roll and a couple of wontons.

"By chance do you have her ID yet?" Peyton asked.

"Mary Elizabeth Bradley. She was only nineteen years old. Why?" he asked.

"I find myself attached to her since I was the one who found the body, and because she rode home with me from the store and is around here somewhere, I'm sure."

"I wasn't expecting to hear you say that." He shook his head and glanced around the room. "No offense but I don't want to see her."

"I don't blame you. My life is full of surprises even to me." She chuckled. "I hope this doesn't weird you out. When I saw her sad expression today, I began to wonder what a victim is aware of after they die. I mean with their life violently taken from them, do they feel sorrow about not having a peaceful end? They say Gettysburg is haunted by the soldiers who died there. Do you think there is a consciousness after death of having died? Do they want those who they love and maybe even the murderer to understand? Because she looked like she understood what happened. Maybe there is more to this living and dying business than we will ever understand."

"I can't say that I've thought much about the victim other than to investigate who killed them. It stands to reason there is a lot we don't understand. Can I just say this is not a light dinner conversation?" He filled his glass with tea.

"Sorry, we can discuss this later if you wish, but I feel sad for Mary and her family."

"I know you do, sweetheart. The fact that you care deeply about others is what I love the most about you." Jaxon leaned back in his chair. "Murder is terrible. The victim and many other lives are destroyed by one thoughtless act. Take you," he said, reaching for her hand. "You have been impacted by every victim you've discovered, and so have I. We are touched deep inside by the personal stories that go along with the people. Maybe that's why we do the job we do. If we don't let the process harden us, we do the job for them."

"I can see that. I want to know about the victim as a person, and like my cousin Jessie, I want to give voice to their stories. Mary Elizabeth had dreams, and I want her story to be told. I need to hear more details." Peyton cleared the plates from the table and placed them in the dishwasher. "You know what I think." She glanced at him. "A nice article in the college paper about Mary, Emily Hart, Sarah, and the other murder victim might generate some information from people too afraid to speak up."

"The other victim is Eloise Morton. She was only eighteen and in her freshman year." Jaxon frowned. "I'll be interviewing her family and students who knew her this week. I still wonder why we had no reports of her missing. You might be right about telling their personal stories could garner more info. I will talk to the college student president and paper editor and see if we can work that out but only if you'll write the article."

"I will, with my cousin's help. She is brilliant with moving folks by the words she pens. I'll ask her and let you take care of the college part of this. Let's get more comfortable." Peyton walked into the living room with Jaxon following.

"Tell me about your interview earlier."

Jaxon told her what he had learned from Larry Hart. "He's brokenhearted. His wife died not long ago. The circumstances are rough all the way around."

"Darn, that makes the story even sadder." She shook her head. "Do you see what I mean? Their story is important. How do you generate thoughtfulness that might stop someone else from doing some awful action against another person? I swear we live in what seems to be a super violent world at times."

"Hey, you're talking to the choir here. I was a homicide detective in a major city and saw enough there and now as an agent. I hear enough to keep me up at nights."

"I'm sure you do."

Jaxon leaned his head back against the couch, and she handed him the remote. Watching the game helped to take his mind off of other matters. Not to mention after a couple of hours of watching punts, passes, and touchdowns his mood had evened out a bit. Nothing like a good, close football game to take you away for a bit. His favorite college team had made the last two hours exciting to say the least.

Chapter 16

Jaxon kissed her good night, then whispered in her ear, "I'll see you in the morning." His breath caused flutters in her stomach long after he was gone. She sighed as she made her way to her room. Turning on her computer, she compiled an email to Jessie to fill her in on what was happening at the college and to her. Peyton had questions that she hoped her cousin could answer. Had a ghost ever followed her home? The one watching Peyton from the corner of her bedroom was making her nervous. Should she be worried?

Peyton finished her note to Jessie and remembered the box she had brought home from the inn. She wished she had opened the darn thing while Jaxon was still here. More than a few scenarios rushed through her mind, making her hesitant to open the box. *Come on, girl, you're no wimp. Just open the stupid box and get over it.* She took a letter opener and slit through the packing tape. Once she opened the box and moved the paper inside carefully, she found an envelope addressed to her. She didn't have a good feeling about what she held in her hand. She glanced at the clock. Hopefully he wouldn't be asleep yet.

"What's up?" Jaxon asked when he answered his phone.

Peyton explained about the box and contents. "What should I do?"

"Don't open the damn envelope. I'll get if from you in the morning and let the lab check it for any substance or fingerprints— Will you be okay?"

Even though he didn't say the words, Peyton was sure what he was asking. "I'll be fine. I am a bit spooked that he knows where I live, but the internet makes that possible with little effort."

"Call me if you are concerned at any point tonight. You know I'll come if you need me. I'll give Dylan a heads-up too."

"Thank you, I know you will." Peyton left the box on the desk, double-checked the alarm, and said good night to Jaxon as she walked into her room.

She stretched out on her bed and turned off the lamp beside the bed. Her night-light in the bathroom cast a soft glow into her room. She could still see the sad expression on Mary Elizabeth's face. She seemed more real since Jaxon had told her the victim's name. She turned the light back on. She wanted to check to see if Jessie had answered her email. She also wanted to see if she could find any information on Mary Bradley in police reports or campus news.

Bingo. She found a few items of importance that she hadn't known. Jaxon mentioned Mary was only eighteen and a freshman at the college. Both victims had some similarities from size to hair color. Reddish brown hair, medium height, and outgoing personalities were descriptions given to both girls and now Emily Hart too, although she was blonde. What would a profiler conclude from those facts? Were they important to the case at all? She wrote down the question to remember to ask Jaxon tomorrow. The pictures she saw of each of the girls seared themselves in her consciousness. Pretty young lives, two gone and the third needed to be found before she became a murder victim too. No wonder the ghost had a sad expression.

These were young girls not political operatives, who maybe stumbled upon some information about a secret society on campus or were simply in the wrong place at the wrong time. Maybe some sick kind of campus initiation ritual of some sort. At this point who knew. Either way, it wasn't safe for any young girls on campus at the moment. She sent an email to Jeremy, hoping he could dig up some information on the girls that she didn't have.

She checked her emails once again. Yay, her cousin had sent a reply.

Wow, cous, it sounds like you have your hands full. To answer one of your questions, yes, I have had a ghost follow me home. She has attached herself to you because she wants your help. Reassure her that you will be there until her killer is found. I know what you mean about never thinking about the crime from the victim's side. Do they feel anything when it's all over? I found out the hard way on more than one occasion and was deeply moved by their sorrow and trauma. I'll never forget the time I saw one young man sitting on a rock near the cove. I heard his weeping and thought he was alive. I called out to him, but he didn't respond. I understood only after I watched his body wash ashore. He looked down at his body with shock upon his face and wept more. I cried with him, and when I heard the story of how he died, it changed everything for me. I knew their stories were important and had to be told. One of the purposes in my life and of course loving my new husband. Peyton could see her cousin smile when she wrote the last sentence.

It also made me want to find the people who had murdered him and help Matt do just that any way I could.

I will be happy to work with you in telling the girls' stories. People want to know the whys. Strange as it may seem, they're not being ghoulish, but the details help in some way to grieve with those who are suffering the loss. It's a part of being human, I guess. We like to believe we can remain untouched by what happens to others as long as we are safe, but that's untrue. We still are impacted by others suffering. That's why people love the stories of the underdog beating the bully. They give us hope, and hope is powerful.

There are a lot of mean bullies in this world who think they can do what they want to whomever they want, but their victims get justice even if it seems to take a long time.

Oh, and before I forget, I'm finding out more about our family. Matt has gotten into the spirit of the search with me. We're having a blast. Pardon the pun. I can't wait to tell you all the juicy details of our family line. Aine O'Flaherty was a character like you. An amazing strong woman and I can see where your strength and endurance has come from. Love you more than words can tell. I'll chat more later because Matt is ready to eat breakfast, and you need to go to sleep.

Sleep sounded like a good plan. If only her mind would cooperate with her tired body. She closed her computer, turned off the light, and snuggled beneath the covers.

"Good night, Mary Elizabeth," Peyton whispered as she closed her eyes.

****

A dark mist swirled around her as she walked. The

place seemed familiar and yet unlike any place she had been before. Straining to see through the darkness, she walked with care, stumbling over obstacles in her path which she couldn't see. When she walked into a clear place, she focused, and what she saw shocked her. Bodies lined the path where she had traveled. She instantly knew they were victims in one way or another. She sat down on a fallen tree to ponder what she was seeing. Had all of these died by the hands of another? The atmosphere around her became charged, and spirits swooped around her from all directions, calling out *remember me* before flying away again.

Startled, Peyton awoke in a cold sweat with her blankets kicked off the side of the bed. The voices of desperation imprinted themselves on her heart. When she hid with her sister, she often pleaded for help and for someone—anyone—to remember them.

Grams often told them when they were young, "You may choose a path you want for your life, but often life's circumstances rise up and call to you. Your purpose is born in that moment." Maybe she had survived for no other reason but to give hope to others who shouldn't be forgotten.

She wrapped her arms around herself and exhaled. "Whew, girl, Blue Cove has done a number on you. All you wanted was to live a semi-quiet life in the Big Apple, enjoy the shows and restaurants. Purpose wasn't a big part of your vocabulary or job description when you thought of your future."

Peyton got up and tried to fix the bed she had made a mess of. She straightened the sheets and rearranged the blankets. As soon as the bed was semi neat again, she sat on the edge with her feet on the ground and tried to make sense of her dream. At least she thought it was a dream. At this point, she had no idea. Mixed in with all the elements she could remember were various colors. Yellow, reds, whites, and purples all whirling around the spirits as they flew in and around her. Someday soon she hoped she would understand what they all meant if anything. Three was way too early to get up. The best she could hope for after the dream was rest. She plumped the pillow behind her head, stretched out, and closed her eyes. Almost like magic, sleep claimed her in a dreamless slumber.

Chapter 17

Jaxon was in a hurry to get to Peyton's house. Little sleep for him if any, after he heard about the box with the envelope inside. His gut told him that Peyton's stalker was upping the ante from phone calls to getting more personal, which didn't bode well for her. Ignoring his phone calls might not have been a good idea, but he understood why she didn't want to hear the guy's messages a number of times a day.

He parked beside her car and walked the familiar path to her cottage. The door swung open as soon as he knocked. "Were you watching for me?" He smiled when he walked past her.

"I was. I want you to open this envelope. It's driving me up the wall not to rip the darn thing open myself." She waved the box in front of him.

"I'm curious myself. I need to do this by the book. There can be no envelope ripping." He chucked her chin. "Good morning by the way."

"Good morning right back at you." She ran her hand down his cheek. "Now open this please." She handed the envelope to Jaxon. "Pretty please."

"I thought about your little gift most of the night. I'm sure there's some form of intimidation involved, but no matter what, this represents a threat, and he's upping the ante."

"Why? I want to hear your theory."

"Because he has proved he knows where you live and that's bothersome to me." Jaxon slipped on a pair of gloves and carefully slit the envelope with a letter opening. "No powder or substance inside, that's a good beginning." Jaxon carefully unfolded the paper and began to read. "Damn."

"What does it say?" she asked, touching his arm. "Is there anything familiar with his handwriting, or is it printed from the computer?"

"Neither. It's cut and paste but gets the message across loud and clear. Do you want to read his words, or do you want me to read them?" he asked.

"I'll let you have the honor." She frowned.

Pretty green-eyed girl, you can run but you can't hide. I will track you wherever you go. We are in a strange dance at the moment, or you can call it a game if you please but a game of chance that I will win. I never lose. I have something you are searching for, but you'll have to hurry if you want her to live. Take my calls—both of your lives and others depend on it.

"We'll that's not a pleasant way to start a morning. I didn't want to hear he has the girl I saw. How does he know I'm searching for her? That's a bit freaky."

"Maybe he does or doesn't have her but knows you want to find her. He could have seen you talking to Kelsey at the college."

"You're right. That's probably what happened. Remember there was a car that followed us until we turned off on the exit into town." She pulled her jacket out of the closet and draped it over the back of the couch. "I'm not happy about him by any means. The fact that this guy knows where I live and that he'll be calling me every day isn't a pleasant thought. I guess that's what I get for taking the wrong path on my run. If only," she mused.

"You can't second-guess yourself. As you told me the day of the murder, she needed to be found. You had no way of knowing the guy would be watching."

"Joe reminded me of that fact the morning I reported the crime." She slipped her arm into the coat he held for her. "I may take this off later, but the temps are always chilly to me in the morning. Where are we headed?"

"I want to drop the box and envelope off at the field office after we eat breakfast. I found a great little place outside of Hanover. I had a quick lunch there one day, and I thought they had great food. The waitress told me that breakfast is their specialty, and they have the best homemade cinnamon rolls around."

"I like breakfast on Sunday mornings. I think it's because I have time to eat at my leisure. Eggs and bacon sound like a good way to start off the day to me. But I wouldn't mind sharing a cinnamon roll with you." She licked her lips and smiled.

He opened the door. "Let's go. I have a hankering for biscuits and gravy." He chuckled. "My dad always said that when something sounded good to him, and then he would pull his pants up above his waist and pat his small belly. All of us kids would laugh. He looked beyond funny to us, and of course, that's why he did the whole routine."

"That's how a family should be and how I want my family to be someday. Grandpa Max and Grams were wonderful, but we didn't get to see them much. I had friends when I was growing up who had normal families, and I loved to go to their homes whenever I could, which wasn't often."

“I never heard you say that before.” Jaxon glanced at her.

“What did I say?” She slipped into the passenger seat.

“That you want your family to be a happy one. At least that’s what I heard. I don’t remember you mentioning wanting a family,” he answered before he closed the car door.

She waited until he settled in behind the wheel. “Maybe I told you once or maybe not. I can’t remember.” She touched his arm. “I’ve only begun to believe that it’s a dream that could become reality. Until Blue Cove and you, I never considered the idea at all,” she told him. “You make me believe anything is possible. We’ll see.” She latched her seat belt.

“I’ll take that as a ray of hope and a challenge.” He smiled and started the engine. “A good one.”

“Why a challenge?” She fiddled with her purse strap.

“I need to prove to you that we can have a happy life together. I’m not promising we won’t face issues but only that we’ll go through them together and have some good times along the way.” He pulled out of the parking space and headed out to the main road in front of the inn.

****

Peyton glanced at Jaxon sitting across from her. She enjoyed being with him. In fact, she was almost ready to tell him how much. The small restaurant was the perfect place to spend a Sunday morning talking. After she took her last bite, she found enough room in her stomach for another cup of coffee and a shared cinnamon roll. Listening to this man who had touched her heart in so many ways, she learned a few new things about him when he talked about how he made his way to Phoenix after college and his somewhat humorous stint at the police academy. His forensics background and investigative ability eventually landed him a job as a homicide detective. He was the lead investigator on EJ Dawson's murder and as he talked about his death, her guy became misty-eyed. The highlight of his story for her was the day when they met at the murder scene.

He was thoughtful and caring. She loved how he tried to help his friend with his wayward son. Their friendship had survived a lot, including the murder and the good news that EJ had made some things right before he died, which was an element of comfort to his father.

No doubt about it Jaxon was a great guy. She couldn't believe how providential it was that they would meet. He restored her belief that there were still some good men out there.

After breakfast he wanted to go back to the field office, and she wanted to spend the rest of her afternoon researching Aine and what the colors in her dream meant. Before she told Jaxon what she had seen, she wanted to have some clue about what to tell him. He promised to tell her anything he found out. Plus, the kiss he gave her when he brought her home still had her fanning her face.

Peyton opened up her computer and moved through the texts of the ancient scrolls she had scanned. She still marveled about how Jessie came to possess them and what they taught about their ancestors. They were the reason their stalwart guardian still remained alert at the bookstore. The spirit was a welcome sight to them now. She and Jessie were from a long line of women who had various unusual gifts that others might find strange if not bizarre, but they were coming to terms with how they manifested in their lives. Hopefully Madison would have her own too. Only time would tell.

Chapter 18

Jaxon had a note of his own to contend with. The person who called him had more information than he had wanted to give him over the phone. The gist of the note's contents was Jaxon was in danger along with the other agents working the investigation. A fact that the young man enumerated many times in the call and his note. Jaxon read through the meat of the note again.

People will die. These folks mean business. They operate under a cloud of intimidation and have created a culture war at the college. A group that likes to call themselves the bros think it's fine to openly harass the girls on campus. They've gone as far as to walk up to a girl and tell her that her body is their choice to do with as they want. Girls are scared but are fighting back and standing their ground. They travel around the campus in groups especially at night. No one feels comfortable walking alone. It's not safe for them or for some guys. Many have joined an anti-dating group because they have no idea which guys are normal and which are part of the brothers or bros as they like to call themselves.

The girls' no-dates policy has created another problem. The guys are becoming angry and looking at ways to retaliate. As you can imagine, that makes for more recruits into their brothers group and is widening the gender gap on campus. Campus security needs help—this is bigger than them. I say that knowing anyone who tries to bring this group to justice is in the crosshairs. There are some powerful people involved.

Jaxon wondered who the powerful people were. Were they campus personnel or outsiders? Were they pulling the strings on campus or off? The underground agents working the case had uncovered more details about the online participants. Their cyber unit was tracking the encoded footprints. A list of active followers was being developed. He couldn't wait to see who was on the list after reading this note. Tomorrow he had another interview with the professor and his assistants. They were among the last people to see Emily Hart before she disappeared.

Jaxon also had an email from Frank Wagner telling him he could meet them on Wednesday with Carlene his tracking dog. Emily Hart stood a better chance of surviving with a bloodhound on the trail. He knew Peyton would be happy to hear the news if she hadn't already.

Jaxon's gut told him that the case was about to blow wide open. According to the note, someone on campus was recruiting girls who would suddenly disappear, and the problem had been an ongoing one for a while. What they recruited them for remained a question in his mind. He wished he could interview the author of the note or that he would call him again. He told Jaxon where the authorities might want to look for more evidence. The FBI needed to see if they had enough evidence for a search warrant. It would take more than an anonymous note.

Jaxon answered his phone. "Hey, Matt. I take it Jessie told you about Peyton finding a body."

"Yes, she did. How's the investigation going?" Matt

asked.

"Your department is on the job and working with us. The girl was kidnapped from the nearby college, and her body was left where Peyton found her. There were some unusual evidence that we are holding close to the chest. The stuff only the murderer would know." Jaxon filled him in on the details he knew to this point. "The suspect watched from the shadows because he's been stalking Peyton by phone, and he upped his game yesterday." Jaxon described the box and the envelope with the note inside. "I find the fact he knows where she lives troubling."

"Jess and I've been thinking about her stalker problem, and we've come up with a logical solution." Matt shared their idea with Jaxon. "What do you think?"

"I like the way you think. How you suggested I ask would be acceptable even to her. I know I would feel a heck of a lot better knowing she was in an undisclosed location. I know better than to suggest my place. She wouldn't be ready for that yet. The inn might also be a possibility, but I like your suggestion better."

"What are you looking at? Do you have a handle on the situation yet?"

"Here's what I've learned so far. We have two bodies and possibly more according to an anonymous tip. There's a missing girl and someone harassing Peyton. Add to that a strange online secret society, and the campus is a hotbed of drugs and criminal enterprise. Most of the students are there to learn, and many of them are afraid. It's hard to know at this point how deep and wide the problem is. The college president and dean seem to think it's only a few students involved, but to my way of thinking, they might have a larger issue on their hands."

"Any suspects?" Matt asked.

"Emily Hart's father, Larry, swears it is one of her college professors. He has a strong alibi that has held up to this point. We'll wait and see. I appreciate your call and tell Jessie that I said hi. I'll run your idea by Peyton later on. Enjoy your honeymoon. We're taking care of the business here."

"I told Jessie all was in good hands, but she was worried about her cousin."

"Before we hang up, Peyton asked Frank to bring his bloodhound with Maxwell's permission of course. Dylan also wants to let him try to track the killer."

"I agree on both ideas. I've seen Frank's dogs track, and they're amazing. What does Maxwell think about Peyton working with you?"

"Right now, he's okay with her working with me under the radar in an advisory capacity only. You understand," Jaxon stated. "The Reynolds girls' ability Maxwell knows well, even if he doesn't understand how. He's seen them at work in other cases with you. For now, she is working with me unofficially. I'm okay with that. I wouldn't want her to become an agent, which Maxwell wants. He's told me on a few occasions in meetings he would like to see her trained and working for the agency, but that's not what I want, and I don't think she wants that either. She loves working with her class."

"I understand. I wouldn't want that for Jessie either after my stint as an agent. We're talking too much stress on the agents and politics at the top involved. Because Jessie was the target on more than one occasion, I sent her through some defense training, and she got certified to handle and carry a gun. I issued a badge for her. Not as an officer but in an advisory capacity. I wanted her to be able to enter a crime scene. I think she might have carried the badge. A few times, she discharged her weapon when a suspect attacked Kip and maybe a few times more. I had to take the gun out of her death grip when she ran into Fred Anderson in our last case, but mostly she keeps the badge in her purse, and I have no idea where the gun is." Matt laughed. "She doesn't like carrying one. Come to think of it, she had the gun near enough to point the darn thing at Fred. I might need to talk to my lovely bride and get the skinny on where she keeps it."

"Something tells me Peyton would feel the same way. Although, the high kick she has is lethal enough." He smiled to himself. "I'm looking forward to seeing Frank's dog in action again. Time is crucial at this point. I'll let you know if we find Emily and whether Carlene has success in finding the murderer in Dylan's case."

"Sounds good. We'll talk again. I'm sure Jessie already knows I called. I can't hide anything from that woman." He chuckled. "I'm not bad when it comes to her trying to hide something from me either. I win a few but let her win more. I want to keep my wife happy. I'll tell her you said hi."

Jaxon thought Matt's idea was perfect for the problem plaguing him. He could only hope that Peyton would think the same way about it. He was still learning to maneuver around unchartered waters with her. He wasn't sure if she would appreciate him interfering in her life, but Jessie had suggested the perfect way to frame the idea to her, and Jaxon considered her suggestion a gift.

He picked up his phone. "Have you had any more

calls, from you know who?" he asked as soon as she answered the phone.

"No. I've actually had a nice quiet afternoon. I've been chatting with Jeremy and reading over the scrolls that I scanned."

"Speaking of those scrolls, your cousin made a suggestion that I think you might like and one that holds a lot of merit."

"Oh, yeah. What's that?" she asked.

"Since we know that our suspect seems to know where you live, she thought you should stay at their house. You can keep an eye on their place, water her plants, and be free to read the scrolls anytime you want. I thought it sounded like a solid plan. What do you think?"

"Like you said, the idea has merit. It would save me having to go after work each day and check on their place. Plus, me being able to read those scrolls anytime I want would be like Heaven. I want to discover all I can while they are still in our possession. We have no idea how long they will be since neither of us knows how this works."

"I can only imagine, but you seem more secure with all the strangeness you experience now than when we were in Arizona where it all began."

"True, our discoveries when we were in Ireland were a major turning point for us. When we learned we have sisters in time who had similar gifts, I made peace with mine. Now I want to learn all that I can about what I have."

"What more do you need to understand?" he asked.

"I had a dream last night, and I saw many things that I'm trying to understand. When I do, I'll tell you all about the dream. At least that's what I think it was."

"We'll meet up tomorrow night and compare notes if that works."

"Perfect. I'll be back at the school tomorrow and close the bookstore so Audrey can go home early. We could go to dinner, and then I could move over to the Parkers' house. Will that be soon enough? I'll pack my necessities tonight."

"Sounds perfect. I will meet you at the store at five and follow you to their place. We'll go to dinner from there. Have a good day tomorrow, babe."

"You do the same."

****

When Peyton disconnected the call, she went back to her computer and began her research once again. She remained sitting there until her back was stiff from being in one place for a long period of time. Her stomach grumbled, reminding her she hadn't eaten since breakfast. She stood, stretched, and walked toward the kitchen in search of food. She had more than enough ideas to push around in her mind for a few hours.

She popped a bagel into the toaster and pulled the cream cheese out of the fridge. Next, she put on the kettle for a cup of hot tea. What she wanted was to give her brain a break with some mindless TV. Preferably a rom-con. The kind of movie with a happily-ever-after ending. She might be serious to those who didn't know her well, but deep down inside she was a hopeless romantic who wanted to believe true love existed and each person could make their world a better place. But if she wanted to be a part of the change for good, she had to do her part to make her small world better.

Jaxon was having a positive effect on her. Peyton

spread cream cheese on her bagel and decided to opt for strawberry preserves on top. Pouring hot water over her tea bag, she carried her food into the living room. Once she found the perfect movie, she nibbled, sipped, and sighed her way to relaxation. The leading man wasn't nearly as handsome or swoon worthy as her guy. It's time to do something about living out her own romance movie.

She topped off her evening with a warm bubble bath. Relishing in the liquid warmth, she sank beneath the bubbles and let her mind wander through the events of the day. Yes, Jessie's and Matt's place seemed like the perfect solution to her. Not only were the ancient scrolls calling to her, but Jessie's beautiful new office was as well. Matt and Jaxon worked on the space, and they did a beautiful job. She closed her eyes and savored the warm watery cocoon for a moment more. From there with a few steps in between and scented lotion which made her smell like vanilla, she stretched out under her cozy blanket and was ready for sleep.

Chapter 19

After dealing with exuberant, active children all morning, Peyton walked out of the school and took a deep breath. The temps were warm for this time of year, but she wouldn't complain. She lifted her face toward the sun, and its warmth caressed her skin. "Glorious." She turned around in a circle. "I need this."

Audrey had texted her this morning and told her not to worry about coming to the store. The day had been a quiet one, and she could handle the closing alone. Peyton wouldn't argue—she could use some downtime. Whenever she did a music day with her class and the rhythmic instruments, her ears could use a moment of silence. A smile lit her face. She loved how her special kids, as she liked to think about them, could bang, clang, and shake those instruments in such abandonment that in no way resembled the song playing on the recorder. Did they care? No, they were happy playing their own version of the melody. The results were chaotic but created happy, musical moments. The joy they found made every bang on the drum and clang of the cymbals worth the noise. But between the music and cleaning up colorful dough off desks and the floor from art projects gone awry, she was ready to get away.

She started her car and turned her radio on to her favorite station. Her ears needed to hear a few sounds that actually went together. Before she drove out of Blue

Cove, she sent a text to Jaxon and told him she was going for a drive but would meet him at the bookstore at five like they had planned. With no destination in mind, she headed toward one of the back roads leading out of town. She hoped Mary Elizabeth was up for a ride too. She glanced in her mirror to see her sitting there.

The fall foliage still vibrant in color had her pulling over not many miles out of town to snap a few photos. The leaves danced in a mesmerizing fashion in the light breeze, and sunlight shimmered back and forth with the sway of the branches. Bright blue skies, white fluffy clouds, and the colors around her were a visual delight.

How difficult it must be for a person who was color-blind not to see the beauty around them. New glasses were allowing some people to be introduced to the colorful world, and she found that fascinating. How did the idea of seeing colors and premonitions work for her? A question she needed to research further since she had been witnessing their purpose in a whole new way.

When she pulled onto the shoulder her ringing phone startled her. "This is Peyton."

"Are you busy, or do you have time to talk?" Madison's cheery voice asked.

"I always have time for you, sis. What's up?" Peyton kept her eyes on a car that drove past her.

"Are you working at the bookstore?"

"No. Audrey didn't need me to come in today, so I went for a drive."

"I hope you're talking hands free," Madison said.

"I'm using no hands and not driving at all. I parked for a few minutes to take some snapshots."

"I wanted to say I'm sorry for how I left last week. I know you worry about me, and I appreciate that you care. I've always wanted to see if I can make it on my own, and the answer is yes. I can."

"I could have told you that. You're one intelligent and strong woman. And, sis, I'm sorry too. I want you to live closer. I realized after you left that I was the one who moved farther away, not you. I love this town, but I know you're where you're supposed to be, doing the work you're meant to do."

"It doesn't mean forever but at least for now. Speaking of work, we've had a lot of gunshot emergencies coming in. It seems like everyone is on edge. The damage these new guns can do to the human body is unbelievable."

"I know. I've seen firsthand their destruction." Peyton wanted to move. She got in and started the car, then put her phone on speaker. "Guess what happened to me right before you left? You know when I went out for my run."

"I have no idea."

Peyton told her about finding the body and what she knew at the moment. She filled in details but left out the fact she was being harassed by the suspected murderer. "It's been an interesting few days. You know how it is, sis—life is a roller coaster ride. Everyone struggles with the ups and downs. All we can do is our best."

"I hear you. I keep trying," Madison said.

"Are you safe working in the ER? Has the fighting on the streets erupted inside?" Peyton asked as she made a U-turn.

"We have a strong security presence at the hospital especially in the ER. If we have a shooting victim, they make sure there are no weapons hidden on the victim when they come in or any of their visitors."

"It's sad how cheap life seems to some of these folks, and they think nothing of shooting someone to prove how tough they are. I understand the anger. Our childhood wasn't easy, but I never wanted to hurt anyone else," Peyton told her.

"As a matter of fact, that's the reason I went into the field I'm in. I wanted to do the opposite and help people, and so did you."

"We're no saints, you and I, but we still manage to see good in our world." Peyton slowed down to make the turn back into Blue Cove.

"At least we'll see each other at Thanksgiving, and I'm looking forward to the day," Madison said. "The idea of someone else cooking sounds appealing to me. I'm sick of my own. I mean how many times can you eat canned soup?" She giggled.

"I'm excited for the holidays. Jessie and Matt will be back, and Jaxon's family decided to join us. You'll love them. They are such a fun family. They are everything I used to dream of when I thought of family."

"We only have a couple of weeks, and I'm looking forward to getting out of the city for a couple of days again. After all the gunshot victims coming into the ER, I could use another break soon."

"Of course, you'll be staying with me. Stay safe, sis." Peyton smiled as she disconnected the call and turned onto Main Street. Maybe she would look for a new book while she waited for Jaxon to arrive. She waved at Audrey and tipped her head to the warrior ghost who remained in his usual place standing watch over her cousin's store. She couldn't help wondering if he remained there when they were gone at night. In her mind she could picture him sitting in one of the comfy wingback chairs with his feet up. With leisure time he could grab a book and catch up on life in a different century. Peyton smiled as she walked to the bookshelf to search for her new read.

"Did you have nice afternoon?" Audrey asked as soon as the customer left.

"Yes, thank you. Time alone was exactly what I needed." She pulled one of the books from the shelf. "I love my students, but some days their energy level is on a whole other level than mine." She laughed. "If I'm having even a slightly off day, those kiddos can eat me for lunch. They keep me on my toes." She took three books up to the counter to pay.

"I just finished this one." Audrey rang up the book. "I found the story intense, but I loved the book. I liked the way the author writes, and the pace kept me flipping through the pages. I read the darn thing fast and had to find another book she had written. I need this job to pay for my reading habit." She placed Peyton's books into the bag. "I think I see that handsome guy of yours getting out of his car. Have a nice evening. I'll take care of closing."

"Thanks. I'll be here tomorrow." Peyton met Jaxon at the door. "I'm ready."

"I'll follow you to Matt's, and we'll go from there."

"Sounds good." Peyton slid behind the wheel and started her car. She would see this as a mini adventure at her cousin's place. Just her, a few ancient scrolls, and time to study them seemed perfect.

She pulled into the driveway beside Matt's pickup. His pride and joy. He restored the truck with the help of his younger brother. Even Jaxon, who loved his sports car, drooled over the truck. Matt loved Jessie's restored sixty-five cherry-red ride too. She couldn't see what they saw in the restored old cars. Personally, she liked the comfort of the new. Peyton's blue sporty model that Jaxon helped her pick out was perfect for her.

Jaxon opened her car door. "Let's get you settled, and then we'll go to dinner." He went in the house first and deactivated the alarm. "Matt said the guest room is all yours until we catch the suspect harassing you."

"I appreciate my cousin letting me stay here. I'll admit I was feeling scared when I thought of the man knowing my address. I can take care of myself, but this guy sounds like a strange fella to me. The way he posed Mary Elizabeth's body with the white rose in her hand is like in his sick mind he was being respectful and kind to her. It's my theory at the moment."

"A possibility and something to consider. He could be a serial killer operating under the cover of all the crime going on at the college."

"I guess we'll know soon enough." Peyton placed her suitcase and overnight bag in one of the guest rooms. "Now that we're here, why don't we order takeout from Anthony's? This is a bigger place than what I'm used to," she told Jaxon when she walked into the living room.

"I wouldn't mind staying in. I'll look up the menu, and you can tell me what you want." Jaxon pulled up the menu on his phone. "Instead of pizza let's do this one." He pointed to a lasagna dinner for two. "The meal includes salad and bread. Does that look good to you?"

"Works for me." She sat on the couch beside him while he called in the order.

****

After a great dinner Peyton let Jaxon listen to another phone message. She was getting tired of hearing from the man. This message was more threatening, which had shaken her when she listened to the voicemail earlier. The threat included his normal warnings of saving others by doing what he tells her to do, but this one also included a death threat to those she loved if she didn't. The list included her grandmother, her friend Destiny, and Jaxon.

"I agree this guy is stepping up his rhetoric." He placed his arm around her shoulders and pulled her tight.

"Will you be okay here alone?"

"Yes, I'll set the alarm and make sure the doors and windows are locked up tight." She leaned her head against his shoulder. "You should go home, you have work tomorrow, and so do I. You can hardly hold your eyes open." She stood and pulled him up beside her. After she kissed him, she walked with him to the door.

"Don't forget to lock up. Here's the alarm code." He handed her a piece of paper. " He pulled her into his arms for another kiss. He deepened it the minute he felt her response. "I should definitely go, or I won't want to."

She watched him until his car pulled out of the driveway. She shut the door, locking it as she touched the numbers on the alarm keypad. She didn't have the heart to tell him she already knew the code because she checked on their house every few days. He was nothing if not endearing. She got ready for bed and pulled out the scrolls from the drawer in Jessie's office. She had waited for this moment all day. Unwrapping the scrolls carefully, she looked for Aine's name and began to read what she could. Searching Gaelic words and translating them on a new app she had purchased for her phone and computer. A slow process but she had several days before her cousin would be back from her honeymoon, and she would make good use of the time.

Aine was married and had four children who had lived. From the way she read the statement, she must have had other children who died at birth or as babies. Peyton couldn't imagine bearing children in the time in which Aine lived. Life was tenuous and vulnerable at best. One group conquered another over the strangest reasons. Times might have changed for the better somewhat, but wars were still fought over the craziest reasons. She placed the scrolls back into their safe place and plugged her fairy night-light into a socket where she could easily see her shining. There was no way she would leave home without her. Climbing into bed, she stretched out and pulled the covers up to her chin. She wondered about the colors Aine had seen and how they impacted her actions.

Chapter 20

Jaxon closed the file he was studying, stretched his arms over his head, and yawned. Maneuvering Peyton into staying at Matt's was much easier than he thought it would be. He could only hope he had made the right decision. After he read the stalker's message, he agreed the guy's threats had intensified. Knowing Peyton, her greatest worry wouldn't be her own safety but that of Sadie, her sister, and others including himself. He would need to keep on eye on her.

He texted her to send him a copy of the text in the morning. He would like to have eyes on her until the guy was caught. Maxwell would have to approve the request or Dylan from his end. He would make his appeal to his superiors tomorrow.

The sound of his morning alarm brought him no pleasure after what seemed like a short night with little sleep. Jaxon jumped into the shower and made short work of his morning routine. He needed coffee, and he would stop by Joe's on his way out of town. Reaching for his jacket, he grabbed the file from the counter and locked the door as he rushed out to his car. He hit the button lifting the garage door and threw his briefcase into the backseat. As he reached for the door handle to open the driver's side, he heard a sound he knew all too well and dove to the ground, pulling his gun from his shoulder holster.

"Damn, that could have been my head." He crawled forward, hoping to get an idea where the shooter was. He noticed a car idling in front of his house. A gun pointed in his direction from out of an open window. Jaxon rolled to his right and fired off a shot as a bullet whizzed by his body and narrowly missing him but hitting the open car door—sending metal and parts of the door scattering in an explosive manner. At least it wasn't his sports car. This one belonged to the agency. One of his dumber thoughts in the last few seconds. His car could be repaired easier than he could. He fired another warning round toward the car. A deep voice hurled expletive-laced threats out the window before the car sped off. Once Jaxon stood up, he pulled his phone out and dialed the police station.

"Dylan," Jaxon said. "Hey, I had someone shooting at my place. You're the local authority, and I wanted to report to you first before I call Maxwell at the agency."

"Are you okay?" Dylan asked. "I'll send my team right over."

"I'm okay, but there's a couple of bullets your team might want to have a look at. I'll hang around until they get here."

"A team is on their way. We'll talk later."

Jaxon called Tom Maxwell. "Hey, Tom, I'll be late getting there this morning." He explained what happened earlier. "Dylan is sending a team over, and I need to wait until they get here and finish up."

"Any ideas who?" Tom asked.

"I'm sure the shooting has to do with the investigation we're working on. I got a note from the guy who called the other day, which I'll show you when I get into the office. Peyton got another message too. This one contained more threats and included me."

"Robert Craft, one of the undercover agents on the investigation, had a visitor at his house today too. He's being treated at the hospital this morning. The bullet grazed his upper arm and narrowly missed one of his kids. He was taking them to school before heading to work."

"Will he be okay?" Jaxon asked.

"He will be fine, but his family doesn't want to stay in the house. His kids are scared, and so is wife. Hell, I don't blame them. I have a team at his house."

"I was going to request protection for Peyton," he told Tom. "I know we're spread thin right now, and if our agency doesn't have the manpower, Dylan might be able to assign someone."

"I'll call and talk with Dylan. I'm sure we can work something out between the two departments. How's Peyton handling the continued harassment?"

"She's staying at the Parkers' while they're on their honeymoon. Matt suggested the idea after she received the box in the mail. Right now, she's good, but with the added threat to her grandmother and sister, she's not happy."

"I can understand. We'll talk more when you get here."

"The fact that two of us were shot at and Frank and his bloodhound is coming this week to look for Emily Hart, we might be hitting a few nerves."

"You're right. We might need to put all of our agents working this case on high alert."

"Sounds like a good idea to me, sir. I need to run, and Dylan's team just arrived. I'll be there as soon as they are done here."

Jaxon greeted Kip and Gary when they arrived followed by Evan to take pictures.

"Sounds like you had a fun morning. I hope you're not trying to follow in Matt's footsteps with shooters coming to town." Kip bent down to get a closer look at the bullet lodged in the door.

"I'd rather not make a habit of dodging bullets. I'll leave you to do your work. I need to change." He swiped at the dirt on his shirt and the side of his pants. "Concrete diving is rough on the clothes."

When he returned to the garage, Jaxon learned they had found shell casings out in the street near where the car had been idling. Kip had dug out the bullet lodged in the door leading into the house. Another bullet was removed that had burrowed into the wall when it ricocheted off the car door.

"With any luck we might be able to lift a fingerprint off this." Kip raised the evidence bag in front of Jaxon's face. "We're done here, so we'll be on our way. I'm sure you'll hear from Dylan at some point."

"I'm sure I will. I need to get to work myself. I'll put in a call to my insurance company on my way. Another item to stick on my agenda for today."

****

Peyton's students were angels today. Always a nice turn of events for her. No yelling, screaming, or fighting. They must have all been tired. Even story hour went smoothly with all the kids being attentive. She had to admit this school day was a pleasant one, which worked for her. Edgy herself she was happy her classroom was calm. Her phone buzzed too many times during class. Each one irritated Peyton until she was in no mood to check her voicemails. Of course, she would if Grams or someone else she knew left her a message. Her phone already blocked unknown numbers as spam, but he still somehow found a way to leave a message anyway.

The bookstore and the mystery book club was just what the doctor ordered for her afternoon. She always loved when she got to work at the store when the group met. Besides reading great books, they knew all the local gossip. Those tidbits got mingled into their lively discussions on their current book.

Peyton rushed to her car and headed to Idle Time Books. If anything could help her forget the crazy threats, some lively, gossipy discussion could. The most troubling part of all this was she knew the guy's voice but had no idea of his appearance. He could come into the store, and she would never know he was there. But then again maybe she would. If she didn't sense his presence, their resident ghost surely would.

She pulled into the parking space at the back of the store, unlocked the door, entered, and turned the lock again. "Hi, Audrey," she said, walking into the front of the store. "Take a break and have lunch if you need to. I'll cover the store."

"Thanks, I could use something to eat. The book club should be here soon, and you know how busy the store gets when they are here. Can I get you something?"

"No, thanks. I brought my lunch." Peyton pulled out her phone. She didn't have to listen to anything at the moment, but she would check her text messages. She had already sent Jaxon what he wanted and took time to answer Destiny's text. *—We are looking forward to having dinner with you soon. I've missed hanging out with you—*

Peyton had two voicemails from the unknown

caller. Duh, he wasn't unknown but a nuisance to be sure. She refused to listen or read one word from him. "You won't ruin my day," she muttered.

"Who are you talking to, dear?" Reba said as she walked from the coffee shop with Grams following behind her.

"Hi. What are you two up to?" Peyton slipped her phone back into her purse.

"We had a delicious lunch and a nice chat. Rumor has it that our Molly is getting close to having her baby. I for one can't wait to see the little fella."

"We didn't come empty-handed." Sadie hugged her granddaughter. "We have treats and wanted to spend some time with you."

"Sounds good. Let's sit in the comfy chairs with the small table. The book club should be here soon, and they take up the big table." Peyton pulled the three chairs closer together so they could talk and hear one another.

"I love that group. They get into, shall we say, interesting discussions if not heated." Reba draped her sweater over the back of the chair before she sat down. "I swear this has been the longest stretch of mild November weather that I can remember. My joints are happy."

"You won't hear me complain either." Grams placed her napkin on her lap. "The dear boy next door promised to bring us our tea when he gets a chance. They are swamped over there."

"You still didn't answer my question," Reba told her.

"I'm sorry. I was talking to myself. I have someone who is leaving me harassing messages, and I've chosen to ignore them. I'm having such a nice day."

"Do you think that's wise?" her grandmother asked.

"Jaxon knows about the messages—he's heard them all. I'll let him listen to these later."

"I'm happy to hear you say that you've told him, because you girls can be too stubborn. But Jaxon's a good young man, and he'll know what to do."

"Yes, he will."

Reba thanked the young man who brought in their tea, sticking a nice tip in his hand. "Ladies, shall we get down to business before the store is filled with noise?" She grabbed Peyton's hand. "You had a dream again, haven't you?"

"Yes, but this one seemed different. I wouldn't call it a premonition. I'm used to having those, but each dream seems to be teaching me more about my gift. Grams, you know how I talked about colors when I was growing up."

"Your grandpa used to tell me all the time you would tell him what you saw. You told him once your dad looked a lot like a thundercloud. He used to be fascinated by you girls. He thought you were wise beyond your years. I always knew you were too."

"What are the dreams teaching you?" Reba asked.

"All the colors have their own unique meaning, and when I see them surround a person, they are telling me something about that person. This way I know when I can relax or be concerned. I can also sense the same without the colors, but colors seem to get my attention."

"What do the different colors mean to you?" Grams asked.

"One example is when Sally first saw the fairy, she described a bright white light. White speaks to me of virtue and purity. When the Indian legends described a black wolf, it was always associated with fear, death, or negative feelings. Do you remember when I talked about the *Black Wolf* when we were investigating the Native American children killed in the boarding schools?"

"I remember. I'll be interested to hear more about what you are learning. I hear the ladies coming in for their meeting. I know you're about to get busy. Sadie and I will sit here and enjoy the atmosphere." Reba took a sip of her tea.

Peyton rang up a customer and placed her books into the bag. "Thank you."

"Oh, you're welcome. I'll be back. I love to read. Is this place always filled with people like this?" The woman picked out a bookmark and stuck it into the bag.

"The group at the table is a book club. We always enjoy when they come in each month. They are a fun group. Do you read mysteries?"

"I do. I'm new in town, and I might like to be a part of a group like this."

"Why don't I introduce you, and you can talk to them? What is your name?"

"Julie Sanford." The woman placed her card back into her wallet.

After she introduced Julie the ladies welcomed her into their group and told her the title of the book they were reading. The sight of people enjoying each other was a happy one. This was why her cousin bought the store to begin with.

Sadie and Grams were enjoying a quiet conversation. She should be thrilled by what was happening around her. Audrey was getting into the spirit of the day. Yet, she sensed a dark foreboding. When she glanced through the doors into Joe's, there was thick gray haze gathering.

Someone was in the coffee shop who was up to no good. Could her stalker be there watching her? The thought sent shivers slithering down her arms. She rubbed her hands together and reached for her sweater to ward off the chill. Not that a sweater would do much good against a supernatural chill. She glanced at the warrior standing guard. He wasn't in his usual place. He was on the move. He now stood in front of the open doors into Joe's with his sword drawn.

Goodness, if the mystery book club knew what took place in this store every time they were here, they might want to find a new place to meet. A testament to the fact that not everyone knew what went on in the invisible world around them. Which was likely a good thing. There were times she wished she didn't.

****

His lunch bore the resemblance of gravel in his mouth. He had no idea why but watching her made him sick. Warning bells went off inside his head. She wasn't what she appeared to be. He rarely was rattled by anything. Heck, he had murdered, and their deaths were a game to him. Did she know he was watching her? He could almost swear she did. She had looked him in the eye more than once in the past ten minutes. She seemed to look through him to his very soul. He shuddered. *Get out of here before you are discovered*, his mind screamed at him. He decided for once to listen. Grabbing his jacket, he slipped out of the coffee shop and took the darkness that surrounded him with his exit. His power didn't seem to faze her.

Chapter 21

The first opportunity he got, Jaxon called Peyton. She'd been in his thoughts all afternoon. Of course, thinking about her was one of his favorite pastimes. But this was different, which usually meant something was up.

When she didn't answer her cell phone, he tried the store's number. "Can I talk to Peyton?" he asked. "This is Jaxon."

"Just a minute, I'll get her," Audrey said.

"This is Peyton. How can I help you?"

"The best way is to tell me that you're okay and then say you'll go to dinner with me."

"I'm okay. It's been another unique day. Dinner with you sounds like the perfect way to put a period on an unusual experience even for me."

"What's all the noise in the background?" He cleared his desk and stuffed a file into his briefcase.

"The book club ladies are chattering before they leave to go home. When they meet, the day goes by quickly. It's a darn good thing they can't see what goes on in this store." She chuckled.

"I can't wait to hear what brought that on. I'll pick you up at Matt's around five thirty. I can't wait to tell you about my morning too. It started off with a bang."

"Depending on the bang, a day could go either way. See you soon. Be careful, Jaxon. I wouldn't want anything to happen to you."

"You do the same, babe."

Jaxon couldn't wait to hear what Peyton thought was noteworthy in her day. He almost hated to add to the stress by telling her about his morning. Love was a two-way street, and he needed her to be aware. Dylan would assign someone to watch Matt's house starting tonight and watch her during the day without an interruption to her activities. Hell, he hated that she was facing another threat. She may as well be an agent, but there was no way he would encourage Peyton in the pursuit.

"Hey, Jaxon." Tom walked into the room. "We are going to meet with the undercover agents by telephone in my office in a few minutes. I want you in there to hear what's going on. They believe their cover is broken. They will bring us up to speed on what they've collected to this point. We'll plan where this investigation is going next." Tom turned and walked away.

Jaxon followed him back to his office. He wondered if there might have been a breach in their cover. The fact that an agent was shot was proof positive someone knew who a few of them were. If that be the case, it wouldn't be long until all of the team's identities would be known. Jaxon wasn't undercover, but others had done the tough, hard work to get on the inside with students. To win their trust and become a part of the group was never an easy feat. A breach could mess up all their groundwork.

After the meeting with Maxwell, all the agents working the investigation, including him, had many questions and a heightened sense of concern. Maxwell was considering changes to protect the agents without compromising the investigation. They were close to getting to sources that could blow the case open. One of the agents on the inside told them today there were former students, graduate students, and a few professors and a couple of politicians in the mix. If they could maintain their cover for a few more days, they should have enough evidence for indictments. Robert Craft would be sidelined.

Jaxon had a lot to think about on his drive back to Blue Cove. If he had his druthers, he would keep Peyton as far away from the college and the investigation as he could. But she was pulled into the case when she came across that body.

He turned off the highway and intended to go straight to Matt's, but since he didn't need to meet Peyton for thirty minutes, he decided to stop off at the PD and see Dylan.

"Hey, Jaxon, what are you doing here?" Kip asked.

"I thought I would check in with Dylan to see if he has any news for me about the shooter this morning."

"He's in his office, and I'm off duty until tomorrow. See you around."

"Enjoy your night off." Jaxon walked past him toward Dylan's office.

After Jaxon knocked on the open door, he asked, "You've got a minute to talk?"

"Sure, come in." Dylan closed the file he was looking over. "What's up?"

"Did you learn any more about the shooting this morning?" Jaxon sat.

"Only that I think the guy means business. I'm not sure if Peyton will approve, but Matt agrees that you should stay at his house too. That way we can keep an eye on both of you at the same time. Besides, don't you have to wait for the insurance company to get back to begin the repairs on your car and garage?"

"I put in my claim and hope to hear from them soon. And if I promise to behave, I'm sure she will be fine. I mean we both are dealing with threats to our lives. Man, bro, we are living in crazy times. I was never threatened like this as a homicide detective in Arizona."

Dylan chuckled. "No offense, man, it's the company you keep. The Reynolds girls attract these guys like magnets."

"I'm beginning to understand how true that is. Wouldn't you know I'd have to fall for the one girl who has a crazy family history. I guess you can't choose your ancestors. I don't know what the women in their family were like, but I sure do like this modern version. She's a keeper as far as I'm concerned." Jaxon stood. "Speaking of my defiant angel, I'm meeting her in a few minutes. I'll run your idea by her. We'll see how it goes."

"Text me and let me know. We're running ballistics, and I hope to have more answers for you. Of course, we are working with Maxwell on the shooting. We should know soon if we are dealing with one shooter or two."

"Thanks, Dylan, I appreciate it."

"I'll walk with you. Katie has dinner waiting for me." Dylan grabbed the file from his desk.

Jaxon talked with him on the way out to the car. Telling him what he could about their investigation at the college. He asked Dylan questions about the Mary Elizabeth murder case. No suspect seemed to be the only major answer they had, and the investigation was ongoing.

He drove to Matt's house with plenty of time to think. He knew he needed to get back to the college and ask questions. He was missing something. Peyton had mentioned Kelsey was afraid, and the guy who called him was too. Intimidation seemed to play a big part in how the crimes had flown under the radar for so long. Bullies seemed to be around in every age bracket. Some simply had a bigger bully pulpit than others.

****

Peyton left the store with enough time to get back to the house and freshen up. Katie called her with the news that Jaxon had a close call this morning. Why hadn't he told her when he called earlier? He liked to protect her from the extra stress…maybe. But he needed to understand this wasn't the big city and any news travels fast through the grapevine in a small town. Something she learned early on when she first moved here. She would rather hear what happened from him than anyone else. She ran the brush through her hair and put on her favorite lip gloss. Reaching for her sweater, she went into the living room to watch for Jaxon's car.

She would never have believed that Blue Cove, such a lovely idyllic town, could produce all the troubles she had seen since moving here. You couldn't ask for a more beautiful location, nicer people, or a perfect place to visit or live. The unseen activities were the issues, but that was true in any town. The trouble didn't seem to be uncovered until Jessie moved to town, and her arrival hadn't helped either. She doubled the problem.

Peyton walked out the door, turning the lock behind her when Jaxon pulled into the driveway. She slid into the passenger seat before he could get out to open her door.

"You know, I like to open the door for you." He glanced at her.

"Yeah, I know. I thought I would save you the

trouble." She smiled. "Hi to you too by the way."

"No trouble at all. My mama taught me you always open the door for the girl. You wouldn't want me to disappoint her, now would you?"

"Of course, not. But I think she'd understand when I told her I was trying to keep you from being a target to get shot at again." She pursed her lips.

"Oh, you heard about my morning."

"Yes. You need to remember this is a small town and news travels fast. I would rather have heard the news from you, instead of Katie, who obviously heard the story from Dylan. Firsthand is always better than a second-hand account. You know straight from the horse's mouth." She latched her seat belt.

"Okay, I hear you. I'll try to remember to tell you before anyone else does." Jaxon told her about his morning and the other agent who was grazed by a bullet that almost hit his child.

"I appreciate you telling me. You know I worry about you the same way you do me."

"Nice to know."

"I'm learning how to do this whole caring thing. This town has taught me a lot about the importance of having the support of people who love you. That's a big deal." She took his hand in hers.

"Not always easy for any of us to do when we've seen the dark side of people," Jaxon said.

"Being closed off from people was easy for me."

"I guess that's something we all do."

"Yeah, I suppose you're right. The whole caring idea made me feel vulnerable, which I didn't like. On the other hand, life without the love and support of others is a lonely way to live."

"I remember telling you the same thing. Working all the time kept me from building any decent relationships. That was what drew me back to living in the east to be closer to home and family," Jaxon told her.

"Where are we headed?" She leaned her head back against the headrest.

"My surprise. Relax, sweetheart, we'll be there in a few minutes."

Chapter 22

Jaxon pulled into an open parking space. He was ready for a nice uncomplicated dinner, and the resort was quiet this time of year. A perfect spot to run Dylan's idea by her. He took her hand and walked with her toward the restaurant. Aware of his surroundings, the warning his boss gave him earlier echoed in his mind. *"Watch your back. Until we arrest a suspect, you and Peyton are targets. We have no idea what we're looking at."*

His shoulders relaxed the minute they walked through the door in one piece, and the host walked them to their table. From their table they could watch the lights shimmering off the water in the cove and view the boats bobbing with the soft ripple of the waves. An idyllic sight until a larger boat came in and the water movement picked up in intensity. Still, for Jaxon the sight gave him a sense of peace.

"I can watch the ever-changing scenes in the cove all day." She sighed. "The lights on the water tonight are mesmerizing."

"I can relate." He gestured with his hand. "This is what I missed most about living in Arizona. I love the ocean and the charm of the seaside towns."

"After my visit to the Phoenix area during a summer heat wave, I knew the desert wasn't for me. The heat was too intense for my liking. Tombstone, Boot Hill, and the Superstition Mountains were interesting places, but I'm a Midwest girl myself but also love the charm of New England." Peyton thanked the waiter who placed her dinner in front of her.

"Tell me about your day." Jaxon took a bite of his salmon. "I think you described it as unique."

"Before I tell you, do you mind if I change the subject for a minute?" she asked.

"Be my guest. I'm sure whatever you have to say is important."

"I've been fascinated by the charms found on each of the girls' roses. In the list you gave me, the colors of the roses changed but the charms or talismans were the same. Why use a symbol for life on a victim you murdered? The idea has me trying to get inside the mind of the murderer. The concept is strange but has me wondering if in his mind he thinks he's freeing them to live somehow."

"Wow. I love how your mind works. A detail only a criminal profiler might think about." He finished the last bite of his salmon. "What else about this case has piqued your interest?"

"With my history, the fact that the charm is a Celtic symbol for the circle of life leaves more questions in my mind than answers. I doubt that the symbol's origin is a coincidence. He must have some ties to Ireland. All these pieces fit together and will make a complete picture in time. I'll keep thinking about how, and I'm sure I'll figure out why soon."

"Speaking of pieces, after the morning Dylan made a suggestion today that I think we should consider." He reached for her hand.

"I was wondering when you were going to ask me. Katie mentioned Dylan thought his job would be easier if we both stayed at Matt's house. Before you say anything else, I know you will behave yourself because I'd make you." She smiled sweetly at him.

"I'm sure you would." He chuckled.

"Do you need to stop at your house for anything?"

"I did earlier, hoping you would understand." He grinned at her.

"I don't want to make their job harder, and truthfully, I'll feel safer with you close by if I need you. Or I could also say I'll be close by if you need to be rescued too."

"As far as I'm concerned, I could do a lot worse than having you rescue me." He stood and pulled out her chair. "Let's go."

When they got to the Parkers', she let him listen to her two voicemails. For the moment they were more of the same. At least he hadn't escalated his rhetoric. To Jaxon's way of thinking, the guy would figure out soon that Peyton wasn't at her house.

"Do you mind if I watch some TV?" He held up the remote.

"Not at all. I want to spend time working on the scrolls. I'll see you in the morning. Thanks for a nice dinner." Peyton left the room.

Dang, he wasn't fast enough to give her a good-night kiss. The fact they would be in close quarters for a few days, it was probably better he hadn't. At any other time, he would have simply jumped up and kissed her. Why was he sitting in this damn chair, second-guessing himself? He flipped through the stations until he found something to get lost in.

****

When Peyton opened her email, she saw a note from

Jessie. Clicking on it, she began to read.

Hey, Peyton. I have a few minutes to write while Matt is out getting directions and ideas from the owner of the inn where we are staying. The two of them connected at dinner last night, and Matt loved all the stories the guy was telling us. One story that captured both of our imaginations is a tour of twenty towns that represent portals to Ireland's magical past. Matt is trying to work a driving tour out with this guy. In Irish mythology there is an Otherworld. Tir nAill which means the other land. As you can imagine after learning about the thin places, this caught my interest big-time. Our storyteller explained the Otherworld is the world beyond the real human experience. The idea is woven into Irish myth and spirituality. One idea that got my interest was he said it is not an afterlife or a land of punishment but rather a vibrant space of magic where one can experience transformation. It is believed to exist in tandem with the natural world. Like the idea of an invisible world that overlaps with our visible world and interacts with it. I hope you see where I'm going. I'm so excited to visit some of these places. He said the idea is the connection between the seen and the unseen and the boundaries between the worlds are fluid. Now, I understand why those paintings carried such powerful experiences for me. Can you understand what this might mean for us? The door in the woods, the fairies, and all the imagery we have come to understand. Our guardian and artifacts for heaven's sake. I will tell you if I experience anything. We aren't strange; we are understanding our Irish ancestors. I'll write again soon. Have a nice rest, and when you get a chance, visit my office and please look at the painting behind my desk.

Love you, cousin.

Jessie's enthusiasm was contagious, and Peyton caught her passion. Peyton typed the words *Irish Otherworld* into her search bar, and a whole world began to open up to her. She had caught the fervor of what research could teach her. She was keen to learn more about their heritage because every time she did, she learned more about herself. Knowledge was freeing. She came from a long line of strong women. Jessie called them her sisters in time, and Peyton related to them the same way. "What would they call Mary?" she mused as she glanced at her ghostly guest.

Reading through a grouping of short articles, she found herself following along the storyline with photos of the ten Irish wonders. This was the perfect way to relax and de-stress after a tense day. When she finally glanced at the clock, she reluctantly closed her computer and got ready for bed.

They had one more day before Frank arrived with his dog, and she wanted to find Emily Hart—hopefully alive. The fact she hadn't seen or heard any more from her was cause for concern. But she didn't believe she were dead yet, because the guy harassing her hadn't let up yet. He was dangling Emily as a way to get Peyton to do his bidding. She wasn't quite sure what that was at the moment. He had made veiled threats and told her she needed to do what he told her to do but never said what he actually wanted from her. Today she knew he was watching her from Joe's. She had no idea who he was, but the darkness she saw made her aware of his presence. Joe's went back to normal when he left the premises. She ought to be more observant of people. She might have missed an opportunity to confront the man. With a store full of people and her guardian blocking her way, there wasn't much she could do.

Tomorrow before Jaxon returned, she would check out the painting in Jessie's office and would continue to research about the seen and unseen world. She had seen a small glimpse beyond the door in the woods. Not a visible door to simply anyone and one she could only see when she was supposed to. Like Reba told them many times the past year, you only see and hear what you do. Anything else is simply something you've made up, which can't help anyone. She also understood that the gifts passed down to her were for the good of humanity and not for personal use. The moment she crossed that line, she would be in danger of moving to the dark side. There were a few examples of that in her family line as well.

Thinking about her cousin seeing all these new wonderful places with the all the beauty and magic of Ireland, Peyton would love to be there. One of the places Jessie mentioned was Cork, which she found out was known for its rebellious spirit. Another trail of interest for her to follow. A glance at the clock told her to stop, but her mind said *no way*.

Cork City was often referred to as the rebel city due to the city's long history of resistance against enemy rule. She found that quite interesting. The same spirit that gave them the name in the fifteenth century of Rebel City was still their strength and tradition of the community today. There had to be something important in that truth. Their history inspired many new generations to fight for their rights and freedoms. The truth of every generation having to choose who they want to be seemed etched in the stories of Cork, and in Blue Cove for that matter. Her ancestors' stories were passed down to her. Now she had to decide what kind of person she wanted to be and how she could make her small corner of the world a better place. Peyton shut off her light. Her mind was free to wander in the dark. When she got a chance, she would check out Killarney and more on Galaway. And of course, to study the painting in Jessie's office.

Chapter 23

Jaxon struggled to wake himself. He must have fallen out at some point. Matt was right about the chair. The darn thing had lulled him to sleep with the TV still on in front of him. He glanced at the time in the corner of the news channel before clicking the remote's off button. He had slept through the night. His day would be another long one, and he needed to get started. *Keep telling yourself to move, Jaxon.* He stretched his arms over his head and unfolded his body from the chair. A brisk walk down the hall was needed to get the kinks out of his stiff body. *Note to self—stretch out in bed tonight.* He turned on the hot water and stepped into the shower, letting the warmth of the water relax his tight muscles.

He hoped Peyton had slept well, and if he hurried, he could make coffee for both of them before they had to go to work.

When he got out to the kitchen, Peyton was already there, and the coffee was hot. "That smells good."

"There are some bagels if you want one. I bought them yesterday for this morning. I need to get on my way. See you later." She carried a mug and walked toward the garage door.

"Wait a minute. I think you forgot something." Jaxon walked after her, carrying a brown paper bag.

"Not mine it's in my bag. I made you a few snacks in case you get hungry during the day." She smiled.

"Well, I wouldn't have wanted to walk over here for nothing." He pulled her into his arms and rested his chin on her head. "You look pretty and smell nice too." He ran the back of his hand down her cheek. "I should at least give you a proper greeting and goodbye. You get two. Good morning." He kissed her cheek. "Have a nice day." He kissed her lips and nudged her through the door he held open for her.

"See you." She rushed to her car and backed out of the driveway.

He could get used to seeing her every morning standing in his kitchen. "Steady, old boy, no need to hurry." He chuckled. He looked inside the bag she had packed for him. Thoughtful and beautiful. He couldn't lose with her.

Jaxon poured the coffee into his mug, twisting the lid on tight, and wrapped his toasted warm bagel in a napkin. He got into his car, noticing where the bullet had hit the door panel. Another sobering reminder of someone out to get him. He couldn't let down his guard, and neither could Peyton. The drive to work was uneventful, which he would welcome any day. With Frank coming, he was on edge. He had no reason to believe their plans were known, but instinct told him something was up. The more evidence they gathered, the tempo of a case usually picked up and the possibility of something going wrong did too. That made him try to cover every base. At least starting tomorrow, Peyton would have someone watching her around the clock.

Jaxon pulled into the parking lot at the field office. He had interviews set up for the day. Besides an appointment with the professor and his assistants, he would also be meeting again with Larry Hart.

"Hi, Jaxon. I came in early to see you. I'm off the case for safety protocols. My cover is blown, but I wanted to talk to you and Tom and fill you in on my part of the investigation." Robert jumped up from the chair in the reception area.

"Sure, do you want to meet in my office or Maxwell's?" Jaxon shook his hand. "How's your arm doing?"

"It'll be okay. But don't let anyone fool you. A bullet that grazes can do some damage and hurts like the devil. I'm grateful the damn thing didn't hit my boy. I get angry thinking about all the what ifs that could have happened."

"I can't imagine. I know how I felt when Peyton was hit, and I thought I would lose her. It makes you wonder about why you do the job."

"I'm telling you, man, there's a lot of crazy stuff happening on that campus. I've followed the money, which led to an online influencer and a podcaster with a huge following. Some of their listeners include some heavyweight names if you know what I mean."

"Hey, you two, Maxwell said he'll see you now." Claire, their boss's secretary, motioned them toward Tom's office.

"Thanks, Claire." Jaxon followed Robert down the hall.

"Come in and close the door behind you. How are you doing, Robert?" He pointed at the chairs in front of his desk. "Make yourself comfortable."

"All things considering, I'm doing good. My wife and kids aren't, though. We're staying at her mother's until this case is done."

"I understand. You had a close call. I want all the

details. We need to know what we're up against." Tom pulled out a notepad and took notes as Robert talked.

"I have a list of all the names I've linked to the online operations on campus. We are closing in on the prime location of the center of operations. The operator has done a good job of covering his tracks, but we have broken through some of the encryptions."

"How many folks are involved besides the creator of the site?" Jaxon leaned forward in the chair with his notepad and pen.

"We started making a list of names so that we could identify from their usernames and follow their online footprints. There are many users, but we are only listing the ones we can see are involved in criminal activity."

"How can you determine that? What parameters are you using?" Jaxon jotted down notes as Robert and Tom talked.

"We have three categories the users fall into. The passives are people who wander onto the site, search, but stay out of the conversations and chat rooms. Next are the braggarts. They talk big and need to be watched in case they move from talking to action. The criminals are already involved in buying and selling or describing acts with posted pictures."

"That makes sense. Speech isn't a crime unless it crosses the line into a threat or a crime."

"What else do we need to know?" Tom tapped his pen against the notepad.

"There are some high-profiled people involved. I've followed the money, and here's another list of some of their names. I've connected them to the group either by donations or payments to them." Robert handed Tom the two lists. "The team is running checks on all the people on both of these lists and will file a detailed report soon."

Tom looked over the list and whistled. "Damn good job. There will be some unhappy people when they're exposed." He pushed the paper toward Jaxon. "To me this looks like the team is covering all your bases. We need to be sure before the possible suspects are interviewed. This guy is a big family values guy. He has a podcast with a large following." Tom pointed at a name on the paper."

"Wow, this could get dicey. Expect some big-named lawyers and lots of press." Jaxon glanced at the list.

"I want to go on record as saying that I think most of the people on campus were sucked into the group out of a need to belong. You know, college kids finding ways to connect and pull some pranks. I'm not sure how much they buy into all the junk they're peddling. Only future interviews will tell us for sure. There's a criminal enterprise going on, and a few are making a whole lot of money, and those who may have got too close to the truth have died."

"There's always someone willing to take advantage of the vulnerable. What else do you have for me?" Tom asked.

"Only that the toxicology report from the lab on Eloise Morton should be coming in soon. We need to compare the findings with the one for the Bradley and Crammer girls. If they're a match, we are dealing with one killer. Otherwise, we might be dealing with more."

Jaxon and Tom pumped Robert with more questions until they were satisfied they understood the complexities of the case. Jaxon didn't want to be caught flat-footed in his interviews later on in the day. The fact they had a missing girl and two bodies made the situation more urgent. They needed to shut it down before the numbers grew if they hadn't already. He was young as far as his career went, but he had seen enough to understand there's a dark side to humanity. Not to say there weren't a lot of good folks too. But homicides were messy and showed him repeatedly what people were capable of.

****

Peyton's morning went by quickly. Before she knew it, the kids' parents were picking them up from school. She stopped by the office to chat with the secretary and grabbed the papers from her inbox. Some routines were worth keeping. She smiled, digging her keys out of her purse. Her phone started ringing as soon as she got into the car. She didn't need to look to know who the caller was, but she had had enough.

"Look, you'd better stop and think before you give me another one of your stupid threats. I'm not going to listen to them anymore. You can keep calling if you want, but I won't respond. I have no idea who you are, but I do know what you did. If you're smart, you'd turn yourself in to the police—they're closing in on you anyway. Leave me alone!" She disconnected the call before he could say a word. She changed the settings on her phone to block all unknown callers.

She started her car. Probably not a smart idea to antagonize a killer, but she was sick of his stupid threats and endless calls. This time her defiance might work against her, but she was sick of doing nothing.

"Hi, Audrey." Peyton walked into the bookstore. "We have only a week and half until Jessie returns. Time is flying by. Have you been busy?"

"Not too bad, but I'm glad you're here. I need a

break, if you know what I mean."

"Go ahead. Take time for lunch while you're at it. I can handle any customers that come in. Don't rush."

"Thanks." Audrey rushed to the back room then made her way into Joe's.

Peyton scanned an email from Jeremy who sent her some material to read on Emily Hart and Mary Bradley. He also had some notes on the web site along with two names he highlighted. He said he had seen their names come up a few times in some of the backroom chats on the site. He wrote *bad stuff* in bold letters in parenthesis. She could appreciate Jeremy's way of warning her this case could get dicey. The names of Markus Cervantes and Toni Vanderhoff were the two he mentioned.

The bell rang above the door, and a customer came in. Peyton wasn't sure what to think of the man. His overly bright smile, polite nature, did nothing to take away from the raging dark colors swirling around him. She studied him as he walked around the store, picking up one book after another. Their warrior friend had moved from his place and followed the man. Stalking him when he moved and never left his side while he stood still. Mary Elizabeth's ghost was watching him from a distance with a sad expression on her face. Her cousin would say simply another strange day in her bookstore. She had experienced her share of them since she moved to Blue Cove a little over five months ago.

When Aundrey came back from lunch, the man left through the open doors into Joe's. Thankfully, the charged atmosphere went with him. Was he the one stalking her? Peyton could tell he was a deeply troubled man from the colors that swirled around him. From dark, stormy, to sunny, and yet not quite light. His nature warred within him. The struggle was visible to her. This must be the man the police were looking for. She reached for her phone to call Dylan as she followed the man into the coffee shop to see if he was still there.

"Joe, this is Peyton."

"How can I help you?"

"I'm not sure, but I think the suspect you're looking for in the Bradley case might have been in the store."

"Are you sure? Is he still around?" Joe asked.

"You know how this works. I have no way to prove the man was the suspect, only what I sensed while he was in the store. As soon as Audrey came back from lunch, he went into Joe's. I followed him as soon as I could, but he had already left the premises. I did get a good look at him."

"Could you work with our sketch artist and describe him?" Joe asked.

"I could. I thought you were minus a sketch artist since he moved on." Peyton went behind the counter.

"Matt's brother is filling in until we hire someone else. But I think we should hire him. He could simply add his hours to taking photos of crime scenes. We don't need anyone full time, but it's nice to have one when we need them. I'll let Dylan know you called, and I'm sure you'll be hearing from him soon."

"Thanks, Joe. I need to get busy, but I'll be around here until we close." Peyton disconnected the call and went to help Audrey carry a load of books from the back room to the table at the front of the store. How would she describe the man to Evan? She tried to remember each detail of his looks. He was tall, muscular, and she noticed scratches on his neck and cheek. She didn't notice the color of his eyes only that they looked lifeless to her.

Dark hair barely peeked out from the red ball cap on his head. An instant reminder to her time in Arizona. The night she was shot. One of the suspects escaped but was wounded. Frank's dog was able to track him from the blood droplets. Jaxon told her the man's name was Edwards. He worked as the janitor that cleaned the offices where Jaxon worked. He was the leak to those outside the department. It was the bullet from his gun that hit her leg. When they found his body, the coroner found something strange. His DNA type matched another man's who had died in the same hospital a month before. The strangest part of the scene was Edwards' signature red hat was missing. No one could remember seeing him without the darn thing on.

As strange as the whole scenario sounded to her now, was Edwards in the body of another missing person? Was he the man who was just in the bookstore? Had he jumped before he died into a new body and took his hat with him? Was it possible? Weird that he would come to mind at this moment, true, but something she needed to think rationally about. She would talk to Jaxon about the possibility later.

Evan walked in with his sketchbook. He motioned her over to one of the small tables and began to ply her with questions as his pencil moved across the page, creating a picture of a man as she described him.

****

He hightailed it out of the store as quickly as his feet would carrying him. The way that woman looked at him was weird to him. He was foolish to have gone into the store to begin with. Something about her pulled at him for a second time, but now he was afraid his curiosity could destroy all his work. He needed a plan to deal with her. No more games. She was a big problem. She could see through him until his actions and thoughts were bare in front of her. He shuddered. Was she a witch? His time might be limited. He would look for his escape as soon as he dealt with her. Reaching into his pocket, he pulled out the talisman and flipped the silver piece between his fingers. The game was about to turn deadly for her.

Chapter 24

Jaxon stopped in to see Dylan on his way home. He had called him and told him about Peyton's visitor at the store. Evan and Peyton spent the afternoon working on the composite drawing, and Dylan wanted him to come by the station to take a look at the possible suspect.

The first thing he noticed besides the hat on his head was the color red. He wondered if Peyton had the same thought he had when he saw the hat. His logical mind didn't want to believe it could be Edwards, the quirky janitor in Arizona, sporting a new body. But anything was possible as he had learned since life with Peyton. He would know soon enough.

"What do you think?" Dylan stood beside Jaxon and studied the drawing with him.

"I can't say that I've ever seen the man before. She used the words tall and muscular to describe the man."

"I noticed she said there were scratches on his neck and cheeks. Which has me wondering if our victim might have fought back." Dylan pointed to the words written below the composite.

"She captured a lot of details, didn't she?" Jaxon studied the face in the drawing.

"I'd say she remembered a lot. As much as you and Matt don't want to hear this, those girls would make great cops."

"Don't I know it, but how could they ever explain

how they came to their conclusions? There are many things I've simply had to leave out of my reports."

"Jessie has told Matt many times she's the heart of their partnership and he's the logic. She loves to tell the stories of the people who are victims, and he loves to logically solve the investigation. They make a good team, the same as you and Peyton do."

"I couldn't agree more. Peyton is newer to this side of her life than Jessie, but I see her being shaped by the stories of the victims as well. Having been a victim herself, she has empathy in abundance."

"A rare commodity these days. Wait a minute, and I'll walk out with you." Dylan thanked Joe when he handed him a stack of papers. "Here's a copy of the suspect for you."

"Thanks. Do you mind if I take a few extra to give out at the agency tomorrow?"

"Be my guest." Dylan walked beside Jaxon out of the station. "I love going home at the end of the day to my wife. She always has a great meal for the guests and for me too."

"Do you like being married?"

"I do. Katie is fun and a complete mystery to me. She keeps me guessing all the time. I'm never sure who will show up. She's strong willed but passionate. As much as she fought Jessie about her new life, she has become her champion. That's my girl and my greatest fan. With Katie Donovon Mitchell there is never a dull moment."

"Sounds perfect to me." Jaxon got into his car.

After stopping by his place to make sure all was cool there, Jaxon headed to the Parker residence. He played over in his mind the conversation with Dylan. He understood no relationship was perfect, but his parents had come close. Their thirty-fourth anniversary was coming up. He, along with his siblings, were planning something extra special for them on their 35th. A romantic cruise around the Hawaiian Islands.

He would love to create the happy home that he knew growing up. He got into his share of trouble, but his parents were always there to support him. Peyton's childhood was the complete opposite of his, and he hoped he could help her to see the possibilities of a better future for herself. One that could be filled with love and happiness.

First, he had to deal with this case and the damn red hat. What was the possibility they had another traveler in a new body? He hoped what he was thinking was wrong because how could it be true? Yet, nothing was beyond the realm of possibility anymore. Still, he knew no one would believe his budding theory but Peyton.

Jaxon pulled up in the drive and saw that Peyton was still sitting in her car. "Why are you sitting out here?"

"I'm thinking."

"Do you mind if you do your thinking inside where you're not a target for a murderer?" Jaxon took her hand when she got out of her ar.

"I'm sorry. I forgot about safety. I guess you've heard about my visitor at work." She waited as he opened the door and turned off the alarm.

"Yes. I stopped at the station to talk with Dylan. He had the composite drawing you made with Evan earlier. Do you believe he's the suspect?" Jaxon closed the door behind them.

"I do. Logically I can't explain why I feel that way, but I could sense many struggles within the man, and I know it is him." She placed her purse on the coffee table.

"Do you think he'll come around again?" Jaxon asked.

"I do. We are destined to meet again. It has to happen. He tried to kill me once, and he will try to finish the job again. The problem for him is I'm not the same person I was in Arizona, but then again neither is he." She plopped down on the couch.

"What do you mean?"

"It was a much smaller man that wore that red hat than the man in the bookstore today."

"I know where you're going with this theory because I was thinking the same thing." He sat beside her. "You think Edwards jumped into someone else before he died. I'm going to try to find out who he is now."

"Was it the red hat? It was a dead giveaway for me." She glanced him when he reached for her hand. "I like how your mind works. Finding out who he is now sounds like a solid plan. But no matter what I believe, you can understand why I say we are destined to meet again."

"I understand, but I don't have to like the idea. I will do all I can to prevent him getting near you again." He squeezed her hand tightly.

She pulled her hand free from his grasp and patted his cheek. "You're sweet, and as much as I want to believe you, there is no way you can watch me twenty-four seven. He'll slip through the crack somewhere, and I'll do all I can to be ready."

"And what might that be?"

"Who knows. I'll figure out my plan of action when I find myself faced with the situation. The plan will depend on how the whole meeting goes down." She stood. "In the meantime, I'm hungry, and dinner sounds like the best option. We should do a little grocery shopping and plan a few meals while we are here."

"I forgot I picked up a few things when I stopped by my house, and while I was there, I ordered dinner. The guy should be here in a few minutes. I hope spaghetti and meatballs sounds good to you. Antonio's had a spaghetti dinner special—buy one, get the second for free. I couldn't pass it up."

"Works for me. I'll be back in a few." She walked down the hall to the room she was using. She didn't have the heart to tell him that Mary was her new sidekick.

****

Peyton changed into more comfortable clothes and sat on the foot of the bed. To be so close to the suspect and not able to get him before he hurt someone else was a bummer to her. Her mind raced back and forth all day about his possible identity, but when Jaxon asked her about Edwards, she didn't have to think before she answered. As much as she didn't want to believe in the possibility, she did. Six months of these strange occurrences in her life weren't going to go away anytime soon. Reba said she needed to work with Jaxon the way Matt and Jessie learned to work together. She would find a way to.

"No more using your past as an excuse and jump in feet first," she muttered. "Too many families need closure, which can only come with answers and time."

She would do her part to bring peace to Mary Elizabeth, Emily Hart, and her dad. With her decision made, she needed to let the past stay in the past and move forward with new vigor. Jaxon would be pleased. Although, she would give him her decision in small doses not to overwhelm him. She wasn't ready for marriage. She laughed. An engagement ring wasn't out of the question though.

"Peyton, dinner is here." Jaxon knocked on her door.

"I'll be right out." She stood. When she opened the door, she saw herself as walking into a new chapter in her life. With her mind made up, she couldn't wait to put her own plan into action.

Jaxon stopped and looked at her when she walked into the kitchen. "No matter what you are wearing, you're beautiful. How is that possible? My sister could take some lessons from you."

"Oh no, you don't. Your sister is beautiful, and being at home among her gooney brothers is a lot different than being by the man she cares for."

"Gooney, huh. Is that how you see us?" Jaxon chuckled.

"Your sister was outnumbered, and she is one of my heroines. She managed to remain sweet and feminine despite you three."

"When did she secure you as her champion? I won't argue with you about her being amazing despite our torture. And believe me we did tease her and any guy that came around to see her." He walked up behind Peyton and wrapped his arms around her waist. "Just for the record, are you saying the reason you always look beautiful is because you care for me? Notice my power of deduction."

"I'll never tell." She pulled out of his arms and reached for a plate. "Let's eat." She flashed him a flirtatious smile.

After dinner they worked side by side to clean up the kitchen. A nice domestic picture which reassured her that she had made a good decision. Yes, they could work side by side and have fun while they did.

"Sweetheart—" He put the last dish back in the cabinet. "—how are we going to keep you safe with this guy roaming around?"

"I've been thinking about the same question all day. Because I can't anticipate how or where I will meet him again, it's hard to plan. He holds the element of surprise like he did today. I was bummed that we couldn't get him today. I should have moved faster. I watched him in slow motion, trying to figure out if he was who I thought he might be. I know that must sound strange, but I think I was in denial."

"You must have been shocked. I would've been."

"At least Frank will be here tomorrow, and maybe we will find Emily."

"I'm hopeful he'll find her if not tomorrow before he leaves town."

"Sounds good. I believe it's possible she is being moved around, which might make finding her harder."

"We can count on it. But I found the suspect who thinks he's invincible does something along the way that gives away his game. Our guy has been getting more brazen. He walked into the store and now realizes who you are. He must be panicking about what he found out."

"I sure hope he is because I was most of the day. Turnabout is fair play." She frowned. "He looks ordinary enough, but something tells me we are dealing with the unordinary when it comes to him."

"I don't want to even explore that possibility at the moment. What do you say we try to relax for a while this evening. I could use turning off my mind for a bit. Downtime often gives me a fresh perspective. By the way, I interviewed Larry Hart and the professor. There's a lot of animosity between the two of them, which is understandable. I'll fill you in while we search for a movie."

Later all the thoughts she had pushed aside rushed back into Peyton's mind. Jaxon had worked hard to make her feel at ease earlier, and she appreciated his effort. But she could tell he was concerned too. There were a lot of moving parts to this case. Somehow, they all would blend together to make a coherent picture, but they weren't to that place in the investigation yet.

Yes, they tried not to talk about the case, but the subject kept coming up all evening. Jaxon was concerned the closer they got in discovery that the speed of the case would accelerate. A dangerous time in any case and people usually got hurt. If he said it once, he repeated the same words over a few more times. This suspect is a real charmer. She remembered smiling to herself each time he said the words. Not because he was being funny, but rather he was using a twist on the man's use of charms. She still found that part of the crime scene odd, and she wanted to understand the idiosyncrasy better. Jaxon was upset by the fact that some of the collateral damage would be young college students who might be caught in the crossfire. She could understand his concern. Mary Elizabeth's ghostly presence always around her was a constant reminder of the damage.

Chapter 25

Jaxon was up early and out the door before Peyton. He had a few meetings scheduled first thing before Frank arrived. Frank had texted him that he wouldn't be there until late in the afternoon, which would put the tracking off until Thursday morning. He thought his dog would perform better with a fresh start after the long car ride. Of course, he was right, but Jaxon was anxious to get started. Time was crucial especially after his talk with Peyton last night.

As much as he didn't want to admit the fact, if she recognized the suspect in his new form, then he must also know who she was. Peyton hadn't changed in looks since Arizona when he shot her almost six months ago. One fact remained true—he wouldn't be writing any of those odd tidbits into any report. A man jumping into another person's body before he died was an anomaly that most people wouldn't understand. If he had learned one thing from Matt after moving to the area, it was that there were ways to fill out a report without sharing the unusual details of some of their cases. Solving a case with a logical path to evidence that could stand up in court made the bosses happy. The rest of the unusual details remained their secrets to carry around, leaving many questions unanswered in their own minds. At least, in his for sure.

Jaxon stopped for a coffee on his way to Hanover.

Joe's was all abuzz about Molly in the early stages of possible labor. Peyton would be excited to hear the baby could be on his way. Kenny had proudly told him one day his little boy would be named after him, and they'd call him Junior.

He sent a quick text to Peyton, telling her about the change in the track time from today until tomorrow and reminding her of their dinner later with Dylan, Katie, and Frank. He also told her about Molly. Wishing her a nice day, he drove to Hanover, ready to get into his morning meetings. Ready but not excited might be one way to describe the meeting. He would rather be at the college working with the evidence he had than discussing the topic.

****

Peyton could hear her phone vibrating on the nightstand. She read the message from Jaxon and was happy he had sent one. The news about Molly brought a sigh to her lips. A baby was such a joyous event, and she couldn't wait to see the little guy. The time displayed on her phone told her she would be late if she didn't get a move on. She rushed through her morning routine and out to her car. She'd be drinking coffee from the teachers' lounge this morning if she had time to grab a cup at all. Depending on who made the morning joe, at times the brown liquid was hard to define as coffee.

Thankfully, this morning there was a special school assembly, which the children always liked, and the special time in the auditorium gave her and her aides a break from their usual strict schedule for about an hour. Established and consistent routine was important for her special kids. They didn't handle change well, but they seemed to love the excitement of being with all the other kids. The key was not to let them get overstimulated. They walked a fine line between too much or too little to grab their attention. But all the teachers said the same thing. Classrooms could get out of control fast if students lost focus. She wholeheartedly believed her kids taught her more than she ever taught them.

The coffee wasn't the best, but she was able to guzzle a cup down. The assembly was worth all the time it took to get the kids settled in the auditorium, and her kids did great despite the big change in their morning. Even with her late start, the morning had been a success. Now if her afternoon at the bookstore went as well, she would be happy. A nice cup of good coffee or tea wouldn't hurt her mood either.

****

Peyton answered her ringing phone and exited her car. "Hi, cous. I'm surprised to hear from you this time of day. Won't Matt miss you not being by his side?"

"Remember it's night over here, and I wore my hubby out. He's sawing logs." Jessie laughed. "How's life in Blue Cove?"

"I just got to the store, but business is picking up the closer we get to the holidays. I think you'll be pleased with the numbers." Peyton stashed her purse behind the counter.

"My store has managed to do quite well. Between business from the year-round tourists and locals, I believe I made a sound business investment. But best of all, I love working there."

"I know you didn't call to just chitchat. What's on your mind?" Peyton straightened the bookmarks in the basket.

"Truth is I've been thinking about you a lot and

wanted to make sure you're okay. Tell me what's going on and why you're in my dreams."

Peyton told her about the man in the store and how he might be Edwards. "I'm not sure, but it's possible he's the same guy but in a different body. Not a wimpy guy like the man who shot me in Arizona, but this guy looks like a body builder. I'm sure we are destined to meet again, because if I recognized him, he knew me also. I believe this time he will try to finish the job he started. But I won't let him."

"Well, darn, no wonder I've been worrying about you."

"Don't. I'm safe, and you're on your honeymoon. Blue Cove with its problems is many miles away. Besides Frank is here and they'll do their best to keep me safe." Peyton updated her on her ghost tagalong and the one standing guard at the store. "He keeps watch over me. He stood between me and the guy when he came in the store."

"He turned out to be a blessing of sorts, didn't he? The old curmudgeon can call my store his home as far as I'm concerned."

"I agree he's a welcome sight. On a lighter note, Jaxon texted me about Molly being in the early stages of labor. Hopefully, her little fella will be here soon."

"How cool is that? I love being here with Matt, but I can't wait to get back to all of you and our crazy wonderful spot of paradise."

"The time will go fast, and you'll be wishing you had Matt all to yourself again. Enjoy what time you have left before you have to fly home."

"You're right of course. I can't imagine sharing him with the whole town, but such is life. Promise to write me with all the news and not a short phone call version. Oh, feel free to purchase new books if you see we are getting low on certain ones."

"Yes, ma'am, I'll obey both of your orders." Peyton saluted. "You've always been a bit bossy." She laughed. "Now, hang up and get some rest while you can."

Peyton and Audrey had an uneventful but busy afternoon at least for a few hours. She ordered some books for customers who requested them. With the holidays coming, she ordered a few more of the titles that seemed to be flying off the shelves like her cousin told her to do.

When she sent the last online order off with the click of a button, out of the corner of her eye, she saw Mary's ghost swish past her. The usual sadness on her face replaced with something a tad more scary looking. Anger perhaps. Peyton tried to discover what had the spirit incensed. Nothing in the store seemed out of the ordinary. She kept an eye on Mary while waiting on customers. Suddenly a rainbow of flashing colors swirled around the store like a rotating color wheel, with no one in the store besides her the wiser.

The air was charged, and shivers started at the base of her neck and danced their way up and down her spine. Mary's killer must be near enough for her to see him even if Peyton couldn't. If ever she was tempted to doubt that a spirit had emotion or knew what had happened to them, she would remind herself of this moment. She moved back and forth, whirling around in circles. With each spin the atmosphere became cold and clammy.

Peyton was grateful Audrey and her customer weren't bothered, but at the same time she was blown away by all the supernatural activity that only she could see. She could understand the ghost's response, because the girl's life was suddenly interrupted. Mary had much more of life to live until it was stolen. Peyton followed her movement into Joe's but couldn't follow her. The warrior blocked her path with his sword drawn.

Life experiences have a way of altering a person. When she had been shot and her life was hanging in suspended animation between one world and the next, she faced many truths about herself. Good and bad. The life-changing moment altered the course of her life. She moved from New York to Blue Cove and found a way to use her degree in teaching special needs kids. Though she liked the results, she would rather not have to learn all her lessons the hard way.

She blinked, trying to stop the tears forming in her eyes. "Allergies," she told the woman. As soon as the woman took her bag and left the store, Peyton walked to the open doors to see if she could see what Mary was up to. She had to help her like so many supported her in her hour of need. Where was Mary? With another customer coming in the door, she wouldn't find out yet.

Mary returned to the store later and remained near her for the rest of the day. Her anger replaced with melancholy that Peyton had come to know. She might never figure out what had upset her or where she had been. With less than an hour until the store closed, she reminded herself to write a detailed email to her cousin. One of her cousin's orders she could wipe off her to-do list. Peyton smiled to herself. Before she typed, she opened an email from Jeremy and found herself caught up in the research he had found on Aine O'Flaherty.

After reading for a while, she came to one conclusion—she got her tenacity and defiance from her ancestors. According to records, Aine was considered a sage by some. The people in her village often sought her out when they needed the wisdom in dealing with people. She had a knack of seeing a person's true colors. Peyton found that particularly interesting. Some were scared of her abilities and steered clear of her for fear she would know things about them that they didn't want to be common knowledge. Those folks viewed her as a witch with mystical powers. Peyton frowned as she read on. Basically, people haven't changed much. Maybe there was less superstition now or maybe not. People often fear what they don't understand and demonize those who they think of as different. A saint or a witch, she was neither. Aine was only a woman trying to live her life and make a difference with the strange gift that possessed her.

Peyton wanted to be thought of as someone making a difference in Blue Cove.

Thankfully most of the residents had no idea what went on in her life or in this bookstore. Both her and Jessie would be run out of town. All of the colors she could see around people were helping her to distinguish who people were. And she didn't see those colors hanging over folks all the time, only when the situation called for them.

At five o'clock she turned off the computer and worked with Audrey to close the store. She needed to get home to change for dinner tonight. Jaxon texted her that Frank and his dog Carlene were already at the house. Dylan was paying for a nice evening out at the Chowder House. If she knew Katie, she'd be wearing something special, and she would too.

Chapter 26

When Jaxon arrived at the house, he found Frank and Peyton sitting in the living room, chatting. Damn, she looked gorgeous. He gulped. "Hey, Frank. Did you get settled in okay?"

"I sure did. I know this place well. I'm sitting in my favorite chair. I made my wife agree to us buying one after hanging out in this one. Although, I have to say Jessie's touches can be seen, and I'm sure there'll be more to come in the months ahead."

"Did you see the office Matt did for her?"

"Not yet."

"Be sure to see the room before you leave. He did a great job. He made the desk, bookcases, and he even bought a painting from an artist in Ireland." Jaxon sat on the couch beside Peyton.

"A truly beautiful and romantic gift." Peyton sighed. "I saw her office when we moved her stuff into his house. I have yet to see the special painting he bought for her. But I will while I'm here. Jessie reminded me again."

"Was the room his wedding gift?" Frank leaned his head back against the chair.

"More like *I want this to feel like your home too* gift. He surprised her." Peyton smiled at them. "To look at him you'd never know that Matt is a romantic, but he is. Especially when it comes to my cousin."

Frank chuckled. "If you'd have seen those two doing

everything they could to fight their attraction for one another in the beginning, you would understand how truly remarkable their relationship is. I had a front row seat and got a lot of enjoyment out of watching the two of them."

"I heard the guys at the department were placing bets on whether they would ever get together." Jaxon took Peyton's hand in his.

"They were, and in the end being the activist that your cousin is, she asked Matt to marry her before he could ask her. Funny thing was she wouldn't wear the ring in public. Matt decided to take matters into his own hands and invited all their friends to the house and surprised her by asking her to marry him among witnesses. They were a trip." Frank laughed.

"I may need to have my cousin tell me more about their strange courtship. I heard about her asking him to marry her, but she left out a few details about how they got past their standoff in the beginning. I wasn't in Blue Cove as long as she was. In the end their relationship worked well because they are now honeymooning in Ireland."

"Are you two ready to go?" Jaxon glanced at his phone.

"Yes, I'm always up for food." Frank patted his stomach.

"Dylan texted and said they are on their way to the restaurant. Let's get on the road."

Jaxon set the alarm before he followed them out the door.

Once their party had arrived, Roger Blackman, the owner, escorted them to their reserved table. Jaxon placed his arm possessively on Peyton's back as she walked in front of him past a table of young men who he didn't like the way they were ogling her.

"Your waiter will be right with you." Roger pulled out a chair for Peyton.

"Thank you."

"How's this big lug treating you, little lady?" He pulled out Katie's chair and pointed at Dylan.

"He is a keeper."

"Nice to know. Enjoy your meal. I sure had a good time at Matt's and Jessie's wedding." Roger gave them each a menu.

"A fun time was had by all." Peyton smiled at him. "Once we got them there," she muttered under her breath.

****

Peyton glanced around the restaurant and was happy to be in such a lovely place with such special friends. She loved the décor, which was a blend of New England and Old Country charm. Perfect for a restaurant on the waterfront with a vista of the boats in the harbor and the ocean beyond. She listened to the men talk for a while but soon lost interest. Katie jumped up after she had seen a friend and was over at their table chattering gaily. Everything about Jessie's best friend Katie was over-the-top energy wise. She could understand why their friendship had lasted as long as it had. They were in a good place now since Katie accepted the strange part of their lives. She wasn't sure, but Peyton thought there might have been a bit of magic to bring that about. Katie could even talk about her Irish heritage with vigor.

"Sorry to leave you alone with these guys talking shop. I hadn't seen those folks in a while, and I had to say hi." Katie sat in the chair next to her. "We need to catch up on all things Jessie."

"Have you heard from my cousin?" Peyton asked.

"Only that they are seeing lots of fabulous places and going through old records. She promised to find out information on my family if she could. I have no idea why, but I'm excited to learn about some of my ancestors. I don't know if you know this, but Jessie's strange life and yours too quite frankly used to give me fits. I would go nuts."

"I know. Jessie always wanted to be careful around you. Your friendship means a lot to her. I'm glad you can share this area with her now. I happen to know that even reluctant acceptance to talk about this part of her life with her makes her beyond happy. You've been friends for a long time. You don't often have friends you keep all your life. Your relationship is a special one."

"We've been friends since our first day of kindergarten. Talk about going through a lot of ups and downs together, we had our fair share. I almost let it slip away until recently and more than one dream reminding me of my own heritage. Believe me when I say I don't want what you have, but at least now I can live with all your strange premonitions and ghosts. I amaze myself when I say I can accept this new side of you both."

"Don't think for a moment that it's been easy for Jessie or me for that matter. We have had more questions than answers for the most part. Yet our trip to Ireland opened up our understanding, and we both are at peace with this part of our lives." Peyton continued to tell her about some of her recent conversations with her cousin. "They are having a wonderful time, and the last thing Jessie told me was that Matt was getting into the spirit of the search through the records. It suits his investigative nature."

"That sounds like Matt. I have one just like him." Katie laughed.

When their waiter placed their meals before them, the table got quiet. Peyton planned on enjoying every bite of the tempting meal in front of her. Grilled herbed chicken on a bed of field greens and strawberries with a drizzle of raspberry vinaigrette to top it off, and the serving was huge. Leftovers would be fine because she wanted one of the luscious desserts on the menu. The meal gave her time to watch the others at the table. Frank and Jaxon talked while Dylan and Katie flirted. She couldn't fault them. She found their obvious love for one another quite encouraging. Still considered newlyweds, the couple's playful banter made her smile.

Jaxon was intense in conversation with Frank, which made him all the more fascinating. His facial expressions, the rise and fall of his eyebrows when he was passionate, and his wonderful grin were visual delights. The fact that he was interested in her was a marvel. The man was handsome, kind, and brilliant when it came to his job. A girl could get lost in his gorgeous eyes. She took a few more bites of the wonderful juicy grilled herb chicken and greens. The next time she glanced at him, their eyes met and he winked at her. She wondered if he had caught her studying him and knew what she was thinking. The blush that followed was the bane of her existence. The red heat on her face testified against her.

When they ordered dessert and they brought it to the table, Peyton eyed the vanilla cream cake with strawberries and realized how full she was. After a couple of bites, which were yummy, she had the waiter box the cake along with her leftovers. The evening and meal were relaxing in every way. She never had to talk about the case once. No one asked her a question or what any of her premonitions might mean. Mary was never far from where she sat. Peyton was used to her being around. She figured when things were settled for her, she'd be gone.

The guys did all the theorizing, and she was free to enjoy a break. One thought led to another, and Emily Hart came to her mind. Why hadn't Kelsey called her? She was hopeful that Frank's dog Carlene would be able to locate Emily alive. Peyton still found the premonitions strange. The way they showed up randomly often without all the information needed was still a mystery. Reba was correct. You can only see what you see. Anything else would be made up. But there were times when she wished she could see a clearer picture. One small taste of chocolate wasn't enough when you could have the whole chocolate bar. She wanted to help the girl and not simply know she needed help.

"Earth to Peyton. Where have you been, pretty lady?" Jaxon stood behind her chair. "Are you ready to go?"

"I'm ready. I'm afraid I was lost in thought. I wasn't paying attention." She stood after the others had.

"If you hear anything else from Jessie, let me know." Katie leaned toward her.

"I will."

"Promise. I have a need to know." Katie giggled. "I do love juicy honeymoon gossip."

"I promise. Although, when it comes to my cousin, I'm not sure how juicy the news will be. She's over the moon in love with her new husband but doesn't talk much about that."

Jaxon opened the car door, and she slid into the passenger seat. She turned to look at Frank in the back. "Did you enjoy your dinner?"

"Oh, my, yes. I've been to that restaurant a few times, and the food never disappoints. My filet was tender enough to cut with my fork. We didn't mean to ignore you tonight. I should have tried to involve you in the conversation."

"I was actually thinking how nice it was to have a break. I see and hear enough. I enjoyed letting you guys talk shop while I people watch. One of my favorite occupations."

"I would have never taken you for a people watcher." Jaxon latched his seat belt.

"You learn a lot about folks by observation. You, as an investigator, already know that I'm sure. Didn't you have a course in reading body language?"

"Dogs and kids are better at understanding the nature of people than most of us will ever hope to be," Frank said.

"That's true." Jaxon pulled out of the parking space. "My niece Emma loves most people, but there are some she won't go to and even will cry when they approach. What did your observations tonight tell you if anything?"

"Well, for one, Dylan and Katie are totally into one another. I enjoyed their banter and playful flirting. And you"—she glanced at Jaxon—"are lost in conversation when you talk about a case. You are in the zone, as they say."

"I can't argue with you there. I wished you had been sitting next to me instead of Katie. I would have loved to have had your input in our conversation. You have a special way of seeing things."

"Thank you kindly, sir."

Peyton was happy to get back to the house and the quiet solitude. She said her good nights and made a beeline for the room and her computer. Her cousin would be back at the end of next week, and she wanted to study the scrolls for as long as she could. Putting on her comfy clothes, she rolled out the scrolls on the bed and started reading. She wanted her ancestors to speak to her through their writings. Aine had many entries on the parchment she was in the process of reading.

Wait, what is this? Peyton pointed at a symbol halfway down the page. The symbol looked a lot like the charm the suspect left at the murder scene. She needed to understand the writings in Gaelic on the page. She took photos on her phone and sent the words to Jeremy to see if he could find out what they meant. She was positive the words held the key to understanding this case for her. She carefully placed the scrolls away and stretched out on the bed. *Emily, I wish I knew where you are and how you're doing. Speak to me if you can.* She shut off the light and closed her eyes.

****

Mila knew her charge couldn't see the golden dust that filled the air around her. She landed softly on the pillow and tapped Peyton gently on the forehead three times and flew back to her home beyond the door.

Chapter 27

He hoped everything was okay with Peyton. She hadn't said much and went right into her room, which wasn't like her. When he walked down the hall, he stopped outside her door. All was quiet. He would check to see if she was good in the morning. Frank fell asleep in the recliner as soon as Jaxon had turned on the TV, and Carlene was in her crate sleeping soundly too. An early night wouldn't hurt him either. He switched on the light in his room and shut the door.

He plumped up his pillows against the headboard and stretched out, leaning his head against their soft texture. Hell, he should be feeling good about how the investigation was going, but his gut told him there were a few bumps ahead. When Peyton explained she was destined to meet Edwards or whoever the guy was again, his heart sank. The whole scenario didn't set well with him. He didn't like surprises even though every case he ever investigated had a few. Not of the supernatural kind though. He was still doing his best to get used to the unusual that came along with his girl. The thought of some ghost hanging near Peyton meant the spirit was somewhere in the house. She had reassured him that the spirit was harmless and needed closure to let go of this life. The whole idea messed with his head, but Peyton seemed to be at peace with the whole scenario.

What could she do about it? She never asked for the

gift that was passed to her from her ancestors, and neither did Jessie. A charm baby, Jaxon shook his head. Thank goodness he was not one nor did he want to be one. Call him boring, logical, and not one to think outside the box, and that was fine by him. But damn, if he hadn't gotten used to the idea of the guardian watching over them at the bookstore, ancient scrolls, and artifacts that magically showed up one day. What did that say about him?

He wondered if Matt ever thought he had lost his mind through the process. He needed to have a serious talk with his friend, not that a conversation would change Jaxon's mind. When it came to Peyton, he was already a lost cause, but he needed to know how to navigate the strange world he found himself in with her. He didn't want to wake up one day and regret a decision he made without logically thinking it through. Did Matt ever have doubts? Surely, he must have.

What Jaxon needed right now was a long conversation with someone who would understand his hesitation to embrace this part of her life. The only person he knew that would understand was Matt. He couldn't help wondering how many plans Matt had to make to keep Jessie safe.

He didn't want anything to happen to Peyton. He had almost lost her once, and he'd be damned if he let that happen again. His girl and her cousin were cut out of the same material. Both strong women with soft hearts which is an amazing combination as far as he was concerned.

The fact the suspect showed up in the bookstore in the middle of the day was a gut check for him. The guy was audacious, he'd give him that, but he'd seen more than one suspect's overconfidence take them down, convinced of their own invincibility. Cockiness could lead to slipups, sloppiness, and getting caught. What foolish thing would this guy do? Even the smartest criminal made mistakes. Contacting Peyton wasn't one of the smartest things he could have done. The man had no idea what he was dealing with. A truth that gave Jaxon some sense of relief.

If he didn't shut down his mind—he would never get any sleep. He reached for the file he brought home earlier to read. There was nothing like working on a report to put him to sleep. He jotted down his notes in the file. He rubbed his eyes and placed the file on the nightstand. Jaxon reached for the light at the same time his phone rang. He smiled when he saw the caller ID. He wouldn't need to call Matt in the morning. He was calling him.

****

When she struggled to sit up, her eyes had to adjust to the dark room. At some point she had kicked off her covers, and her legs were freezing. The house was quiet. Frank and Jaxon must be sleeping. She glanced at the clock. *Three a.m., of course they were sleeping as you should be.* But vivid images of needles, vials, and the cries of people still haunted her mind. Wide awake now, she tried to make sense of what she had seen before something pulled her from her nightmare.

As she recalled the dream, it was filled with disjointed images, places, and faces all surrounded by constant movement with one scene melting into another. Emily's face was among those calling out in her dream, and she was one being moved from place to place. Seeing her face gave Peyton hope that she was still alive.

Added to the mix was the deep sound of a man's voice and the blurred face of a woman with long dark hair. Were they somehow involved? This was not the man she saw in the bookstore. She was sure of that fact. How she knew was another question she couldn't answer. The one fact that stood out was there seemed to be crimes going on and crossing each other.

She covered her cold body with the blanket and closed her eyes. Sleep might not come easy, but at least she would rest. Another busy day awaited her once her alarm went off. Hopefully Jaxon would have the coffee ready.

****

When all her students and aides were gone, she sat alone in her empty classroom, and she was hesitant to leave. She wasn't quite alone because her ghost companion Mary watched her from the corner. The ghost's sudden agitation and her own instinct told her something wasn't right.

Jaxon hadn't called or texted her about the track. She had no idea how the search was going. She scrolled through her messages again, hoping she had overlooked one from him, but no such luck. Why was it when you anticipate something like she was, time seemed to move at a snail's pace while on other days the same time seemed to simply fly by? Time was time. There were sixty seconds in a minute, sixty minutes in an hour, and twenty-four hours in a day, which never changed, but watching the clock on the wall sure made it seem like it did.

Her up-and-down night had left her listless and tired, but she needed to quit stalling and get to the store to help Audrey. She stood, reached for her purse, and shut off the classroom light. Her phone buzzed an incoming text.

—Carlene found several places where the girl must have been and recently moved. The dog needs rest, and we'll try again later. Love, Jaxon.—

—Not what I hoped to hear but I'm not surprised. I'll tell you why later. Love you back.—

She locked her classroom door and strolled toward the office. This was one of the routines in her day that she always enjoyed. Grownup contact after a morning of rambunctious kids served to remind her why she loved her job. The staff was accommodating and encouraging, especially when she told them one of her success stories of a child who read a whole page or colored a picture just for her. They celebrated the special milestones with her. She wasn't in a hurry to leave for some reason, and she followed one of the teachers into the lounge. Where she listened to two teachers talk about their hectic morning.

When the bell rang signaling lunch was over, teachers went to get their classes, and she knew it was time for her to get to the bookstore. She had no idea why she kept dragging her feet. She dug her keys out of the bottom of her purse and stuffed her phone into her pocket as she made her way out of the school toward her car.

When she rounded the corner of the building toward the parking lot, she thought she heard someone behind her. Before she could turn to look, someone grabbed her. A large hand with a white cloth covered her face. She tried to fight, but her legs buckled beneath her, and her arms went limp before the darkness overtook her.

****

He noticed the playground attendant glance at him. Damn, but people get suspicious of a man near children playing at a school. As if he was interested in one of them. He pulled his red hat down, shielding his eyes, and when she quit watching him, he slipped behind the bushes. Pressing himself into the soil, he waited, listening to the giggles and screams of the children. He couldn't ever remember a time when he wanted a kid in his life. All they did was cramp the lives of most adults. Little rug rats every one of them. He had plenty of time to wait.

The vial in his pocket contained the magic elixir to make his job easier. Unwrapping the clean white cloth, he poured the liquid onto the cloth and placed the soaked material into the plastic bag. For the past few days, he'd studied her movements. She was late leaving the building, but he was patient. Time was something he had plenty of.

When the bell rang and the kids filed inside, along with the old biddy that had stared at him, he jumped to his feet and positioned himself. Like a wolf ready to pounce on his next victim, he tensed with anticipation. He didn't like being in such a public place, but he had no choice. The presence in the book store gave him the creeps.

Yet, now, Heaven was smiling down on him. His operation had worked to perfection with no one the wiser. He closed the trunk, making sure she was still out. Sweet dreams, he chuckled. He knew when he awakened this morning, he needed to act fast. She could mess up the nice operation that he had going here. Tired of jumping from one person to another, he finally found a spot where he could do what he liked best. Hell, he had to deal with her a second time. What was the presence that surrounded her? Confidence radiated from her, and he wasn't able to intimidate her. Stronger, yes, but there was something more, and he feared that unknown. He could tell she knew him even in his new and improved form. How was that even possible?

There was no way he was ready to move on yet. This time he would take care of her like he had so many others. This was his domain, and she would leave one way or another. He would take her back to be with his other treasure, and the two of them could rest in peace together. He smirked.

****

When Jaxon pulled into the PD parking lot, followed by Dylan's cruiser, Jaxon and Frank got out of the car and stretched their legs. The track hadn't gone the way they wanted, but Carlene was finding all the places where Emily had been—which was a good sign.

Kip approached their group. "Audrey called from the bookstore and said Peyton hadn't arrived yet. She said the school called her when they found her keys and purse lying on the ground. Her car is still parked in the school lot, but she seems to be missing."

"What do you mean she's missing?" Jaxon hands fisted at his side.

"No one can find her, and her purse on the ground seems to suggest maybe someone surprised her. There is a team on the scene now."

"Damn, I'm headed that way too. Frank, do you want to come?"

"Count me in. Looks like we'll be tracking two instead of one. I wonder if the same suspect has both of them."

"I'm telling you there are too many moving parts on this case. We have a serial killer, drugs, and some kind of secret society operating on campus. I'm sure we have more than one suspect. Hell, this is a mess."

Chapter 28

Jaxon arrived at the school after pushing back the panic rising inside him on what seemed like an endless drive from the station. The one thought repeated in his mind that pushed all others aside was he couldn't lose her. Not now, when she was beginning to trust him and their love was blooming. The thought of the suspect touching her made his stomach churn. She knew they were destined to meet, but his ego couldn't let him believe her. That same pride wanted him to rush off to save her and bash someone in the process. Not a good plan on his part. He clenched his fist.

"Hey, Jaxon, you need to hear this." Gary motioned to Jaxon. "This is Mrs. Potter. She has something of interest I think you need to hear."

Jaxon nodded at her and showed her his badge. "Did you see something that might help?"

"I saw a strange man lurking around the school. I always keep a keen eye because of the kids, you know. It's my job."

"I'm sure you do. Can you describe him to us?"

"I thought he looked strange with his dark hoodie and red cap. He was a big man, which made him worth watching. His cap was pulled low to shield his face. I can't tell you much more other than when he saw me watching him that he seemed to disappear. Good riddance."

“What do you mean he just disappeared?” Gary asked.

“I mean he was there, and when I turned to look again, he was gone. The bell rang, and I went inside along with the kids. As for the man, I don’t know where he went, but I don’t think he was up to any good. At least, that’s my take on him being near the school. He looked suspicious to me.”

“Thank you, ma’am. You’ve been helpful,” Gary told her.

Jaxon went to talk with Dylan and Frank. He repeated the conversation he heard from the woman. “The size of the man and the red cap sounds the same as Peyton’s description of the man she saw. I’m not happy to hear he is one and the same.”

“We don’t know that for sure.” Dylan frowned.

“You’ve been around these ladies long enough to know how accurate they are.” Jaxon folded his arms across his chest.

“Sure, but hell, I don’t want to believe the possibility of travelers and ghosts. The whole damn idea messes with my brain. Yes, I’ve seen them in action, but I’d rather go on as if I hadn’t. I’m not sure what that says about me.”

“I hear you, but I don’t believe we have any choice. They make us look good as Matt always says. He lets Jessie be herself, and he works a case the way he knows how. You know what that means, Frank?”

“I sure do. We are no longer looking for one but two.”

Jaxon took Peyton’s keys and purse. He drove her car back to the house with Frank following him. When he checked her purse, the one thing he noticed was her phone wasn't among the contents. If the phone was still in her possession, they could get a signal and a possible location. He had to trust her strength. She wasn't the same woman he met in Arizona. Somehow, he knew she would survive. What he wondered was how the guy was able to surprise her. That would be a story for another day. She would survive, he told himself many times as he walked into the house.

****

Peyton stifled a groan when her body landed hard on something and bounced upward. She needed to be quiet, her brain kept telling her. *Don't move.* She could smell his breath when he leaned close to her. He slapped something over her mouth and moved away mumbling to himself. She had to wait for the moment to present itself, and she knew the time would come. He came to the bed to check on her and the person next to her more than once. She tried to remain calm, but it seemed like he took an eternity before he settled down, and she could hear his even breathing and occasional snores. He did plenty of mumbling in his sleep. She glanced to her right and saw the motionless body next to her. When she touched the girl's hand, Peyton felt the slight movement in response to her touch. The girl was still alive. That's all she needed to know—her mind started designing a plan to get the two of them out of there to safety.

With any luck, Jaxon knew she was gone, and along with Frank they would search for her. In her heart she knew she couldn't remain here for them to find her. By the time they arrived, he might move them or kill them. She shuddered at the thought. A fact she didn't want to face but one she needed to consider to keep her motivated to fight.

A snore assured Peyton her captor could still be sleeping. She looked around and spotted him on a cot near the door. Not good, but not impossible to get by him either. Next to the bed on a small table was the white cloth that she remembered covered her nose and mouth, along with a vial containing a clear liquid. The same liquid that put her to sleep. She moved her hands, thankful that he hadn't tied them together like the girl's beside her. Her plan to get away had to include the girl. If that cloth soaked in the liquid knocked her out, maybe if she got close enough to him, that liquid might guarantee he slept long enough for them to get away. Once outside she had no idea where to go because she didn't know where they were. As she saw the situation, as far away from him as they could travel would be good. If she ever needed a bit of magic and a perfect execution of a plan, now was the time to believe.

The next time Peyton glanced at the girl, her eyes glistened with tears. She understood the emotion and closed the distance between them to reach for the girl's hand, wanting to reassure her. She could understand the fear she read in her eyes because the same sense pulsated through her. But as Grams always told her, courage wasn't the absence of fear but to stand in the face of that fear. *Well, Peyton, this is your moment to put her words into action.* Any movement she made from this point on had to be made with caution. She rolled slightly to her side and paused to listen. Steady snores and even breathing were music to her ears, as she lifted the small vial and poured some of the clear contents on the cloth. *Please, oh please let this stuff work on him the way smelling the cloth did me.* Any progress she made would have to be done as silently as possible. She could only hope the guy was a solid sleeper.

Peyton placed her finger to the tape covering her mouth and glanced at the girl again. Swinging her legs with care over the side of the bed, she pushed up to a sitting position. She paused when the man snorted and turned his face toward the wall. She sighed inwardly before she gained the courage to move again. She held the cloth as she stood and stealthily moved toward the sleeping man. When she crept close enough to him, she placed the soaked cloth over his face. His arms flailed, and his fist hit her hard, almost knocking her backward, but she braced herself against his attack until the man's arms went limp. She rubbed her cheek where his fist had connected and ripped the tape off her mouth. He slept with some kind of book under his pillow. She wanted to take it, but she couldn't carry anything and help Emily too.

She rushed to the girl and untied her legs and arms. They had to hurry, and she hoped the girl could walk. She helped her into a sitting position. Holding on to her so she wouldn't fall.

"Do you think you can walk?" She pulled the tape off the girl's mouth. "Emily?"

"Yes. Who are you? Can I trust you?" she whispered as they made their way to the door.

"Yes, you can trust me. I promise I will help you. I hope if we hurry, we can get away from this guy."

Once outside the shack where he kept them, the sky was dark, and Peyton had no idea where they were. Nothing looked familiar to her. She had no idea how long she had been in the trunk of the car. For now, she would follow the road and find a hiding place if she heard a car.

She reached her hand into her pocket, taking out the

phone, she had stuffed in there. Thank God she had. She tried to call Jaxon, but she had no service. Darn, where were they? If she could get to a higher place or out from under the canopy of the trees maybe.

"Are you doing okay?" She glanced at Emily struggling to keep up.

"Don't worry about me. I will keep moving if it kills me. I've seen what that man is capable of, and I would rather die trying than by his hands. How did he get you?"

"It's a long story, and when we are far enough away, I will share the details with you. I met your roommate Kelsey who was worried about you. I also saw you in a dream and knew we were destined to meet. I wasn't sure how or when, but here we are." Peyton kept walking down the road. She linked her arm through Emily's, helping her as much as she could.

"Who is that man? I never saw him around the campus. Although, there is some crazy stuff going on there. I was writing a major article that would have exposed a few people. I thought for sure he was sent by one of them. He seemed to be a bit of a loose cannon."

Peyton could see more lights in the distance. Hopefully they were getting close to people, and she picked up her speed. She checked her phone again, pushing Jaxon's number and hoping that this time maybe the call would go through and maybe he would answer. Sounds of a car coming on the road had them moving to hide in the trees with the idea of a phone call pushed to the back of her mind.

****

"Have you picked up her phone signal yet?" Jaxon paced around Gary's office.

"Not yet. I had to work through the channels to get

the okay, and now I'm trying to get a signal."

"What would that mean?" Jaxon frowned.

"Maybe he found her phone, or she dropped it somewhere. The other possibility is she is out of the signal range. Don't fret, Jaxon, if the phone is anywhere near her, we will get the signal eventually."

"I know, but this guy will kill her given the chance. She's strong and smart, which is in her favor, but even she understood he meant business." He leaned his shoulder against the wall and folded his arms across his chest. "Any sign at all?"

"Not yet, I'll let you know the minute we see something."

"Okay." He pushed away from the wall and sat in one the chairs outside Gary's office.

"We'll find her." Dylan sat down beside him. "Frank's dog will be ready to go soon. He assured me she has tracked at night many times. Catch me up-to-date on what else is happening at the college."

"There seems to be three major areas the agents have uncovered. I'm sure there will be offshoots of those three that exposure will discover." He told Dylan the details from his last meeting with Maxwell, and recent interviews with families. "The truth is there is a dark side to social media and online activity."

"As Matt has told this department often, we need to get with the times. Criminals seem to be one step ahead of those trying to arrest them. If you can think of a scenario, I can guarantee someone else has and has implemented it." Dylan said.

"I'm finding that to be the truth. We are talking college students here, and they understand the cyber world in ways I never would have imagined. Take artificial intelligence, which is a whole new frontier we will have to deal with. It wasn't on the radar when I was in college. The alarms are being sounded from the top, but some are already warning we're too late to put the rules in place. AI will control us in a few years."

Gary called out from the office offering his take on the subject. "We're in a hell of a mess. Our discoveries meant to improve life could ultimately destroy us, along with those who benefit from the steady doses of fear fed to us by those wishing to divide and control us through propaganda."

"Those of us who work this side of the law can see what we're up against, and that knowledge can be hard to deal with on a daily basis," Dylan said.

"I hear you." Jaxon shifted in the chair.

"Matt and I often talk about rethinking our job. The events leading up to his wedding had us all wondering if our jobs were worth the price of our physical and mental health. You never know who from your past might want to seek retribution." Dylan shook his head.

"Yeah, Frank told me the same thing. He's seen crime scenes he'll never be able to forget, but he's also seen the upside too. Finding a missing child alive or bringing closure to a family is one good way to erase some of the bad."

Jaxon continued to talk to Dylan and with Frank who joined them. Between pacing and sitting down with a foot he couldn't hold still waiting for an answer to come. When no answer came, time in his mind seemed to stretch out before him.

"I think Carlene is ready to track if you want to try." Frank interrupted his thoughts.

"Anything is better than waiting here and feeling

helpless." Jaxon stood.

"Bingo. Jaxon, come look," Gary called to him.

He pointed to a small faint dot on the screen. "This is faint. Her battery might be low, or the place has little to no Wi-Fi service. She might be at this location, or this could be where her phone was discarded, but at least it gives you a starting point." He handed them a paper with coordinates on it. "My rough guess is this place is in the middle of nowhere about forty minutes from here."

"By nowhere you mean?" Jaxon asked. "We live in a densely populated area of New England."

"There are plenty of abandon houses and areas off the beaten path. You know, near towns and yet they seem to be out in the country. There are reservations, public lands, and forests. In other words, there are plenty of hiding places."

"Thanks for this, Gary, if she's out there we'll find her." Frank took ahold of Carlene's leash.

"We'll be on our way. Call for back up and give them the coordinates you gave us. I'll keep an open channel." Dylan walked with Jaxon out of Gary's office.

****

He awakened groggy with a massive headache. Damn, what had happened to him? When he tried to sit up, his pounding head and numb limbs made the simple seem almost impossible. After his first feeble attempts he accomplished his goal while he tried to focus in the dark and quiet room. He reached for his phone and turned on the flashlight, shining it toward the bed.

Hell, they were gone. How did they slip past him? He stood on legs that were a bit wobbly, and that's when he saw the cloth near his pillow. She used the same drug on him that he had used on her. Why hadn't he tied her legs and hands? She had been out when he checked the last time, and the other one wouldn't dare to move a muscle without help. She was his fearful little mouse. His hand reached under his pillow. Relief filled him that the book and the testament to his work was still there.

Her days were limited, he raged. Damn, women. Now he had to go search for them. They couldn't have gotten far. He'd go as soon as his head settled down, and his legs would move on his command. He knew this one could be trouble if he didn't get her first.

When he finally made it out to the car, he had to search on instinct because he had no idea which way they would go. His brain still foggy from the drug kept him in a daze and restricted his ability to function. If he could clear his head and think correctly, his abilities to locate them should kick in. At least the night was a dark one, and they had no idea where they were nor how to find their way out of the area. It was a bit of a maze even for him. He'd find them all right, and when he did, he'd take care of the problem once and for all.

Chapter 29

Peyton had kept her ears tuned to the noises around them, and as soon as she heard the car in the distance, she knew they needed to hide. She held Emily up and pulled her along beside her to a hiding place off the road among the trees.

"Will you be okay?" Peyton glanced at her. "We may have to be here for a while and make little to no sound at all."

"I can be still. Right now, resting here will be easier than walking. My legs have had little activity for the past several days. I have no idea how long I have been tied and unable to move. Long enough for me to be wobbly on my feet. I guess."

"You did great. I'm not sure how far we got or even where we are at, but we've at least made his job harder. If we put out heads together, we can make it even harder for him."

Peyton tried to encourage the girl while she tried to think of a plan to stop the guy. He wasn't an ordinary man. He managed to survive, who knew how many decades, by jumping in other bodies, and who knows what else could be named among his abilities. Help from an unlikely source is what she needed. Something to block their location until she could figure out what they should do. She couldn't explain that to Emily sitting beside her. The girl was wrung out, and every sound around them caused her to get agitated.

"I want to hear more about the story you were working on when you're able to tell me. Your roommate was concerned that was the reason why you went missing." Peyton rubbed her arms, trying to ward off the chill in the air. She wasn't dressed to be out in the cold night air, and neither was Emily. She wondered how many times he had drugged her and how many times he had moved her since he kidnapped her. Was he toying with her or getting ready to kill her? Maybe his plan was to kill Emily in front of her because she hadn't played along with his plan. Emily was in a dress similar to the murder victim she found, and the charm was still wrapped around her hand. The only thing missing was the single rose.

A few cars had passed their hiding spot, but thankfully not one of them had stopped. They were safe for now. Peyton studied the charm on Emily's hand. The minute she reached over and unwrapped the talisman from her arm, she could feel a dark sensation rush through. "We need to get rid of this. I'll be right back."

"Please don't leave me alone." Emily began to cry.

"I promise I'll only be a few minutes. Stay hidden." Peyton cautiously walked out of their hiding place, searching for landmarks to find her way back to Emily.

She crossed to the other side of the road and bent branches and took the charm and threw the darn thing as far as she could. She couldn't help but think of the Irish legend of the pooka. Believed to be a spirit. The pooka was a fairy that was capable of assuming another form like a horse or wolf. She learned about the pooka in one of her cases. The pooka could assume a human form but had some form of animal characteristics. They could do both good or evil and assist or harm the communities in which they operated. The charm had her thinking that all this was somehow attached back to the battle of her ancestors and the battle for the minds in their time. The pooka legend didn't seem to fit this case, but she knew there had to be one that would.

Research was first on her agenda if she ever got out of the mess she found herself in. She made it back to the road and listened and waited until she felt it was safe to make her way to the other side.

"Emily, it's me. Are you okay?"

"Yes," she cried out. "I was scared he would come back before you did. Where did you go?"

"I went across the road and sent that charm on a journey, and I hope I bought us a bit of time. How are your legs? Do you think you can walk a bit more?"

"Yes, I believe I can. I want to get away from him." She stood.

"We'll walk in the shadow of the trees and keep heading in the direction toward the lights. Hopefully we can stay safe under the cover of night."

****

Jaxon answered his phone. "What's up, Gary?"

"Keep this line open, and I'll keep you up-to-date on what's going on."

"Okay, sounds good. Do you still have a signal?"

"I do. I've been watching a strange pattern. The signal seemed to stop in the same spot for a period of time. Then she must have changed her direction and went a completely different way, but she came back. Now she is tracking in the same direction as the original coordinates. It'll be up to you to ask her why she changed course."

"I'm sure she had a good reason, and we'll know soon enough. How close am I to the turnoff?"

"You're about twelve minutes out."

"Let me know if she changes directions again," Jaxon told him.

"I will. I'm tracking you both. That's some woodsy area, and you'll need the dog's help for sure."

"I'm glad we have Frank and Carlene. With any luck we'll get both of the ladies home safe and sound." Jaxon glanced at Frank sitting beside him in the front seat. "I take it you heard all that."

"I did. Knowing the Reynolds girl like I do, I'm sure she had a darn good reason for changing her direction the way she did."

"I thought the same thing. The fact that the signal is moving means she is still alive, and the phone wasn't simply tossed out the window somewhere, lying on the ground. It gives me hope."

"I agree. Our turnoff should be coming up soon."

If Peyton were lucky enough to get away from the guy, he hoped they found her before the man did. His girl was resourceful, but she seemed concerned about the size of his body. Still, she knew that they would have to meet. What that meeting entailed, he wasn't sure if he wanted to know. But if he knew Peyton, she was planning and putting pieces together in her mind as they were coming to her rescue. Something told him they would find her, but she had already rescued herself in some inventive way. Peyton was not one to sit on the sidelines and cry. One of the strongest women he'd ever known, she never failed to impress him.

"Hey, Jaxon, take the next right. The signal is still moving in the same direction, and it's getting a bit stronger." Gary's voice came across the line. "Can you see the turn? On the map the road doesn't look like much."

"I can see the turn. Once we turn, keep me informed if we are moving toward or away from the signal."

"I will. Although Carlene, with that amazing nose of hers, should easily move you toward Peyton's scent."

"You're right about her. She won't lead us the wrong way."

Jaxon pulled off into a gas station that was closed. Dylan's car pulled in beside him. Frank got Carlene out of her crate and put her line on her.

"This looks look like a good launching spot. Let's roll."

Frank placed a sweater with Peyton's scent on the item. "Find her, girl. Let's get to work." Carlene started moving and pulled Frank with her. "She is picking up something."

Jaxon was always fascinated by the way the dog worked. Between her ears sweeping the ground scooping the scent to her nose and her picking the scent out of the air, she wouldn't stop until she found Peyton, or they stopped her.

"Keep heading in the direction you're going," Gary said.

"Will do."

****

He sat in the car for what seemed like an eternity to him, waiting for his head to clear. The charm was talking to him, and he needed to move in the direction of the call. He was glad she hadn't taken the damn thing off. What girl didn't like a shiny bauble or two to keep from her time with a real charmer? He smirked. From the day he walked into that bookstore, he knew she would cause him trouble. If he didn't find them soon, he would have to start all over again grooming his next girl. What a nuisance.

He drove back and forth down the road a few times toward the charm's call. He couldn't see anything in the darkness. When he drove by a certain area, the call of the talisman grew louder, and he knew they couldn't be far. He drove all the way to where the small-town post office and gas station were to turn around and make another pass. The town rolled up the sidewalks after five and shut off the lights, which suited him fine. He noticed two police cars at the gas station, and he was ready to get the hell out of Dodge. Not wanting to be found, he turned around and drove back toward the shack to gather his stuff. He didn't want to get caught, not that they could catch him, but he didn't want his operations to be messed up. He decided to live and play another day. He knew the area, and he would be back when the cops were gone. The elements might take them before he could, but either way they'd be gone. Although he would miss out on the fun. He would go underground for a few days or better yet look up his brothers. Many years had passed since the three of them joined forces. They had taught him well in their heyday, and there was something of them in him and he in them. They would have been nothing without their mother.

He threw his meager possessions in the car and chose to go in the direction the cop cars were parked in defiance of them. They couldn't stop him, but he'd like to see them try.

Chapter 30

Peyton was stumbling forward, holding Emily up, who was fast running out of strength. She knew she could never tackle the guy while she tried to keep Emily safe. "When was the last time you had anything to eat?"

"I don't know. I've been sleeping most of the time. I could hear him mumbling to himself from time to time. Mostly he gave me drops of water and replaced the tape covering my mouth. When I moaned or cried out, he would place that awful-smelling stuff over my nose and I would be out again. I tried to remain still and quiet. But then he would come close and breathe on me with his stinky breath. I had to fight to keep from gagging. His breath smelled like sulfur."

"I can attest to that. He could've used some strong mouthwash. Do you need to rest, or shall we keep going?"

"I want to keep going. I can't think of him finding us or ever going back with him." She stumbled and fell to her knees. "Don't stop! We have to keep moving," she said when Peyton helped her to her feet.

"We won't stop, but maybe we can go a little slower." Peyton eased the pace and continued to let Emily lean on her.

She couldn't image what this poor girl had gone through. Jaxon and Dylan would have to interview her with care after this ordeal. She needed to be checked out at a hospital and pampered for a while. A good therapist wouldn't hurt either. When had life got so complicated?

She had grown up with evil and knew what abuse was, but she also understood there was plenty of good in this world too. Frank had told her of some of the awful crime scenes he had come across with his dogs. They left an indelible mark upon his life. Light and darkness, good and evil always seem to be a war in the human race. The choice wasn't always easy. When her dad would be in one of his abusive moods, she wanted to strike back at him. Instead, she hid and protected her sister. In many ways hiding had protected her from the hate that could have overtaken her. It took years, but she learned to forgive him with the help of others. Letting go of her anger toward her parents freed her. Jaxon's steady character was showing she could trust and even love a man. To her that was a big deal. Emily could come out of this time strong. One could hope.

Peyton's legs buckled, and she had to shift to stand upright. "I think we have to stop for a few minutes to rest. I can't go on."

"I'm sorry. I'm slowing you down. You should leave me here and get away." Emily sighed and swiped at the tears filling her eyes. "I'm cold and numb."

"I'm not going to leave you. We're in this together. I won't go on until we're both ready." Peyton sat beside her, scooching as close to her as she could. She wrapped her arm across Emily's shoulders. "Now that we've settled that, let's do our best to keep each other warm."

"Thank you." Emily leaned her head against Peyton's shoulder and closed her eyes.

Peyton knew the moment Emily went to sleep. She stopped fussing, and her breathing became soft and even.

She searched the heavens stretched over them like a canopy for a sign of hope. That's when she saw the small light flittering above her. She lifted her hand to swat at what she thought was a bug and stopped midway when the tiny face of Mila came into view.

"Now, now, no hitting or swatting I'm a friend after all." She smiled at Peyton. "Celeste has sent me to you. I can't stay long, but I'm here to tell you an old Irish legend that holds a great truth for you today. Elida and Basil send their warm regards." She landed on Peyton's arm, instantly warming her. "You know nothing is as it seems. There's a bit of magic in all of life, and the invisible world is as real as the one you see."

"I'm learning that to be true."

"There are many notable characters found in our Irish legends from the banshee to pooka. One of them is Carman the warrior and sorceress. The story goes that she was from Athens and tried to invade Ireland along with her three sons. Carman manipulated Dub, Dother, and Dian, whose mission together was to cause destruction. She used her magical powers to destroy the fruit of Ireland. The belief was widely held that she and her sons wreaked havoc on the land using their magical powers."

"What does that have to do with me or this case?"

"Well, you know, my dear, when you and Jessie are involved, there is more than meets the eye. Carman was known for her strength and resilience. She has evolved over time, changing with societal norms although she was chained and imprisoned. The most important part of the legend for you though is her sons. Dub, whose name means darkness, Dother, who is evil, and Dian meaning violence. When they were cursed, her sons were banished across the seas never to return to Ireland. Their spirits have found homes in each generation, at different locations for all these many years. You are dealing with one of their essences now. Celeste believes he is hoping to join up with his brothers, which would not be good. My job along with Elida's and our third wheel Basil's will be to do all we can do to prevent this from happening. You won't see us this time, but we won't be far out of your sight."

"Which one am I dealing with?" Peyton scowled.

"You will come to that piece of knowledge on your own as you see the manifestation of his crimes. Every people group from Native Americans to my own Irish home people have their own legends and ways to deal with the darkness they see around them. But remember, dear, the magic is in you. With knowledge comes defeat. To my way of thinking like Aelfric, the three of them have been hopping around and using whoever was willing to do their bidding for way too long. In my opinion they need to be banished forever, but they were destined to roam far from their home, and that's what they do. Leaving darkness, evil, and violence in their wake."

"I might be wrong, but from where I am sitting, it seems like all three to me."

"I imagine they have influenced each other over the centuries. But dealing with one is not the same as having to deal with all three. There is strength in numbers, dear."

"No, I imagine not." Peyton shook her head. "What's next?"

"Well, my dear, that will be up to you. You might have to be a warrior on the right side to tackle this. Remember the scrolls and the dagger from your ancestors. Mostly, remember who you are, and the strength has passed down to you from the women in your family line. Ta-ta, my sweet girl. I hear the sound of people looking for you. Rest while you can, and they will find you." Mila blew her a misty kiss, and with the swirl of her wand, she was gone.

Peyton pushed her hair out of her eyes and behind her ears. Her parents would have a conniption fit if they got wind of her talking to fairies. Mila was more of a friend than magical creature. With the sisters on the job, even if unseen, she could breathe easier.

She would rest only for a few minutes. She would wake Emily, and they could start walking in a few minutes. She shivered, rubbed her arms, moving closer to Emily, and closed her eyes.

****

Jaxon followed Frank and Carlene. The dog pulled on the line hard, keeping Frank moving at a fast pace. He was amazed how Frank managed to stay on his feet as the dog tugged him forward. He had no idea how far they had walked. To him, the miles seemed to be piling up, which also meant they would have to walk the same distance back to their cars.

"Gary, are we still headed in the right direction?" Dylan asked.

"Yes, the signal has remained in the same place for a while. You should be there soon. I have no idea why there's no movement. I've sent Kip out with a car. I figured you might need an extra transport. You were quite a distance from the signal. I figured you've been walking a few miles. Once you let me know the area is secure, I will send him on the road close to you."

"Thanks. I was thinking we would be walking back

the same way we came. I wasn't relishing the idea." Jaxon chuckled. "I'm impressed with how Frank keeps up. I bet he'll sleep good tonight."

"I think we're getting close," Frank called back to them. Carlene pulled them off the main road toward the cover of the trees.

"Frank, hold up a minute. We need to cover for you. We have no idea what we're walking into." Dylan walked fast to get in front of Frank and the dog.

Jaxon pulled out his Glock and stood next to Dylan. They moved forward slowly with one going to the left and another to the right. Frank couldn't hold Carlene back anymore. She rushed into the area and sat in front of where the two women leaned against a tree side by side.

"They are over here," Frank said.

Jaxon rushed to Peyton's side and checked for a pulse. The minute his hand touched her neck, she jerked awake and started to swing. "What the?"

"It's okay, sweetheart," Jaxon told her. "You're safe now." He was rewarded when she jumped up and headed straight into his open arms.

Frank handed her the sweater he had used as a scent item. "You must be cold."

"Freezing. Once the sun went down, the temps dropped." She placed the sweater on Emily's shoulders.

"We have a car coming so you won't have to walk anymore." He glanced at Emily. "She hasn't moved. Is she okay?"

"She's exhausted, been drugged a lot, and hasn't eaten in a while. I think she needs to be checked out." Peyton took ahold of Jaxon's hand and squeezed it tight. "Thank you for finding us. I don't know why he hasn't."

"We'll figure that out once we get you to safety." Jaxon pulled her into his side. "I'm relieved to find you okay. I want to ask you a lot of questions, but I'll wait. You need to get warm, and you both need to be checked out." He saw her shake her head. "Yes, you too if he used a drug on you."

As soon as Kip pulled up on the road close to where they were, Jaxon walked Peyton and Emily out to the car and rode back with them to get the car. He told Kip to take both girls to the hospital to be checked out. He would get there as soon as he got Frank back to the house with Carlene.

Jaxon leaned in the open back door and whispered in Peyton's ear, "I love you, sweetheart. I'll be there as soon as I can."

"Okay." She reached for his hand. "Thank you for finding us. I let Emily lean on me until we both got too cold and tried to go on." She touched his face. "I love you too."

Jaxon got into the front seat and rode back to where they had parked the cars. He got into Frank's SUV with Carlene's crate in the back. She would be more than ready to get a treat and get into her crate and rest. As he drove up the road, he passed a car that he had seen before. Maybe the occupant lived somewhere up the road, but he wondered. Could he be looking for the girls? The thought didn't set well with him. He knew the guy wouldn't give up and was tied with the college case somehow.

He couldn't wait to hear what Peyton and Emily experienced. He picked up Frank, his dog, and dropped Dylan back at his cruiser, and headed back to town. With

Frank at Matt's house, and Carlene fed and asleep, Jaxon made his way to the hospital.

Chapter 31

"Where are they?" Jaxon walked into the waiting room and stood beside Kip.

"In the examination room. The doctor is with them, and the nurse just told me he would be out in a moment. Peyton seems to be okay, but the Hart girl might be admitted. I'm waiting to hear. We might need to place a guard outside her room if she stays. I already notified Dylan of the possibility."

"I was hoping to talk to them tonight while the details are still fresh in their minds." Jaxon leaned his shoulder against the wall. "I guess we'll see what the doctor recommends on that subject." He clenched his fist at his side as he continued to talk to Kip.

"Are you the officer who brought the patients in?" The doctor walked out of the examination room and approached Kip.

"Yes, sir, and this is Agent Kincaid." They shook hands. "How are they doing?"

"We are admitting Ms. Hart. I know you both need to question her, and as soon as Ms. Hart is in her room, you'll be free to go up. She's been through a major ordeal and will need some recovery time. Do you know of next of kin that we can notify that she is here?"

"Yes. I'll call her father right now." Jaxon reached for his phone.

"That would be great. She's been asking for her dad.

Both girls were dehydrated, and we are giving them IV fluids. Ms. Reynolds will be free to leave as soon as her drip is finished. Make sure she eats a little something and watch her closely. She didn't get as much of the drug in her system as the Hart girl has, but she could still experience some nasty side effects."

"Thank you. We'll keep an eye on her," Kip assured him.

"The staff is getting Emily Hart ready to move. You can go into the exam room as soon as they're done."

"We are going to station an officer outside of her door, and other than police, medical staff, or her father, no one else will be allowed in the room unless accompanied by one of us."

"I'm sure that will be reassuring to her. I'll alert the hospital staff to the protocol. We know how to observe when a patient is under protection. I'm glad you found those two. This story will have a happy ending for their families."

"We're glad we did too." Jaxon shook the doctor's hand again and thanked him.

Jaxon called Emily's dad. And as soon as Emily was moved from the exam room, he went in to find Peyton sitting in a chair with the IV drip in her hand. "How are you?"

"Besides a massive headache, I'm processing. It's been an eventful and long day." She smiled at him. "How did you know where to look for us? I tried calling, but I couldn't get a signal."

"Gary was able to pick up your phone's weak signal after many attempts. At some point you must have got in range of a tower."

"I never thought to try again. All my energy was

focused on getting us away from the shack he kept us in."

"Which brings me to the two questions uppermost in my mind. How did he take you by surprise, and how did you get away from him?" Jaxon pulled an empty chair up close to her and sat.

"I was coming out of the school, he grabbed me from behind, and all I remember after that was a foul-smelling cloth over my nose and mouth. Whatever was on the rag dropped me like a limp doll." She pursed her lips and shook her head. "I didn't have time to react. The whole thing happened fast. My training kicked in a minute too late. I tried to fight, but it was useless once the drug was introduced."

"They're designed to knock a person out." He stroked her fingers, careful not to touch her IV. "I never liked these darn things."

"You and me both. Oh, gosh, I hope somebody found my purse and keys. What about my car?"

"We have your personal items, and your car is at Matt's."

"Of course, you do. Thank you and thank everyone else."

"Not to change the subject but do you know how Emily was abducted?" He leaned forward in the chair.

"I haven't asked her. She was in no shape to talk. Emily will need help getting through her ordeal. I believe he meant to kill her in front of me and then do the same to me. Fear can be a paralyzing useful tool." She went on to tell him about how she waited until he was asleep and used the drug on him. "I'm not sure it could have worked more perfectly. He left the vial and cloth on a table beside me to use on me again if I awakened. We made our escape by following the road and buying some time."

"Weren't you concerned he would come looking for you?" he asked.

"Sure, we both were, and because we had to go slow, I felt sure he would find us. Remember this guy is in no way ordinary. I realized the importance of the charm he placed on his victim. Emily had one wrapped around her wrist, which dangled between her fingers almost like a rosary. Do you remember when Jessie got her pendant, when she touched the necklace charm, a warm sensation shot through her?"

"I wasn't there, but Matt told me about the artifacts and her pendant."

"Well, when I touched this charm, there was darkness and evil associated with it. The charm itself is a symbol of the circle of life, but his usage of the talisman is for evil. I took it off her arm and went across the street into the trees and threw as far as I could. I believe he could track us while she wore his accursed charm."

"Fascinating, another oddity I can't put in a report." He smiled at her. "You make my reports a tad more difficult to write these days."

"If you find that strange, that's only the tip of the iceberg. I have a whole lot more to tell you that will blow your mind. We can talk later. You should go up to see Emily. Her dad should be here soon, and keeping her awake may not be easy. At least she can sleep safely."

"I'll check in with her. Don't go anywhere. I'll be back soon." He reached over and kissed her cheek. "I'm not ready to lose you."

"You're my ride. I won't be going anywhere without you." She stroked his cheek. "I'm happy to still be here myself."

Jaxon stood. "You do know this tiny interview was

only preliminaries. There are a lot more questions to come."

"I know." She sighed.

****

Peyton watched Jaxon leave the room. Since she met the man and they had gotten past their determination to not like each other, he had been there for her. She could let down her guard around him and rest. He had proved himself to her repeatedly. How on earth would she tell the man who waited for her return when she was pulled through a book or listened to her theories of a bad fairy who shifted into a black wolf with raised eyebrows but no judgment, there would be more crazy stuff to come? How he must question his sanity around her at times. And now there were Dub, Dother, and Dian the three brothers who had wreaked havoc in Ireland and among the nations. She needed to tread softly, which didn't come natural to her, and do her research before she told him about the three brothers.

Maybe the scrolls would unlock the mystery of the brothers or their mom, or better yet, she could ask Jeremy to see what he could find. Maybe Jessie could ask some of the locals in Ireland about the legend. She'd love to be involved. Peyton smiled to herself. Finally, she had a plan, something she could sink her teeth into. She wanted to understand what was happening at the college and why there seem to be such an anger building against women.

She could be wrong, but it seemed the moment women found their voice and were no longer afraid to speak out for themselves, the problem escalated. The idea made no sense to her. Men always had their place in the world, but women were only beginning to emerge from the shadows, not to take someone else's place but only to find their own. Did competition have to rule everything? Matt and Jessie had found a way to complement each other. How rare was that?

All her musings fit into this case in some way. She needed to talk to her cousin and her mentor Reba.

"How are we doing in here?" The nurse walked into the room with a smile.

"I'm good. My head still hurts, but the doctor said that might be the case for a day or two."

"Drugs can have residual effects. Especially, in a case when a person doesn't administer correct dosages." She checked the drip line. "You're almost done. I say in about ten minutes we can remove this line and sign you out of here. You'll be free to go home and sleep."

"Sounds perfect to me. Will Emily be okay?"

"Physically she'll be fine soon although more time will be needed for her to heal mentally." The nurse headed toward the door. "I'll be back to remove this and have you sign release forms in a few minutes."

"Okay, thank you." Peyton leaned her head back against the chair and closed her eyes. She could imagine the meeting between Emily and her father. It was easy to visualize because she could see the relief on Jaxon's face, and she had only been gone for hours not days.

Chapter 32

Once the release papers were signed, she was ready to go to the house. There was a bed there calling her name, and all she needed now was her ride.

"The doctor told me to give you this for your headache. And you should see your doctor if the pain persists. His recommendation is to go home and rest, which means no work today. Everything will be better after you get some sleep. You're free to stay in this area until the agent comes back. You've had a stressful day."

"Thank you, again." She smiled at the nurse. Sleep would be perfect if her mind shut down long enough to get there. Her foot tapped under the chair as her hand reached for the phone on the table beside her. After the day she lived through, idleness wasn't sitting well with her. She sent off a text to Jeremy asking him to research the legend Mila had told her about. There was something in that information that was too important for her to forget. While she was in the mood and still semi awake, she went over each aspect of the day that she could remember. Trying to etch into her memory how her abductor looked and acted in the time she was with him. She also needed to remember to tell Jaxon she had seen the man's car drive up and down the road a few times searching for them after she had thrown the charm away on the other side of the road.

Hopefully, the drug dose she gave him made him

feel as bad as they did. She doubted he would be at the shack any longer. Knowing his nature from the round in Arizona, he had gone underground. Somehow, he was tied to the college if only to find his next victim.

"Hi, beautiful, the nurse told me you are free to leave." Jaxon walked into the room.

"Yes, and I'm beyond ready." Peyton stood and took his hand. "How is Emily?"

"She answered a few questions, but once her dad came in and hugged her, she went right to sleep."

"Were you talking to him?"

"Yes. The man fell apart once he realized she was going to be okay. I sat with him for a while. I could only imagine how relieved he was. Emily will have a lot to tell us once she gets her strength back, and so will you, I'm sure." He opened the car door for her once outside. "The nurse told me that you should not work today, and I promised to make sure you didn't."

"You won't have to try too hard. I don't think I could teach those lively kids even if I wanted to, which I don't. I want to sleep beneath a warm cozy blanket."

"A good plan but only after you have something to eat, which also were among the nurse's instructions from the doctor." He glanced at her. "Relax, we'll be home in a few minutes."

"If I get any more relaxed, I won't be able to walk into the house. I'm happy to be away from that man, but I don't think he's gone for good. We will meet again, but next time I'll be ready." She rubbed her temple. "I guess I'll need to call work in the morning."

"Your principal told me yesterday he would get a substitute teacher for today. Of course, he had no idea what had happened to you. You might want to call him later in the day to let him know that you're okay."

"I will."

"By the way, Dylan said they checked out the place where he held you both and he wasn't there."

"I was sure he wouldn't be. He's gone underground, but he'll be back. As much as I don't want him to."

"We'll do our best to prevent that scenario. The crime team is going over the shack with the help of the agency. Kidnapping brings in the FBI. Dylan is happy to have the extra hands."

"I know he appreciates the help. Blue Cove has been challenging for the PD lately."

As soon as Jaxon pulled into the driveway and stopped, he got out and opened the door for her. "You get ready for bed, and I'll bring in something to eat."

"Give me time to shower." She walked down the hall.

"Are you sure you should?" he called after her.

"Yes. I want to wash away the memory of his touch from my body." She closed the door.

He could understand her reasoning. Jaxon heated some water and took a tea bag out of the cabinet. He popped a bagel into the toaster and fixed a tall glass of ice water. The more he envisioned the man touching her, the angrier he became. Tonight, Peyton proved she was capable of taking care of herself, but he wouldn't mind hitting the guy a few times just because. He wouldn't though. He was no better if he couldn't abide by the same laws he swore to enforce. His training drummed into him many times over that no one was above the law. That no one included him.

He filled a cup with boiling water and put a tea bag in with a bit of honey and a lemon wedge on the side.

When the bagel was toasted, he spread cream cheese on the surface the way she liked it. He even scrambled an egg and arranged the food on a tray the way his mother trained him along with his siblings to do. She always told them being able to cook was something everyone needed to know, for themselves or to care for someone else. He smiled at the memory now but groaned and complained when she made him have a turn at doing the cooking.

He knocked softly on Peyton's door. "I have a little something for you to eat." He entered when she told him to come in. He placed the tray on the nightstand. "Are you doing all right?"

"Much better, now." She placed the brush on the bed beside her.

"Be sure to finish all the water. We have to keep you hydrated. Doctor's orders." He smiled and bent close to kiss her cheek. "I'm proud of you for what you did tonight. You used your head and were resourceful. In the process you saved Emily's life as well as your own. My theory is you caused this guy to act ahead of schedule because you wouldn't do what he wanted. You're one strong woman."

"A desire to live is a good motivator, believe me. Thank you for making this. I'll do my best to eat it before I sleep."

"See that you do. I'll be back to get the tray."

"You'd better get some sleep. You have to work."

"Yeah, I guess I'd better. I'm happy you're safe. Sleep well, sweetheart." He kissed her and left the room.

****

She picked up her cup of tea. Jaxon was thoughtful, and she appreciated the sweet touches he added to the tray. Especially, the note telling her to drink all of the water, and the lemon wedge. He remembered she liked lemon in her hot tea. She took a bite of the bagel and tried hard to hold her eyes open while she chewed. Sleep descended on her like a heavy weight too hard to fight against. After her first sips from the glass, she gave in to the sensation threatening to overtake her. She pulled up the blanket and snuggled beneath the covers, cocooning herself in its warmth. Sighing with contentment, she closed her eyes, relishing the sensation of the tension ebbing from her body.

She walked along the shore near the marina in her dream. The boats swayed and bobbed with the ripples of the water while other boats stirred the water as they came and went in the cove. The scene before her was idyllic but seemed to have an undercurrent she couldn't yet see or understand. Someone followed her movement though they remained unseen. The cove suddenly erupted with motion, and waves splashed high against the boats and made their way onto the shoreline, crashing over the docks and boardwalk. A spirit flew from one side of cove to the other and there joined forces with another spirit. The two were soon joined by a third, and the destruction that followed was deadly.

Blue Cove was reeling as the three destroyed what was in their path. When their work was done, they moved on, but the devastation they left behind would take years to recover from. The face of her captor came in and out of view throughout as she walked, ran, and hid in terror. When she awakened, she had her proof that her abductor was attached in some way to one of the spirits she saw wreaking havoc. All the while he laughed and sneered at her as if he thought he had won. Not true, the battle had only begun. She wasn't a pushover, and she would do all she could to keep the three brothers from joining forces.

She pushed herself up against the headboard and stuck a pillow behind her back. Jessie had mentioned to her once that each generation must determine what was worth fighting for. Once she was out of her father's house, she had a fairly simple life. Sure, there were the normal ups and downs that most folks went through, but she never thought about what if anything she could do when it came to the bigger picture in life. No wonder all the different countries had stories and legends that surrounded their existence. The who and why behind their country's demise or hard times. Blaming one another was easier than working together against drought, famine, plagues, or wars and the powers that led. And of course, there is always someone who is willing to exploit others for the sake of power.

She sipped her water and finished her bagel. Her trusty fairy night-light casting a lovely glow in the room filled her with the same warm sensation she had from the first time her grandmother gave the light to her. She needed to seriously consider the words of Mila and look into those three brothers. Her curious nature, once engaged, wouldn't be satisfied until she answered some of the questions rolling through her mind after her dream.

Chapter 33

Jaxon awakened when he heard Peyton cry out. He went in to check on her, but she was sound asleep. He checked the tray. She hadn't eaten everything but enough. He stood looking at her as she slept. So beautiful, he mused. His heart swelled with a deep emotion that he had experienced only once before in Arizona when he thought she would die before he could tell her how he felt. The past day was a reminder once again how quickly life can change. He didn't want to miss a day loving this woman. The important could be lost in the urgent that pressed for attention on a daily basis. She had captured his heart, and he still wasn't sure if she understood how much she meant to him. Love could be odd. The emotion could sneak up on you and take you by surprise when you weren't looking for a relationship.

He had no idea how long he stood there, but he moved when he heard her stir again. He reached for the tray but left the food, hoping she would eat more. He backed out of the room, closing the door quietly behind him. Tomorrow at some point he needed to ask her if she had a dream.

Jaxon had just climbed back into bed and closed his eyes when the alarm rang. A shower and strong coffee would be the only way to get into his day. First item on his agenda was a trip to the hospital to check on Emily.

He wanted to hear her story along with Peyton's. The interview might be more productive if they were questioned together.

He rushed through his morning routine, checked in with the agency, and made his way to the kitchen to make coffee, but Frank had arrived before him, and Jaxon could smell the dark brew.

"I thought you might need this after the night you had. When did you get home anyways?"

"Sometime between one thirty and two. I had to wait for them to release Peyton and listen to the nurse's instructions."

"How is she doing?"

"Other than the headache last night, I think she is good. She ate a bit when she got home, and when I checked in on her, she was sound asleep. That's the physical side for her but who knows how this affected her mentally? The same is true for Emily although she is facing more physical recovery time."

"Has either one of them told you much about their ordeal?"

"Not yet. Maxwell told me to work with Dylan on interviewing them both today while details are still fresh in their minds. We might like to take Carlene out to the shack where they were taken and see if we track the guy to a new location. It's a longshot but might be worth the try." Jaxon opened the fridge. "I don't know about you, but I'm hungry. How about some bacon and eggs?"

"Sounds good. What can I do to help?"

"You can make some toast." Jaxon tossed him a loaf of bread. "The butter is in the fridge."

Jaxon's stomach growled as the smell of bacon sizzling on the griddle filled the kitchen. As soon as the bacon was finished, he poured the grease into a can and wiped the griddle. Next up were the eggs. For some reason cooking felt almost therapeutic to him this morning. A rational way to deal with his anger at a man he had never met.

"Good morning." Peyton walked into the kitchen carrying an empty glass and a plate with food still on it. "You should still be sleeping. Doctor's orders." Jaxon flipped the eggs. "You didn't eat much."

"Well, if you wanted me to sleep, you shouldn't have cooked this morning. The wonderful aroma coming from the kitchen called to me, and I answered the call. Last night I wasn't hungry." She smiled.

"Here's a plate." Frank handed one to her with a piece of buttered toast on it. "Fill her up. There's coffee too, unless you're like your cousin. This is not decaf."

"I can drink the real deal with cream." She reached for a cup, and Frank poured the strong coffee along with some cream. She walked over to the table and pulled out a chair.

"Relax, I'll fill your plate." Jaxon took her plate and moved back to the stove. "Here you go." The plate was brimming with eggs and five pieces of bacon.

"Though this all looks yummy, you might have given me a tad too much." She set aside three slices of bacon and picked up her fork and took a bite of the egg. "This looks more like a plate meant for you. For once I'm simply happy to be able to eat leisurely without having to rush off to work." She took another bite and closed her eyes. When she opened them again, the two men were staring at her. "What?"

"Call us curious. We have questions, and we're waiting until you're ready to talk." Jaxon smiled at her.

"I was hoping you'd feel up to talking along with Emily later."

"I can do that, but right now I want to enjoy breakfast. And when I'm finished, I need to call the principal and let him know I'm okay and should be there tomorrow."

"Fair enough." Jaxon took a bite of the bacon and egg sandwich he made. "Before I forget to tell you, Lawrence dropped flowers and a note from Reba with a promise to hear the whole story from you soon. The vase and note are in the living room."

When they were finished, he watched her head back toward her room. She was quiet, but he knew she was putting all the pieces she knew together in her mind. He couldn't wait to hear what those moving pieces were.

****

Peyton had a nice conversation with her boss. He was happy to hear she was okay. The whole school had been worried about her. Nice to know people care, she smiled. He encouraged her to take the rest of the week off because her class was covered. He told her he would see her on Monday and not a day sooner.

She loved living in Blue Cove. The people had been welcoming and supportive since the beginning. They were the family she always wanted and never had. She wrote a quick email to her cousin and asked her to call when she got a chance. She didn't want to write about the events of the past few days in an email.

She got dressed and now was ready to go with Jaxon. He'd given her space and hadn't asked many questions. But she knew he was itching to. She might as well get the interview over with. He seemed accepting of all the crazy stuff she often shared with him. Maybe he would take this idea in stride along with the others.

She walked back into the kitchen after stopping to see the flowers and read the sweet note from Reba. "I'm ready when you are."

"You don't have to go today. You're supposed to rest. I'm not keen on placing you back in the crosshairs until you're ready, but you know I always appreciate your take on a situation."

"I know, but I would rest better if I can tell you what I know and hear Emily's story. I've been trying to reach Kelsey and haven't been able to get a hold of her. That has me worried about her safety."

"Keep trying." He took her hand. "I don't want to rush you, but I believe you have important information. You experienced his actions firsthand. I would like to get this guy and close down the illegal operation at the college. At least, that's my goal." Jaxon's phone rang. "Sorry, I have to take this."

"Go ahead." She went into her room to get her laptop to take with her. He was still on the phone when she came back into the kitchen. He sounded grim. Something was up. "Is everything all right?" she asked him when he hung up.

"It's bad news. I'll tell you when we get in the car." He motioned toward the door. "Hey, Frank, I will check in with you later. You'll be going to the crime scene."

"Sounds good."

Peyton slid into the passenger seat and latched her seat belt. She glanced out the window as Jaxon pulled out of the driveway and started down the street. From the set of his jaw, the news must have been pretty bad.

"We have another piece to throw into the mix. Two male victims were found on campus this morning, which seems to broaden the scope of the nature of the crimes we are investigating."

"That's awful. You don't send your kid to college to be murdered."

"They worked on the campus newspaper like Emily. Maybe she will know more about them than we have at the moment."

"I wonder if they were working on the same story as she was. If not there must be something that connects them to the facts we know at the moment."

"We'll see." He drove past the bookstore on Main and got into the turn lane.

"I thought we were going to the hospital."

"Dylan called, and Emily is being released this morning. Her father is going to bring her by the station before they go home. He knows we need to interview her." He turned onto Blue Cove Drive, heading toward the station. "I hope you don't mind, but we might be here for a while."

"I brought my laptop. I'll be fine." She turned to look out the window again. The dark clouds building over the ocean might mean they were in for a storm of some kind.

She knew today might be tough when the details of Emily's ordeal came out. She needed to let her mind dwell on a few pleasant topics before the stark reality set in once again. Matt and Jessie would be home next Friday. She couldn't wait to see her cousin and hear about their honeymoon. The following Thursday was Thanksgiving, which would be her first one among her friends at the cove and Jaxon's family. With Molly's baby due anytime, this would be an exciting few weeks.

"You got quiet. Is everything okay?" Jaxon pulled

into a parking space at the station.

"Yeah. I wanted to spend a few minutes thinking about some of the nice events coming up before we have to dig into the seedy side of life with this case."

"There's an element you need to add to the moving pieces. The two males were in a relationship and well liked among their peers. We're not sure if this is a hate crime or being made to look like one to throw us off track."

Jaxon opened the car door for her, and she walked beside him into the station. She followed him to the coffee station and fixed herself a cup. When she saw Kenny, she stopped to talk.

"How's Molly?"

"The doctor told her yesterday that the baby could be here any day. She's had some pre-labor pains. I can't remember what the doc called them. Anyways she can't wait."

"Bless her heart. From what I've heard, the last few weeks can be hard. I am excited for you both."

"When she isn't waddling around the house, she is sitting with her feet up. But at least the nursery is ready for our little fella's first day home."

Eventually, Peyton made her way down the hall to Dylan's office where Jaxon stood in the open door. She leaned against the wall and listened to them talk until she lost interest in what they were saying.

"I'll be in the lounge area when you need me."

Jaxon nodded. "Okay, I'll come for you when we're ready."

Chapter 34

Peyton opened her computer and checked her emails. Jeremy was happy to do some research for her and would get back to her soon. He sent her what he had found on Aine and her sister, then she spent time reading the links he sent. Her cousin promised to call the first chance she got.

While she waited for Jaxon to come for her, she read what she could find on the legend of Dub, Dother, and Dian along with their notorious mother. One thought led to another. From Cara Cassidy's diary in one of their cases, she had learned how her Native American friend's tribe believed when a white wolf appeared, it was a good sign, but a black wolf meant trouble. Aelfric the fallen fairy had taken on the form of a black wolf when he was about to strike. Of course, none of that went into a police report, but she knew the truth.

At some point she would tell Jaxon about her conversation with Mila. He obviously loved her enough to take what she told him with a grain of salt. Where had that old English idiom come from in her head? He would be skeptical, but at least he would listen to what she told him and analyze her ideas logically. She loved that about him. She wasn't sure if she were him, if she could do the same.

"Peyton, they are ready for you in the interview room." Kip tapped her shoulder.

"Okay. Will it be okay if I leave this here?" She closed her computer.

"Sure thing."

When she entered the room, she went to sit by Emily. "How are you?" She reached for her hand.

"I'm not sure. One minute I'm good, but when I think about the past several days, I want to curl up in a ball and never leave the house again."

"I can understand your range of emotions."

"This is my dad," Emily introduced him. "She is the one who helped me get away."

"How can I ever thank you? I don't think I could've survived losing my little girl." He swiped at the tears in his eyes.

"No need. We saved each other." Peyton looked up when Jaxon and Dylan walked into the room.

****

The interview began with each of the girls telling their story. Emily had been working on a major story that would have exposed a secret society on campus that was running an illegal operation. She was on the verge of putting together how the online male group and the society were working together. She thought she had gotten a break when she was contacted by someone who said he had information he knew she wanted. He told her he was working on the same story. He arranged for them meet at the coffee shop a few miles from the campus where they could talk without interruption. She was skeptical, but in the end he convinced her to come when he told her Leo and Vance would also be there. She knew Leo and Vance from the school paper. When she walked into the coffee shop, they weren't there, but she waited to see if they would come. They never did.

"Leo and Vance wouldn't have stood me up like that, which makes me wonder if they are all right. I learned the hard way you have to careful on campus right now."

Jaxon glanced at Dylan and pointed at something on his phone. "Please continue. What happened next?"

"I drove back to the campus and parked my car near my dorm. The last thing I remember is being grabbed when I walked toward the door and something covering my nose and mouth. The smell of that cloth, I will never forget." She paused to wipe her nose. "Every time I awakened, he would use that cloth again."

She told them how she feigned sleep to keep him from using the drug on her. At some point he had put her in a dress and wrapped a charm around her hand. When she told them about him dressing her, she lost control and cried. Peyton placed her arm around her shoulders and handed her a box of tissues.

"I'm sorry to make this any harder on you, but I would rather you hear this from us. Leo and Vance, your friends, didn't make it to the coffee shop because they were murdered." Dylan pushed a photo toward her. "Is this them?" He pointed at the two smiling young men holding hands.

She sobbed and nodded. "They were two of the nicest and kindest people I know. Who would do this them?"

"We are going to do our best to answer that question and put them behind bars."

After Jaxon prompted her, Peyton told them the story she had already shared with him. From the time she was taken at the school to the point where they found her and Emily where they rested.

"Emily, I want you to work with our sketch artist. We could use a composite of the guy. We want to see if he matches the one Peyton gave us days ago."

"That won't be necessary. I took a picture of him the day he came into the store." Peyton texted Jaxon the photo. "I should have shown you earlier, but I forgot I had taken the picture. At the time, I wasn't sure if he was the man or not. But I snapped a photo just in case."

"Bob, why don't you take your daughter home? This photo will work," Jaxon told him. "Peyton, I want you to look over some mug shots to see if you get anything. In the meantime, Gary can run a check on the photo and see if he comes up anywhere in the system." Jaxon walked the Harts out of the building.

When he returned, he found Peyton sitting in the lounge in front of her computer. "I want to hear the rest of the story."

"What do you mean?" She glanced at him when he sat beside her.

"The part you usually have to spoon-feed me in small doses so I can handle the oddity of what you saw. You can start wherever you want."

"When we stopped to rest, Mila our helpful fairy came to visit me while Emily was sleeping. She told me about an ancient Irish legend of the Celtic Witch Carman and three wicked sons Dub, Dother, and Dian. They wreaked havoc in Ireland and destroyed their crops. In the end Carman was imprisoned, but her sons were banished across the seas."

"What has that got to do with us now?"

"I asked her the same question." Peyton told him about what she had learned of the three brothers. "Mila told me in every people group there are legends to fit what happens to them. The essence of their spirits can continue to cause trouble wherever people let them. Every generation fights their own forms of darkness, evil, and violence. One is bad enough, but if all three join together, you have dark times indeed. Basically, that's what my dream was about last night." She told him about how one spirit joined a second and they were joined by a third and together they left destruction in their wake. "The name of the three sons mean darkness, evil, and violence."

"Again, how does this apply to us?"

"I don't know, but I believe we are about to find out."

"I don't like the sound of that. Will you be all right here for a while? I'm taking Frank and his dog out to the shack to let them see if they can get a hit on where the guy might have gone from there. I would prefer you stay here and not be alone at the house." He stood. "Unless of course, you want to come along with us."

"No thanks, I don't think I could stomach that place again. I'll be fine. I'll look through the mug shots. Gary brought them up online."

"Let me know if you find anything."

"I will, but if I do, it's bound to be bizarre, being as this guy might be a jumper."

"Yeah, I forgot that small piece of information. Do your best." He leaned close and kissed her cheek. "Wait for me."

"I can't go anywhere. You brought me." She smiled, and he kissed her again. No simple kiss on the cheek, but a lingering one on the lips.

Chapter 35

Peyton went through the photos in front of her until all the faces started blending together. She stood and stretched her arms over her head. Her stomach was growling, maybe she could have lunch delivered since she had no car.

"Peyton, Jaxon made me promise to get you lunch." Kip walked into the lounge area. "What would you like? I'm headed out on a food run."

"If you tell me where you are going, I'll check out what's on the menu."

"I was thinking of Sally's because it's close to the station. And we all love her burgers."

"That's fine. A cheeseburger sounds good to me."

"Fries or anything else for you?"

"An iced tea would be nice." Peyton sat back down. "I'll be here looking at all these lovely faces." She waved at Kip as he left.

She couldn't help but wonder what poor man became the host to this criminal. He wasn't that old. How had he died or had he? Did the traveler simply take up residence in his body? She didn't have a clear idea how this worked only that it did. She had seen the results at least two times since she started on this unusual journey. She found all of the magical and supernatural aspects of her life hard enough for her to accept, much less try to explain the madness to others. The more she read about

Aine and Brigid, the more she came to understand that she was only seeing the tip of powers that came with the gift of the women in her family line. And now here she was trying to figure out how to live with the knowledge she was learning and of course, Mary who seemed to be forever by her side. Did the suspect ever sense a ghost was nearby? She was his murder victim after all.

Would she exchange any of the gifts to live a normal life, whatever that meant—of course, not. As strange as the past twenty-four hours had been, she was safe, and so was Emily and that was the result of the gift in some regard. How else would she have known that the charm on Emily's wrist carried a power? The man was able to track them as long as the charm was around her wrist. Not unlike her jeweled dagger and Jessie's pendant. Now all she had to do was figure out how the deaths of Leo and Vance played into the crime wave at the college. Mary Bradley still was around, and she was waiting for her murder to solved and for justice to be served, or at least that's what Peyton reasoned. Which made her wonder, were Leo and Vance wandering around too?

"Peyton." Gary rushed into the room. "You're not going to believe what I found on the guy."

"Oh, yeah. What?"

"His name is Lewis Buckner. He was an up-and-coming body builder who died six months ago in Arizona."

"Of course, he did," she muttered under her breath. "How is that possible?"

"That's what I said, but I figured you or Jessie would understand. We all know about your reputation." Gary chuckled. "You two are legends in this department. Of course, we keep it under wraps."

"Who would believe you anyway?" She laughed.

"All of us around here, for sure. Now tell me, how is this possible?"

Thankfully, Kip chose that moment to come in with lunch, and all the guys who ordered rushed into the room to pick up their food. She unwrapped her burger and took the first bite. The growl of her stomach reminded her of how hungry she was. No doubt about it. Sally made a great cheeseburger. She didn't indulge often, which made the times she did all the better. She took a sip of her tea.

At least she understood why Lewis looked like a body builder. He had been. How sad he was nothing more than a criminal now, or was Edwards the real criminal? Wait until Jaxon heard about this. He had experienced the traveler jump a few times with her before, but she knew the concept wasn't easy for him to grasp either. She took another bite of her sandwich. All this thinking outside the box had to blow his logical mind. Still, the man found a way to work through the unusual to get to the facts that would be acceptable in a report.

"You didn't think I was going to go away without you answering my question, did you?" Gary sat beside her with his lunch. "This is one explanation that I've got to hear."

Peyton tried to explain a concept that she herself was only beginning to understand. She did her best to tell him. "I will give you some copies of medical reports on two of the jumpers. Maybe that will help you understand. Those reports helped me a little. I'm not saying I still understand the how or even why. I've come to accept the possible concept is all."

"I would like to see those reports when you get a chance. I'm a big sci-fi fan, and this fits in my wheelhouse. Quantum leaping, time travel, and two dimensions get me thinking any day. When you see the possibilities of AI and where the techno world is going, you can assume anything is possible."

"I didn't know that about you, Gary. No wonder you're so creative. I will definitely get you copies. I think you'll find them quite interesting."

"I know I will. I'm fascinated by both you and Jessie. I want to understand how you came to have this ability that you have. Does your sister have the same gift?"

"I don't know, yet. I think she probably will come into her own at some point." She told him about the first time she experienced seeing a spirit and her first premonition in Arizona. "I was there on vacation, but that's how I met Jaxon. I think he thought I was a bit of kook at first."

"I can imagine. But hey, look at you two now. You work cases with him. Even Tom Maxwell is a believer from a distance and under the radar." He laughed. "Tell me, what do you think of this case?"

"Right now, I'm not sure. There are a lot of moving parts, and they are all tied somehow to an old Irish legend with a modern twist. Throw in a cursed talisman and you have a story that would make a good novel. I should know. I've edited books for years."

"I want to talk more to you, but I need to get back to work."

"Anytime." She watched him pick up his trash and leave the lounge area. She typed in the name Lewis Buckner. His world opened up to her, including how he died. She jotted notes and wrote down the hospital. Jaxon might want to follow up on the information listed there. Maybe the attending physician could give them some added information. The problem was the body couldn't be found. He seemed to simply disappear. Better yet maybe Jeremy could get into the investigation records and find out some interesting info. Lewis seemed like a likable character with his whole life in front of him until it was cut off in what was being called a road rage incident. No wife or children but his parents were devastated, which was understandable. Lewis deserved justice too. Eye witnesses said a car came out of nowhere at a high rate of speed and pushed his car off the road into the lake. The other car crashed into a tree, and the driver died on scene. The driver might have died before hitting the tree from a gunshot wound. She found that noteworthy.

Lewis seemed to have lived a decent and kind life. He raised a lot of money for charity. Peyton felt sad thinking about how the traveler had ruined the image he spent his life building. He certainly didn't resemble in actions the man written about in this article. Was the traveler living in him or a spirit? The timing was about the same time Edwards died. Only time would tell. She couldn't help but wonder if his parents knew what happened to him. The article simply said his body was never found when they fished his car out of the lake. Divers were never able to locate him.

How sad this must be for them. Never knowing where their son was and what a shock if they saw him in the news as a murderer. She shuddered to think about them. How many others have been victims of travelers who needed a body to continue to live on, or as they learned in the last case, the need for a human to do their dirty work? Was it possible the real travelers were spirits to begin with? Something else for her to think about.

“Hey, girl.” Jaxon leaned over her shoulders. “What’s got your attention? You didn’t hear me coming.” He pointed at the photo on the screen. “Is that our suspect?”

“Yes, and he’s an interesting character. I think we need to follow up with some of the information here. Meet Lewis Buckner, body builder extraordinaire, with a kind heart, and generous spirit.”

“I’m not sure I want to hear this story. Carlene couldn’t track him beyond the highway where he turned.”

“Here’s the problem—whether he is a traveler using someone else’s body, or a spirit using a human to do his dirty work, neither will be easy to take down. I’m not sure which we are dealing with at the moment. I intend to find out at some point. I mean the charm had some kind of power. He was using the darn thing to track us.”

“How exactly do you intend to find out?” Jaxon sat next to her.

“Since I’m sure we’ll meet again at some point, I will have ample opportunity to figure out what we are dealing with. Even if I have to try a bit of magic of my own with the help of the guardian to find out. He reacted when Lewis came into my store, which makes me wonder if the guardian already knows him somehow. At least the spirit inside of Lewis that our warrior ghost once battled a long time ago—maybe.”

“Well, so much for thinking this would be an easy case. How could I think this would fall into the realm of a normal investigation? How do you think Lewis falls into what is going on at the campus?"

"He's using what is going on there as a cover, but I think he's doing what he wants. Lewis used Emily's story to lure her to the coffee shop, so he's keeping tabs on what they're doing and using the information he gets to promote what he wants. Killing girls is not all he's here for. I think he's biding his time and creating an atmosphere of fear on campus. Fertile ground for a spirit."

"Dare I ask what more could he be here for?"

"I'm sure we'll find out soon. But if my dream is correct, he's hoping to meet up with his brothers and work their devastation before they move on again."

"How are we supposed to stop that from happening?" Jaxon shook his head.

"You do what you always do. Don't you think in some way all the destructive crimes that happen are dark and evil? Each time we read about something heinous that one person does to another or vile acts in the time of war, that it's like a mirror is held up to us as humans, and we have a choice to make. I believe that choice is repeated many times in our lifetime."

"I see where you're going with this, and you give me something to think about. I just never thought about someone doing another's evil bidding by living inside of them until moving here. I admit it takes some getting used to for me. If you don't mind, I'll leave that part to you, and I'll still search for clues the old-fashioned way."

"Sounds perfect. I believe that's what you're supposed to do. Maybe just maybe if we learn to work together, we'll be as good as Matt and Jessie someday." She smiled at him.

"I can live with that. Now, all I have to do is figure

out who Lewis Buckner is and how I'll deal with that knowledge when I do. I'll be back. I need to run something by Dylan."

"Take your time. I'm not going anywhere. You're my ride." She waved him on.

****

He couldn't stay hidden forever, nor would he. Damn, he still couldn't believe that woman outsmarted him. There was something about her and that store. He sensed the presence of an old enemy there, which didn't seem possible. In the world in which he lived, he'd made plenty of enemies. Most never knew what they were fighting. They thought of him as a bad person, and in someways he was. But like everything, there was more to him than met the eyes. Still, he wondered how she possibly got past his defenses. He should have known what she was up to. He scratched his head. What kind of witch was she?

This time he would win. He had met plenty of women like her before. The setup he had going for himself here was worth fighting for. He wasn't through playing yet, and he wouldn't leave until the right time.

He studied the face of the young girl smiling from the computer page. She would make a perfect play toy to keep him busy for a while. He didn't really like to kill them; that's not what this was about. He enjoyed the fear he saw in their eyes. That look was food to him. The ability to control his victims, toy with them, and prolong their agony made him feel like there was nothing he couldn't do.

Their terror took him back to the days when people feared his name. When battles were won by sheer strength. That's what he loved about finding this body.

He was like the warriors of old, lean with muscles to spare. Strength emanated from his persona. He had no problem attracting girls, looking like this. They didn't fear him. They were enamored by his looks. Yes, he had a good thing going here, and he wasn't going to let her screw it up.

Damn, why did she bother him so much? He had met her once, but she wasn't like this, but then again neither was he. Still, her strength reminded him of someone he'd met long ago. Many years before her time. Was she a traveler? In his world anything was possible. There was an aura around her, and she could walk past his defenses. He shuddered. Maybe he should leave her alone. He laughed at his own joke. The challenge appealed to his ego, and if he knew her, she was already figuring out who he was. If she hadn't discovered his identity yet, she soon would. For that alone she had to die. A shame really but her death was the only way for him to remain here until his time was up, or he decided to move on.

Chapter 36

Peyton had given him a lot to think about earlier. Dylan added his perspective. His grumbling stomach reminded him he was on a mission.

"Are you ready to go home?" He leaned over her shoulder. "You've been here long enough. We can talk on the way home."

"I'm ready." She turned off her computer and slipped it into the carrying case.

"I thought I'd take Frank and you to dinner tonight, if you're not too tired." He took the computer case from her hand.

"How was your afternoon?"

"Not as productive as I would have liked. I was hoping we could find the guy during the track but no such luck."

"I'm not surprised that you didn't, but I hoped alongside of you." She followed him to the car.

"Why is that?"

"Because he's not normal but that doesn't mean he can't get caught. His ego might get in the way or his overconfidence. You'll get him. I know you will." She touched his cheek.

"Thanks for your confidence in me." He opened the door for her and placed her computer into the backseat before getting into the car himself. "Keep believing, I need all the support I can get for this one. I have more questions than answers right now."

"That's always the way a case is until the pieces start coming together. Matt and Jessie will be home soon, and something tells me this one is about to speed up. Hold on, I think we're in for a wild ride."

"Investigations seem to move along at a turtle's pace until the right evidence comes along, then the case moves at warp speed. That's what I love about my job. Working to outsmart the guys who think they are above the law, and their genius will keep them from being caught. That ego is usually their downfall as they become careless, thinking they're being clever." Jaxon pulled out of the parking lot. "My gut tells me some of the actors are getting sloppy and the jig is almost up."

"How do you feel about the professor? I know Emily's father was sure he was involved. Has he been ruled out?"

"No one has. He didn't kidnap Emily or kill Mary Bradley, but he might be guilty of something else. There are too many moving parts, and I don't know if he is innocent. There are obviously a few of the staff members involved in the secret society at the school. We believe they are trafficking in some valuable artifacts. All we need is the evidence to prove this side of the case. Emily was getting close to naming names and had a source who is missing. We don't know if the person went underground or if they are dead." He glanced at her. "Speaking of Mary, is her ghost still hanging around you?"

"She comes and goes. But never seems to be far away." Peyton fiddled with the strap on her purse. "How about Emily's roommate Kelsey or her boyfriend Greg Taylor?"

"No one has been ruled out. Her boyfriend seemed too vague for my liking when we questioned him. He's being watched closely by an undercover agent. I find the fact he never called her dad while she was missing suspect, but that's not evidence for a conviction."

"No, I suppose not." She rubbed her temple and laid her head back against the headrest.

Jaxon caught her action out of the corner of his eye. Damn, he forgot she had gone through the whole ordeal and was supposed to be resting today. And what had he done? He'd kept her sitting down at the station all day. She looked tired, and the dark circles under her eyes accused him of neglect. He should've made sure she got home to rest. Her discharge nurse would have his hide if she got wind of how he treated her.

He would find a way to make the rest of the evening easier for her. Maybe dinner at home would be better than going out. Yes, that's what he'd do. Order in and let her put her feet up and rest. He pulled over to the side of road and made a few phone calls. Thankfully, she slept through the calls.

When his head got involved in a case, he often forgot to eat much less think about someone else. Love demanded more from him. He needed to keep that in mind for the future. Somehow Matt and Jessie wrestled these issues out and found a way to make their relationship work, and he could too.

Caring for another person or family was never easy especially when his job would often consume him, and when you add into the equations his girl was unconventional, there could be a few hurdles. Learning how to be present and take her needs into consideration would be important to their relationship. Loving Peyton was easy, but living with what came with her might take work on his part for as long as they both lived if he let his heart take him where it wanted to go. Yes, that's where he wanted to go. He loved her and couldn't imagine his life without her. He pulled into the driveway. When he shut off the car, her eyes opened.

"I'm sorry you were at the station all day. You were supposed to be resting." He stroked her cheek. "I wasn't sensitive to your needs."

"No need to apologize. I didn't get tired until a few minutes ago. You know how I get when a subject to research gets ahold of me. I don't want to stop until I find the answers I'm looking for."

"Still, I promised the discharge nurse that I would make sure you rested all day. I think she would consider my effort a total failure. But that changes now. I've order dinner in, which should be here soon, and you will put your feet up and rest."

"Hey, I'm a big girl, and if I want to stay up, I will." She chuckled.

"I've noticed you're all grown up." He waggled his brows at her. "But I don't want to have a nurse accuse me of failing to keep my word. I'd have a hard time explaining to her if something happened to you because I hadn't followed her instructions." He opened the door and took her hand.

"Won't Frank be disappointed that we are going out for dinner?"

"Not at all, he's already claimed his spot in the lounge chair, and he's happy to stay put there the rest of the evening." He led her to the couch. "Now sit and rest. Dinner will be here soon."

"What's that all about?" Frank asked.

“Beats me.” She shrugged.

“You choose. A touch of guilt or a wakeup call.” He smiled at her already closed eyes.

“How about a little of both. As long as you feed me, I don’t care.” She opened one eye.

“You’ll get no argument from me, and as I said, food is on the way.” He went to the door when the bell rang.

Jaxon carried the bag of food into the kitchen and set the table. He hoped they were hungry because he ordered enough for many famished people. Never go to the store when you’re hungry, a rule that should apply to ordering takeout.

“Dinner is ready,” he called from the kitchen.

Jaxon pulled out a chair for Peyton. “I hope you see something that looks good to you.”

“I love Italian, and right now the salad looks really good to me. I’ll start there and move to the lasagna and garlic bread next.”

“I’m with you, Peyton.” Frank dished up salad on his plate. “This looks good. Thanks, Jaxon. I’m happy not to have to go out to dinner. I have a TV show I like to watch at home. If you all don’t mind, I’ll watch it tonight after dinner.”

“TV sounds like a good plan to me. But not for you.” Jaxon pointed at Peyton. “You are going to rest and be ready for work tomorrow.”

“Yes, whatever you say.” She saluted him playfully. “Jessie is supposed to call me tonight, and I can talk lying down, daddy.” She laughed. “Enjoy your power guilt trip, but I have other plans myself.”

After dinner Jaxon told her to sit down while he cleaned the kitchen. Gary gave him a sheet of info on Lewis Buckner. He needed to call the attending physician in the morning. There was more to the story than he read on the death certificate. Lewis, at no point in his life, was a predator—if anything the opposite was true. He used his body building and strength as an opportunity to reach young men. They saw a sense of purpose in him. Jaxon found the whole sordid story sad. More men like Lewis were needed today as role models. He had many questions and couldn't imagine how to find the answers. Did Buckner die in that crash and the travel jump in, or is he alive and being used by a dark unseen force? They never found a body, and the family still held hope he was alive somewhere with amnesia. The more he thought about it, the more perplexing the situation became.

Whoever Lewis was, did he have some power that protected him or gave him supernatural powers? Any way Jaxon looked at it, this case was headed in the direction that was once again outside the box of a normal investigation. Who knew, what he thought of as abnormal was the real normal never noticed by most.

****

Peyton went into the living room and sat on the couch. She picked up her computer case with the thought of heading to her room to wait for her cousin's call. She found herself watching the TV and not moving. She really needed to get going, but she was done in. Frustrated with herself, she forced herself to stand and move toward the hall. She stopped by the kitchen to thank Jaxon one more time.

"Sweetheart, you look exhausted." He walked over and took the computer case out of her hand. "I'll carry this to your room."

"Thank you. I guess the last few days have caught

up to me." She walked into the room.

Jaxon placed the case onto the foot of the bed. He turned her around and kissed her forehead. "Sleep would do you a world of good. I'll check on you later." He closed the door behind him.

She sat on the edge of the bed. What was she going to do about him? In her heart she already knew, and now she needed to act like what her heart was telling her. No one except her grandparents cared about her well-being the way Jaxon did. His love and caring made her vulnerable, yet safe and secure. How is that even possible? She slapped her hand to her forehead. She had to be tired—nothing she was thinking made any sense.

Stretching out on the bed, she plumped her pillow under her head. Jessie told her once before she could finally see her way to marrying Matt, she had to believe they could have love that would last a lifetime. She found the answer among their ancestors, and of course their grandparents. Max and Sadie had a swoon-worthy love as Jessie liked to call it. Unlike both of their parents who were cold and indifferent at best. And that was on a good day for her parents.

Grams had assured them more than once no relationship is perfect, and each one takes work. To be in love was risky at best, but to never love would be a sad life indeed. She was willing to take a risk believing in ghosts, fairies, and magic. How could she not take a risk with her heart? She knew if she opened her heart to Jaxon, he would take care not to break it. She hoped she could say the same thing about herself. And that was her real fear that she could be more like her parents than she wanted to acknowledge. She closed her eyes, sighed, and rolled over onto her side.

Chapter 37

Jaxon watched the program that Frank seemed to be enjoying. He found himself laughing along with him and relaxed for the first time all day. During a commercial, his phone rang.

"Jaxon, why isn't Peyton answering her phone?" Jessie asked. "Is she all right? She told me to call her tonight."

"She's fine but sleeping." Jaxon stood and walked into the kitchen. He explained to Jessie what her cousin had gone through in the past few days. "I imagine that's what she wanted to talk to you about."

"Oh, gosh. Is she okay? I mean that's scary. She told me about the ghost following her and the strange phone calls. I will send her an email, and we'll connect another time. I want to hear all about what she's gone through. Sometimes we can see things differently when we bounce them off one another."

"I know you work well with each other, and you can help her. I can't imagine how these events affect you both."

"How are you doing?"

"I'm okay. But I can't help wondering how Matt dealt with all of this. I mean I want to crush this guy, but I can't. I have to uphold the law when I can't even explain what is happening half the time. And the suspect is nowhere to be found. So, there's that."

"You sound a bit overwhelmed. I know Matt would understand. I'll tell him to give you a call. In the meantime, your suspect will show up again because he has to deal with Peyton. His ego will compel him to. That's the reality we live in, but she'll be ready, and I'm sure she'll have a bit of help. The other part she asked me to look into was about the three brothers. I will send her the information that I've found. Hang in there. You'll see things right themselves at the perfect time, and you'll walk away looking good if history is any indication. You guys put up with us, and we make you look brilliant in the end."

"I don't know about brilliant. I'd settle for solving the crimes before you get home. Tell Matt I said hi. He doesn't need to call. This is still your honeymoon. Enjoy."

Jaxon went back into the living room and finished the TV program he had been watching. When Frank went to bed, he turned to the sports channel. He thought about his conversation with her cousin Jessie. She had a way of making questionable stuff seem reasonable. Not unlike Peyton who made him seem like he knew what he was doing all along. He raked his hand through his hair. His girl was a wonderful surprise who walked into his life, and he wanted to enjoy her. As strange as her world seemed to him, Peyton was perfectly normal except for when she wasn't. He chuckled. He needed to go to bed—he wasn't making sense even to himself.

He stopped in front of Peyton's room. The light shown under the door. He knocked lightly and then opened the door a crack. She was asleep, still wearing the clothes she came home in. He took the computer off the bottom of the bed in case she kicked the case and sent it flying. Lifting the throw draped across the bed, he covered her, careful not to wake her. He jerked his hand back from stroking her lovely face. Too many emotions crowded his mind. He loved this woman. Complex and perplexing, yes, but there had to be a way for them to crash through the baggage and reservations that they each had. Didn't every relationship come with struggles? Of course, theirs might be a tad more unconventional but not impossible.

Man, you need to get some rest. You're thinking way too much. He closed her door and walked down the hall to the room he was using. He got ready for bed, shut off the light, and stretched out. Love made him vulnerable. He never questioned his decision-making this much before. Tomorrow was another day, and he needed to have his head in the game. His gut told him that a big break in the case was getting close, and he didn't want to miss any piece of the evidence.

While he waited for sleep to overtake his tired body, he went through the details of the investigation as he knew them right now. He couldn't do anything about the suspect in hiding until he showed himself, but the deaths of Leo and Vance seemed to fit a pattern that was emerging on campus. He could sink his investigator teeth into that part for now.

****

Peyton was ready to face her kids. They were *her happy place*, and she loved being in the classroom with them. Principal Avery told her not to come back until Monday, but Friday was close enough, and she wanted to jump back into her job. No way would she let fear rule her life and keep her from her responsibility and her indisputable enjoyment at the same time.

Coffee was ready, and there was a note from Jaxon on the counter. She poured herself a cup and put a slice of bread into the toaster. While she waited, she read his note.

Sorry to rush off without getting to see you, but I have an early meeting this morning. Maxwell said there have been some new developments at the college that the team needs to know about.

I hope you slept well. If Frank stirs before you leave, tell him I'll be back to get him soon. We would like his dog to work a few sites at the college.

I have much I want to talk to you about soon. I hope we can manage to find some time in the next few days to have some alone time together. Stay alert and on guard, sweetheart. Things seem to be heating up, and I don't want anything to happen to my girl. Love you, Jaxon.

"I love you too." She reached for the toast that popped up and buttered the slice. The man was always thoughtful. His mother raised him well. Jaxon must have been the one to cover her at some point in the night. She didn't remember anything after she laid her head down. She never even changed her clothes for heaven's sake. What must he think of her? Maybe she was tired was the first answer that came to her mind. Funny, but she was okay knowing he had come into her room while she slept. He made her feel safe, and she rarely used the word man and safe in the same sentence.

After she cleaned up her small mess, she left a note for Frank by the coffee pot and rushed out the door to work with Jaxon's warning in the back of her mind. She wouldn't be caught off guard again.

She noticed Mary's ghost in the backseat. Strange how she randomly showed up. She needed to pay attention—maybe Mary was trying to tell her something. When she glanced in her mirror again, there were three. Mary was joined by two others. Her life constantly surprised her. How long would the three of them be with her? "Leo and Vance, I presume." She shook her head. Jaxon was right— things were escalating.

Her morning had flown by. The kids were especially good today. Who knew why, but she would take it as a win. Principal Avery walked her to class, and she had sympathetic glances from the teachers and office staff. More than one person told her how happy they were that she was okay after the abduction. She was thankful to have such a warm and loving group of people to work with.

Principal Avery's concern didn't stop with walking her to class, now he had to walk her to her car to make sure she got there safe and sound. After he closed her car door and waved, she drove to the bookstore with her backseat of ghostly passengers. She sighed. Something was definitely up. She wondered how long she would have to wait before she found out the details.

Chapter 38

The store was busy when she got there. Audrey waved at her when she walked in the door. Everywhere Peyton glanced, there were customers. Sitting in chairs, looking at books, and talking in small groups around the tables. Jessie would love the beautiful sight.

"Boy, am I glad to see you. The store has been like this all morning. Fall tour time and the holidays fast approaching make for more customers than normal."

"Point me in the right direction. I'm here to help." She laughed. Peyton followed where Audrey pointed. "May I help?" she asked the customer near the book table.

As the afternoon progressed, the action did too. The three ghosts joined their store guardian on the stairs, and news came that Molly was in labor and on her way to the hospital.

The excitement of Molly's news was followed by Reba's arrival at the store.

"Hello, dear." Reba gave Peyton's arm a squeeze as she passed her. "You have quite a strange committee hanging out on the stairs."

"Yes, I know." Peyton followed her to her favorite spot. "Audrey, take a break while you can."

"I don't mind if I do. I'll be back before you miss me." She waved at Reba. "Take a breather while you can too," Audrey insisted as she walked through the open doors into Joe's.

"What's up with the trio on the stairs with our friend?" Reba asked.

"I do seem to be collecting them, don't I? I believe they are three of the recently murdered students from the college. At least that's my best guess."

"Aww, yes, that makes sense. They must know you can help them find closure. I find the situation almost comical in how they are getting on with our not-so-grumpy ghost. I do believe he has lightened up since being here."

"I think you're right. Did you hear Molly is on her way to the hospital to have the baby?"

"That's exciting news. A new life is just what this town needs. Into the crazy up and down of living comes something as special as a new person to remind us that life can be amazing even when trying."

"I was thinking something along the same lines today at work. The past few days were rough at best, and yet the people I work with and my kids, of course, wrapped me in warmth and love. I'm happy to live in this beautiful town. There is no place I would rather be."

"I couldn't agree more. I want to hear what happened to you."

"To make a long story short, I was abducted by the guy I've told you about." Peyton gave her the details of what happened. "I know we will meet again. We have to."

"Did he have anything to do with their deaths?" Reba leaned close to ask when someone walked into the store.

"Mary Bradley, I believe. She was the body I found. But not the two males. I'm not sure why they are here to tell you the truth."

"I'm sure you'll know soon enough. Didn't they find another body at the school?" Reba glanced at the stairs.

"Yes, why?"

"Because the group grew by one more." Reba lifted her chin toward the stairs. "Seems to me they are gathering for a reason. You know how this goes."

"I sure do." Peyton placed her hand to her forehead. "I wonder why they are with me."

"Because, my dear, you have the key that will unlock all of this. The one major missing piece that will come to you. Keep your heart open and listen to your ancestor Aine." Reba shifted in her chair. "I will work for you tomorrow. You need to go to the college in the afternoon. As you walk around the campus, you will see more than you've ever seen before. The acts done cloaked in darkness will be made visible in the light."

Peyton couldn't get Reba's words out of her head. She couldn't use the store as an excuse not to go. Reba already told Audrey she was helping her tomorrow. What would Jaxon say when she told him she wanted to go to the college? She would find out soon enough. Whenever she was involved, he seemed to take whatever she told him in stride.

They closed the store at five, and Molly still hadn't had the baby. Audrey reminded her that childbirth could take time. The whole idea didn't sound fun but a lot of work to her. Obviously, she wasn't ready to be a mother. She wondered if she ever would be. If there was even a remote possibility she could turn out like her mom, there would be no way she would want to bring a child into the world.

****

"Frank, that went better than I expected. I think we should follow up tomorrow. What do you think?" Jaxon turned out of the college parking lot onto the street.

"I agree. Carlene indicated a few areas, which means you need to investigate the area more."

"Between your dog and the other agents' findings, we're getting close. There is something we're missing. It's the one piece that completes the bigger picture. We're almost there but not quite."

"I know you'll find what you're looking for. You should take Peyton. She might see what the others can't."

"Frank, you're a genius. Of course, Peyton. Perfect." He turned onto Main Street, heading back to Matt's place.

"You've had a long day," Peyton said when they walked in the door.

"Frank's dog was great as usual."

"I wouldn't think otherwise. I've seen her in action." Peyton handed them each a glass of tea. "Did you hear that Molly is in labor? Hopefully, she's had the baby by now."

"Thanks, this is what I needed." Frank took another sip. He held the cold glass up to his head.

"Peyton, I was wondering if there is any way you could go with us to the campus tomorrow."

"Funny you should ask." She reached for the tea pitcher to fill her glass. "Reba stopped by today and told me I needed to walk through the campus." She smiled as she explained the conversation they had. "She even told Audrey she would work with her tomorrow while I was gone."

"Well, I guess we've settled that issue, eh, Frank?" Jaxon went to the sink to wash his hands. "Something smells good."

Frank inhaled. "I was thinking the same thing about both subjects. If I don't miss my guess, some kind of chicken dish is about to grace the table."

"You're right. Your nose is almost as good as Carlene's." She laughed.

"Let us help." Jaxon reached for the serving bowl filled with salad and came back for the hot dish that smelled delicious.

Jaxon was amused by her stories of the ghosts and her day at the store. She made the school staff sound like saints the way they supported her. Things couldn't have worked out better for their trip back to the campus tomorrow. Dinner was superb. It had been a while since he had Tuscany chicken, and he might have eaten a bit too much.

"Thank you, Peyton. There's nothing quite like a homecooked meal. Whenever I'm away from home, I miss my wife's cooking." Frank picked up his dish and took the plate to the sink. "You cooked, so I'll do the dishes." He came back for her plate and utensils too.

"There are brownies from Joe's. And, speaking of the café, Molly had her baby. I just read Kenny's text he sent to all of us." She waved her phone in the air. "I can't wait to see the little fella." She went to the counter to get the brownies arranged on a small platter. She grabbed the milk from the fridge on her way back to the table.

"Frank, you can count me in to help with the dishes too." Jaxon poured milk into his glass and took a big bite of the chocolate gooey brownie. "Before I forget to tell you, Peyton, Jessie called you last night, and when you didn't answer she called me. I told her what had been going on. She promised to call you tonight."

"Yeah, she texted me earlier."

"Thanks for dinner, sweetheart. We'll take care of the cleanup."

"I bid you good evening. I have some scrolls to look at in Jessie's beautiful office. I'm going to take advantage of every minute I can get in that beautiful spot." She waved at them with a smile as she walked out of the kitchen.

Chapter 39

Peyton opened the door to Jessie's office and turned on the light. Every time she walked into the room, an overwhelming sense of peace washed over her. The paintings depicting some of the thin places in Ireland drew her in, and she could get lost in their beauty. She understood why some of the Irish people believe that the thin places are the spots where Heaven and Earth meet. She had seen beyond the door and had glimpses of the invisible world. Different cultures had differing ways to say how that world looked, but most of them had stories and legends to back their beliefs. These paintings gave her an almost spiritual experience every time she studied them. She could remain in that spot, immersing herself in their beauty, but she had work to do and only a few days to research the actual scrolls and to understand this gift that was passed down to her. Tomorrow would be nicer for her if she could actually put more of her knowledge to work. Aine could see and understand the motives of people by the colors that surrounded them. *Let's go, Peyton.* She couldn't make the colors happen, and she didn't see them all the time, thank heavens.

She took the key from its hiding place on the desk, unlocked the drawer, and pulled the scrolls from their safe place. She opened them with care on the desktop. She unrolled the layers until she reached Aine's entries. Every time she touched the living pages, a warmth enveloped her and wrapped around her like a big hug. Her sisters in time were speaking their words of wisdom in writings from one generation to the next. She would always remember the day the precious writings showed up with the artifacts in the store's attic along with the guardian who had adopted them as his own to protect. One of the many life-changing moments in her life. She smiled at the memory.

Between the emails with Jeremy containing some interpretations of the words and phrases on the scroll, the information Jessie relayed to her, and her own research, she was beginning to understand what this unique part of her gift entailed. The gift came with its own set of warnings. At the top of the list, she was never to use any aspect of her ability for personal gain or harm. Only for the good of the others was easily understood and used often through Aine's entries. Many who had the ability had gone astray and lost their way in life, bringing a curse upon them.

Another takeaway was people's emotions are a veritable rainbow of colors. Passions can range from happy to angry many times even in the same day. Most people had, even if the aura around them was dark, a light that filtered through. Like the silver lining in a cloud. Only in a person who had sold themself to their dark side, no light seemed to penetrate, and there would be complete darkness surrounding them. The hardest and perhaps the most deadly person to figure out according to Aine was the one with a rainbow of colors surrounded by darkness. One side of that individual could be charming, generous, and fun to be around. They appeared as light to deceive, but that glow was shrouded in darkness. They often appeared as a friend who promised the world as they reeled their subject in, but the flattering lies would fade when the person was no longer of value to them. From charming in one moment to an unrelenting need for retribution in the next, this strange one who could remember every wrong said or done to them over a lifetime with a willingness to destroy by whatever means they could find whether lawful or not. The warning Aine gave was that people like this are few and far between, but they exist. Their egos drive them, and they can't be satisfied or happy in life, which makes them an enemy for a lifetime.

I'm such a newbie. How will I ever figure this out? She rolled up the scrolls. Sure, she had seen colors around people. Not all the time, of course. Most of the time she was oblivious to what went on around her. As a child she knew when her dad was angry, but gosh, that had been years ago. Maybe the colors were a way of helping her see what she normally wouldn't. Seeing the ghosts of Mary, Leo, and Vance was more about understanding their plight for closure in this life and the reality of an invisible world. Truthfully, she had been happy to hang out in the visible one well enough. But hey, she was here now and trying to understand how to deal with what she saw. Not every day but with enough regularity to make her question her sanity at times.

She placed the scrolls back into the drawer and turned the key in the lock and returned the ring to its safe place. She paused in front of the painting behind the desk. Her cousin told her that the artist had captured one of the thin places in Ireland. Peyton found herself drawn into the painting. A warmth filled her body and a sensation of peace. In her heart she knew somehow everything would be all right. Which meant she would be too. She was a part of the spiritual journey of her ancestors. She glanced around the beautiful office one more time before she shut off the light and closed the door behind her.

Once in the hall she could hear the guys talking and the TV blaring, and she made her way toward the sound. She sat down on the couch beside Jaxon. Frank had his favorite spot in the lounge chair.

"Hello, there. What have you been up to?" Jaxon grabbed her hand.

"Taking a deep dive into the scrolls while I still have time." She glanced at the TV when Frank laughed.

"Sorry, but sometimes I think the commercials are funnier than the shows. That was one of the dumbest ones ever." He laughed again when he explained what struck him as funny.

They settled into watching the TV show. Settled might be a bit of an exaggeration because Jaxon's thumb stroking her hand was driving her nuts. She glanced at him. The smile on his face told her that he knew exactly what he was doing to her. She tried to pull her hand away, but he grinned and held on tighter. He jumped when her elbow poked him in the side, and the jab was her reason to smile at him.

"Hey, you two, behave." Frank laughed. "Don't you pull a Jessie and Matt. I watched those two spar, knowing all the while they were fighting their attraction for one another."

"You hear that, babe. You can't resist my charm. You might as well give up." Jaxon draped his arm around her shoulders and squeezed her tight.

She rolled her eyes. "Charm my foot. Don't fool yourself." She tried to slip under his arm, but he wouldn't let go. “Be serious, would you?” She playfully slapped his hand.

“I’m very serious. You won’t be able to resist my charm when I turn the full force on you. Peyton, my dear, you may as well give up now.” He leaned closer and kissed her.

Peyton was stunned by the kiss. Not sweet, not chaste, but hot and delicious in front of Frank, Carlene, and the blaring TV in the background. She could feel the kiss down to her toes and would be thinking about the darn thing the rest of the night. As a matter of fact, Jaxon had whispered in her ear that she would.

“I’ll leave you both to your evening. Jessie should be calling me soon.” She stood.

“Good night,” Frank said.

“Yes, sleep well.” Jaxon mouthed the word chicken at her.

She saw that as a challenge. She framed his face with her hands and kissed him, leaving no doubt this was payback. “You sleep well too.” She strolled away, swaying her hips as she went. She could hear Frank’s laughter as she did.

Peyton rushed down the hall to her room, flipped on the light, and leaned against the door after she closed it. What had prompted her to react like that? If she was truthful, she wanted another kiss. The first one had affected her a lot. She sighed. That man could charm her socks off among other things. She was way out of her league trying to out-flirt him.

She got ready for bed, got comfy with her open computer, and waited for Jessie’s call. Peyton read through a new email from Jeremy about what he had learned about the legend of three brothers who were vanquished across the seas. He had much of the same things she had learned about them and their mother in stories told in Ireland, but she learned a couple of new tidbits that might help her to determine if an ancient spirit of one these boys was at work here and now and what would transpire if the three spirits joined together. History taught that when darkness, evil, and violence joined together that lives were left in ruins.

Carman their mother was a sorceress who was not afraid to use her magical powers to wreak havoc on Ireland. The legend says Carman was destroyed by the Tuatha Dé Danann, a supernatural race in Irish mythology. In early Christian writings they were thought to have represented deities with magical powers. At times they were depicted as fallen angels not wholly good or evil, and others saw them as an ancient people who became highly skilled in magic. Thinking of the women in her family line, she could see that possibility. The Tuatha Danann became fairies in later writings. Peyton found this most interesting. Her fairy friend Mila told her about Dub, Dother, and Dian, knowing there was a way to defeat them. Although, she didn't tell her how to. What she found the most fascinating is that in every culture there seemed to be a way to describe good and evil. The battle between the two seemed to be the one constant that never changed.

Even with all the scrolling through her computer, she hadn't forgotten that kiss. Darn that man. She wouldn't have minded a few more. She sighed and reached for her ringing phone.

"Hi, cousin. How's married life?" she asked when she answered the phone.

"I'm not an expert by any means, but right now I

would give the institution of marriage with its benefits a perfect ten. Of course, who is to say what my man might be like in ten years?" She laughed.

"Tell Matt I heard him. You really shouldn't tease him that way. You'll give him a complex." Peyton found herself laughing along with them.

"On a more serious note, Jaxon told me what happened to you. Are you doing okay?"

"I'm fine, but I won't let down my guard anytime soon."

"Why is the guy after you?"

"I'm only speculating at best." Peyton stretched out on the bed, leaning her head on her arm. She described a few of her ideas. "I have no idea how he fits into what's going on at the college if he does at all. I'm sure we'll have the answer soon enough." She went on to describe about what she had learned tonight. "You know what this reminds me of?"

"No, what?"

"When you told me about sitting on the floor in Palm Springs, singing the song you learned in Sunday school to dispel the dancers and the frightening things going on around you."

"That was some night. You know, Peyton, we should really get paid for all the time we've put in and the strange stuff we've had to endure to find our way to why it's happening to us."

"Sounds good but remember not for gain. The gifts can only be used for the good of others."

"At the very least, there should a clause for injury suffered while on the job." She laughed.

"I hear you. Tell that man of yours good night and I promise not to keep you much longer." She heard Jessie repeat her message and his comeback.

Their talk grew serious for a few minutes more while she discussed going to the campus tomorrow and what she was hoping to see. “I’ll do my best to keep your words of safety in mind. Love you, cousin. Go be with your husband and enjoy your day.”

She got under her covers and shut off her light. Her finger touched her lips, and her mind traveled to the man who had kissed her and made her feel loved.

Chapter 40

He smiled as he walked the hall back to his room. She had certainly surprised him. He could live with those kinds of surprises any day. No light coming under her door meant she was sleeping. If Frank hadn't been there, maybe he would have given her a few more kisses. Slow and steady was working, but his patience was being tried. When this investigation was over, he knew he would take this cat-and-mouse game to the next level. If he was going to dance, he wanted her in his arms while he did. A nice thought to end his night on. He stretched out on the bed and closed his eyes.

Light filtered through the small opening where the curtains didn't meet. He could hear Frank and Peyton talking. Was it morning already? He rolled out of bed and got ready to go. When he got to the kitchen, he reached first for the coffee to fill his mug and sent a text that he would swing by the house to pick her up later. He didn't want her to be alone at any time on campus. Of course, he was smart enough to not tell her in those exact words.

"Good morning, Peyton needed to leave early, and I promised to tell you goodbye from her. Goodbye from Peyton." Frank smiled. "I've officially done my job for her."

"That was a wasted text. I'll be sure to let her know you told me when I text her again. Are you up for another long day?" Jaxon took a sip of his coffee.

"We both are. Carlene and I slept like babies. We're ready to get to work when you are."

"I'll pour this coffee in a to-go mug, and we'll be on our way."

They arrived on the campus and met up with a couple of agents already on location along with campus security. They were near the site where Leon and Vance were found. The college was an old one with historic buildings and beautiful grounds. Recent new builds had to keep the integrity of the original look. Jaxon glanced around the area, saddened that such a beautiful setting could be cover for more than one terrible crime.

Before they got to work, Agent Brown filled him in on Robert Craft and how he was doing. The news he was still recovering at home was a nice way to start the day. They needed to move the investigation along before the next undercover agent could be outed. While he talked with Brown, he received a text from Peyton telling him she would drive herself to campus. He could meet her in the parking lot if he wanted to.

"We can start the dog here and see where she leads us." Agent Brown walked up to Frank. "I've heard nothing but good about your dog's ability. I look forward to seeing her on the job for myself."

"Well, let's hope she is having a good day. She usually does."

"I requested these scent items from the coroner's office. They are a part of the young men's personal effects." Jaxon handed Frank the sealed bag.

"I'll give you control of the items as soon as Carlene scents off them."

Jaxon walked over to Agent Brown. "Do you know

if they've had time to comb through the boys' computers and phones?"

"Tech is going over them as we speak. I haven't heard what they've found if anything. It's a damn shame about them. They were young and had their whole lives ahead of them. This job sucks some days. You know what I mean?"

"I do."

Frank let Carlene sniff each of the items, and she got to work by going to the area where their bodies were found. Then she proceeded to their room and down to the basement of the science hall where she hit on a small droplet of blood in the corner.

"Is this a possible murder site?" Agent Brown asked.

"It looks like the floor was recently cleaned, but this droplet made it through. We need to have the drop analyzed and the floor sprayed with luminol." Frank pointed to where Carlene indicated.

They watched the criminalist spray the mixture in the area near where the blood drop was found. The men knew blood could cling to surfaces even if the crime scene had been cleaned, and they were hopeful this might be their lucky day.

"If they didn't use some heavy-duty cleaning materials, evidence will remain if we're lucky." He sprayed another large section of the floor and turned off the lights. "Bingo." He pointed at the bluish green light. "There's the glow we were hoping for." One of the members of the team pointed at the glowing spot.

The lab photographer videoed and photographed their findings on-site to study the patterns. Another from the team took samples to determine if the blood was human. "We should know if this is where the boys were murdered soon enough," Charles from the crime lab told them. "We need to search the area for shoe prints or any possible evidence. Including the stairs."

"I'm impressed. That small drop of blood could have been overlooked, and we would have missed this as a possible site. We could use one of these dogs as a part of our team," Brown told Frank and Jaxon.

"I'll let you know as soon as we have our analysis done on the sample and if it matches one of the boys' blood types. We might have more to add to the evidence file as we build this case," the lab technician told them.

"Sounds good. I have an interview with a couple of frat boys, and then I need to meet Peyton in the parking lot. I don't want her wandering around the campus alone. I'm not sure how I'm going to pull it off without her knowing what I'm doing. She thinks she needs to walk the campus by herself to get a feel for what's going on."

"She's right you know. Like her cousin often would do to gain perspective. Maybe we could have someone follow from a distance and let her go where she needs to. The person could be close enough in case she ran into a problem but not close enough to disturb her process."

"I think you're right, Frank. I know who to ask to follow her. Here's the keys to the SUV if you need to get something for Carlene or she would like to rest in her crate. There's a great small café across the street. My treat. I'll tell Peyton to meet you there."

"Works for me." Frank took the lead line off Carlene and put on her leash.

****

Peyton received Jaxon's text as she was leaving the school. She knew the place where he asked her to meet Frank. She didn't mind eating a bit of lunch with her friend. The anticipation had built all morning through class. She was ready to see where her new understanding would take her. Jaxon mentioned they might have had a major breakthrough in the case. He seemed hopeful. At least two pieces of the investigation might be on their way to being solved. Who killed Sarah Crammer, Eloise Morton, Leo, and Vance? Were there any more missing students who might be fatalities? Questions she hoped could be answered in the next few days.

She still hadn't heard from Kelsey, which had her concerned. Hopefully, she could find out more about her whereabouts too. Peyton enjoyed the drive up to the college. The trip gave her time to think about what she had learned last night. Aine's entries that she understood were enlightening, and she was closer to understanding what the colors she sometimes could see around people meant.

She pulled into the parking lot at the college, got out of her car, and crossed the street to the café. She waved at Frank who sat at an outside table with Carlene by his side. When a young man held the door open, she stepped inside of the super popular café filled with college students. She took her place at the back of the long line and listened to the students chatter to one another. College memories were some of her best, but she never had to worry about a murderer on campus. These students seemed to be unfazed by what was taking place. No coats, only tee shirts, and shorts gave everyone a sense of giddiness and wanting to be out and about. It was also possible they didn't know the details of what was happening on campus. A lot of students were getting ready for break and finals. The murders may not impact them personally but could after the next school paper came out.

As soon as she ordered her lunch, paid, and filled her cup with tea, she went outside. She couldn't help being caught up in the day, which was a nice warm one. Indian summer the forecaster had said on the radio earlier. She was inclined to believe him. The temps were in the seventies, which was quite nice for the weeks before Thanksgiving. Many colorful leaves still were clinging for life to branches, which made the day seem absolutely perfect. She inhaled the air and sat down.

"The day is a beautiful one. I doubt we'll have too many more quite so nice." Frank smiled at her.

"Enjoy the warmth while we can." She agreed. "From the sound of it, Carlene did an awesome job today. Of course, she did." Peyton petted to dog who sat quietly. "Hi, sweet girl." She patted her head. "You must be so proud of her and to be a part of helping solve crimes."

"I've always said bringing closure to the families is what it's all about."

"Does any of what you've seen bother you? I would have nightmares."

"I've had my fair share, and believe it or not, Carlene is bothered by what she finds too."

"I bet. I couldn't have gotten along without talking to a therapist. There can be a dark and awful side to humans. I have a sick feeling that we are going to see some darkness when we see this case resolved. I'm saddened by what I know already."

They talked all through lunch and soon were joined by Jaxon when his interviews were done. He ate the half of her sandwich which she had wrapped to take home.

"Well, kid," he said. "It's showtime. You can walk

the campus and tell us what you see or any premonitions you get." He touched her hand. "Frank, Agent Brown wants you to try something else if you think she can do more work today."

"She'll do fine." Frank patted Carlene's head.

"Let's go." Peyton stood. "I'm excited to get started." She took ahold of Jaxon's hand and tugged him to move him along.

He stopped her forward progress. "Whoa, hold up, sweetheart, I do have some ground rules. This is for your safety and the integrity of the investigation."

"You never mentioned rules when you asked to come today." She frowned at him. "I hope you are not talking about someone to babysit me because if you are I will get in my car and drive home now." She pulled her hand out of his.

"You will be free to walk the campus on one condition there is someone out of sight but close enough to help you should you run into trouble. I believe that's more than fair." Jaxon reached for her hand again. "He won't talk to you or bother you. As a matter of fact, you'll only know who he is, so you don't worry about someone following you."

"You promise he'll only follow from a distance." She saw him nod his head. "Okay, then. Are there any more rules?"

"Only one." He lifted her chin. "If you sense danger at any time, call for help. Agent Huddle will be close by and can summon others."

When they crossed the street, Jaxon introduced her to Agent Huddle and gave him his instructions. She waved at Jaxon and started walking away from him.

Chapter 41

She couldn't have asked for a nicer day to be walking through the beautiful old campus. Kelsey still hadn't returned any of her calls, which troubled her. After walking for a few minutes, she came across the first set of crime tapes. She stopped and glanced around the area. In her heart she knew Leo and Vance were found in this location. She typed in her phone's notepad what she saw as landmarks. Jaxon would be able to confirm if she were right or not. Tears welled up inside her when she saw Leo and Vance's spirits sitting together on a mound of dirt with a sad expression on their faces.

Her cousin told her on more than one occasion that she believed murder victims were overwhelmed by events surrounding their deaths and needed to find closure along with their families. Seeing the two of them at the scene of their murder and the makeshift tribute of flowers and notes placed nearby brought home once again how one life is impacted by another.

The notes, flowers, and stuffed animals were testaments to the two young men. She never met the young men, but as she stood reading each of the posters, she came to know them. A heavy darkness washed with a sense of foreboding took hold of her. Across a grassy expanse she saw the same dark color over the building. Compelled, she followed the sidewalk to the doors. The science hall—something horrific had happened inside the building. She saw Leo and Vance being tortured and murdered there. Another entry was typed into her notepad.

"Can I help you find something?" a young man asked.

"I'm simply taking in the detail of this old building. They don't make them like this anymore." Peyton noticed the darkness around him with hardly any light shining through. "My name is Peyton. Thank you for asking."

"Terrance Haraway." The scowl never left his face. "If you need me, and figure out if you want something, I'm one of the assistants to Professor Blatner and Professor Muller."

"Thank you." Peyton followed the sidewalk around the building and came to the main building on campus. The president's and dean of student's offices were inside along with other student resources, including the larger of two libraries on campus. Another beautiful building but if the tumultuous darkness that surrounded the facility was any indication, there was something else that was going on in there as well. A picture of items covered with sheets in a dark room took shape in her mind.

She followed the path, looking for Emily's dorm building. As she rounded the curve in the walkway, Peyton passed a building where a lot of young men were standing. Colors were flashing with a dark core on the outside and something akin to lightning appeared along the dark edges. Jaxon definitely needed to question some of them. When they caught sight of her walking by, two or three made crude remarks. She didn't stop to figure out who. She would never admit to anyone, especially Jaxon, she was glad her shadow was nearby.

Peyton learned more about herself during her walk than she could have imagined when she started. She believed she had some helpful information for Jaxon and his team. After making the trip across campus to the student union building with the second library inside, she went inside and sat down at one of the tables. Students were busy studying or chatting quietly, depending on whether they were in a group or alone. She was aware of her surroundings one moment, and in the next she was not.

Kelsey had her hand on a book, ready to pull the tome from the shelf. The book was a thick textbook and not light reading. How she wanted Emily to return soon. Besides being her friend, she helped her make sense of the words in books like this. College classes didn't come easy for her, much to her parents' frustration. How many times had she heard the questions and lectures from them? "Do you know how much we have paid for you to go to school? Could you put in a little effort?" They would follow the questions with the proverbial guilt trip of how hard they both worked to give her this opportunity. As if she didn't know what they had done for her. She wanted them to be proud of her. She worked hard, but there were too many shiny objects around her to divert her attention. Since Emily disappeared, she found herself looking over her shoulder. Not to mention the notes threatening her to keep her mouth shut as if she knew something. Well, maybe she knew more than she let on. Peyton smiled at memories of her own conversations with herself. Was she seeing something real happening now or in the past? She watched Kelsey flip through the pages. Peyton saw at the end of the aisle where Kelsey stood unaware wrestling within herself a darkness moving toward her with slow deliberate movements.

Peyton cried a warning which could not be heard. A hand reached out of the tumultuous dark cloud and pulled Kelsey into the midst of the storm. Did they kill her? Who took her? Peyton found herself following the dark figure through a maze until she saw Kelsey sitting in a corner tied to a chair. Her head hung to the side, limp, but Peyton could see Kelsey's chest moved as she breathed. There were many statues and paintings around her that showed when the light flashed through the darkness. Someone with long dark hair watched over her. "Find me," came a voice filled with fear.

Peyton glanced around the library. No one looked at her strangely. She needed to find Jaxon, and they needed to find Kelsey while she was still alive. Emily needed to tell them more about what she had stumbled upon because her friend's life now depended on the information. She would find him when she was done. She circled back around the way she came, and her first observations were accurate as far as the colors told her. She could see the effects on the Dub or darkness. This campus was filled with darkness, which seem sad to her. She couldn't help but wonder how her college would have appeared if she could've seen behind the scenes of the students rushing here and there. She waved at Agent Huddle when she walked past where he leaned against a tree.

"I thought for a minute you might need my help, but you seemed to do fine on your own." He smiled.

"Still, knowing you were nearby if I needed you was quite nice." She shook his hand.

"Seems like you two got along well." Jaxon draped his arm over her shoulders.

"Yes, we did. He left me alone, and I thanked him." Peyton smiled to herself. *I do believe he's jealous, and I like the feeling.*

****

Damn, if he didn't want to yank her hand out of Huddle's hand. Could he be any more lame? He needed to keep his mind focused on the case. Peyton saw something, and he wanted to know what.

"Do you care to share with me what your walk showed you?" Jaxon fell into step beside her after he dismissed Huddle.

"I went to the place where you found Leo and Vance's bodies. I'm sure it's the location not only because of the crime tape, but because the two spirits sat on the mound of dirt at the site." She showed him the picture. Did she take the picture?

"That's right." He nodded. "Where'd you go next?"

"I followed the walkway to the science hall." She shuddered. "I think they were murdered there. A darkness hovered over the building, and a guy who gave me the creeps asked me what I was doing there basically." She went on to tell him about the door and the group of guys who made crude remarks at her and her visit to the building that housed the president's office. "Something not good is going on there as well. There is a room with some important items hidden inside."

"Is there anything else I should know about?" He found her insights helpful and knew there was more. She never failed to surprise him.

“I also saw what happened to Emily’s roommate Kelsey. Someone is holding her captive. A woman seemed to be watching her or at least someone with long hair.”

Her premonition captivated him. “Do you think she is still alive?”

“I do, and she’s somewhere on this campus. We need Carlene to search for her.” Peyton stopped and sat on a bench with a view of the campus. “It’s hard to jive this beautiful place with the terrible crimes that are taking place here.”

“I know what you mean. I’m sure Frank wouldn’t mind doing another track in the morning. I will need to get a warrant for the dorm area.”

“The sooner the better. I’m going to go home now unless you need me for anything else.”

“You’re good to go.”

“I’ll write you an email with what I wrote at each stop along with pictures and send my findings to you. I think you need to question Terrance Haraway who claimed to be Professor Blatner’s and Muller’s assistant. There is something definitely off with that guy.”

“Him along with a few other young men on this campus.” He took her hand and pulled her up. “Let me walk you to the car, and I’ll catch you back at the house later.”

He watched her drive away and made his way back to where Frank was working with Agent Brown. He was happy to hear they had made considerable progress. He told them about putting in for warrants for the dorms and the student library building. Tomorrow he would talk to Terrance Haraway. He also had Gregory, Emily’s boyfriend, on his list to talk to.

By the time he was driving home with Frank, he had a good feeling the college part of the case was getting close to being solved. There would be a few shocked parents, regents, and professors as well as a few prominent members in the community and state. If Emily's finding proved accurate, there would be more than a few people going to jail.

He glanced at Frank who had fallen asleep, his head laid back against the headrest. Carlene was snoring in her crate in the back of the SUV. He could relate. The day had been a long one.

Chapter 42

Peyton hadn't heard them come in last night nor leave this morning. She read the note Jaxon left for her before she left for school. Being with her kids would help her while she waited to hear if Carlene found Kelsey. She also wanted to know what else Frank's dog had been up to all day yesterday. From the sounds of Jaxon's note, the pieces of the investigation were coming together rapidly, and the picture was clearer today. He had an informant that was working with the agency, which was helpful.

She answered her phone. "Hey, Grams, how are you?"

"I'm fine, dear. I know you've been busy with the store and school, but I was thinking we should plan a party to welcome the honeymoon couple back to Blue Cove next week. Are you willing to help me?"

"Of course, I'll help. Do you want to make it a large affair?"

"No, because we'll be doing that the following week on Thursday. I was thinking of a lovely dinner for when they get home with only a few of us because they'll be tired. I want them to know we missed them."

"Sounds perfect, Grams. I'll stop by after the store closes, or you can come by the store if you want. Either way we'll make our plans." She pulled into the parking lot at the school. "I'll talk to you later. I'm at school and need to get my classroom ready for my students. And just so you know, dear lady, I'm never too busy to talk to you. Love you."

"Love you too. I want to hear all about how you escaped your would-be abductor. You didn't think for a minute I wouldn't hear about what happened to you. Peyton, you are my dear sweet granddaughter whom I love. I need to hear about it from you and not learn about the issue from others."

"Sorry, Grams. I didn't want to worry you."

"And why not? Life is mostly about the concern we feel for those we love. You'll see me at the store, and it will be to catch up on your life and not simply to plan a party. Oh, I love you too, dear. Now get to your class and have a good day."

Peyton rushed into the school, waving at those who greeted her as she walked to her classroom. The morning went by in a rush, and a few hours later she was in her car on her way to the store. Sadie hadn't sounded too pleased with her this morning. She wasn't used to telling people about her troubles, but when it came to Grams, she had better get used to telling her. Grams and Grandpa Max had been the one stabilizing factor in her life. She owed them for more than she could ever repay, but her grandpa would want her to do her best where Sadie was concerned.

When she walked into the store, her grandmother and Reba were waiting for her. It looked like a gray-haired gang up to Peyton with another one of their cryptic messages or warning. She took a deep breath, sure she would get scolded for not telling them about being abducted.

"Hi, ladies, before you get started, let me say I'm

sorry for not telling you, Grams, but in my defense, I had a few down moments when I wasn't thinking too clearly."

"I know, dear. Reba got the details from Jaxon. We are here now to get you ready for round two with the guy. He will be back, you know."

"I know, but what can I do?" Peyton shrugged her shoulders.

"First we eat lunch, and then we plan." Reba smiled at her. "Sit up straight, dear. You don't want to get rounded shoulders. That nice young man of yours came to your defense with us. He was quick to assure us that he would make sure we had details when it comes to you in the future. Jaxon's a keeper, dear. Lunch should be here in a moment. Johathan the nice cousin of Molly's said he would bring our order to us." Reba placed her purse on the table in front of her.

Peyton kissed her grandmother's cheek. "I love you, Grams. I appreciate your patience with me. I'm learning that love is a two-way street. A whole new concept to me."

"I know. I think your Jaxon would appreciate knowing how strongly you feel about him."

"You're probably right." She sighed. "I'm not very good at telling or showing my feelings, but I'm learning."

"You can help Audrey until our lunch arrives." Reba patted her hand and leaned close to her. "I think you're wonderful, and Jaxon thinks the same."

That wasn't as hard as she thought the conversation would be. She noticed the stairs were a bit crowded at the moment with the five ghosts who she'd gotten used to. But there was another one with them, which could only mean one thing.

She would tell Jaxon later about the new ghost and any plans that they talked about at lunch. Right now, a chicken salad sandwich was calling her name.

****

Jaxon arrived on campus early in the morning with the warrants he needed in hand. Frank and Carlene got right to work in the area as soon as the warrant was served. A team of agents, campus security, and local PD were working side by side in each of the areas where Peyton suggested they take another look. She was spot-on. They were gathering enough evidence that arrests would soon follow. He knew people would be shocked by the some of the people on the list. Hell, he was.

When they took a break for lunch, they still hadn't located Kelsey, but they had found another body. A student activist, who had been missing for the past couple of months. Aspen D'Anna had trained Emily Hart and turned over some of her notes to her. Emily was the one who reported Aspen as missing. When Peyton told him that all the pieces were interconnected, she wasn't kidding.

"I found more than a few points of interest in the Science Hall. We need to go through a couple of the areas carefully." Agent Brown took a swig of water.

"I've been with campus security in the building housing the president's office and library. I know you all need to see what we found. I wouldn't believe it if I hadn't seen the find with my own eyes." Huddle stood beside the group. "Not only were there priceless art pieces, Ming Dynasty vases, and valuable jewelry but there were a cache of weapons legal and illegal. Makes me wonder what their plans are or were."

"Maxwell said to put our reports together and go back through each of the buildings." Jaxon repeated what Tom had said. "I talked to some young men in one of the dorms, and with the help of an informant, I knew who to target. I can't wait to see what the techs find on their laptops."

"I don't remember college this way. We usually drank too much and skipped classes. I attended a few protests and thought I was a badass. Hell, I'm getting old." Brown shook his head. "I'm not sure we've discovered all of the issues yet. For the sake of the students here to learn, we need to take them all down."

"I agree. Let's get back at the job." Jaxon followed Frank and Carlene. "Show me what you've found."

Jaxon found himself driving home after another long day. The investigation was nearing the end, and he had yet to figure out how Lewis Buckner fit into the story. Lewis kidnapped Mary Bradley and killed her. He also abducted Emily but not because of her story. How did that fit into the problems happening on campus? Peyton, he could understand, because she was the one to find his victim's body. The man saw her and tracked her phone number when she called the police. But there was more to the story—he was sure. Lewis Buckner wasn't Lewis at all, or was he?

He had texted Peyton earlier that they would be late and catch dinner when they could. He smiled when she texted a big thank you back for coming to her defense with Sadie and Reba. She said she had a nice lunch with them, and they came armed with plans for her on how to deal with Lewis. She also mentioned a new ghost, and he understood why. He hoped that no more would show up. The stairs would become way too crowded if they did.

Chapter 43

Peyton was half asleep when Jaxon, Frank, and Carlene came in. She muted the TV and sat up. “You guys must be tired.”

“You’ve got that right.” Frank told her good night and headed to his room with Carlene.

“That man amazes me. Carlene tugs and pulls him, and somehow he keeps up with her. I swear I get tired just watching them.” Jaxon sat beside her.

“He loves what he does, but I know it’s not easy on his body. I can’t imagine how many crimes his dogs have helped solve. I know he has a great reputation among local PDs, tribal police, and any other organization he has worked for. Prestigious organizations like Necro Search and a group who does canine scent work.”

“All I know is his dog did her job the last few days. I will fill you in once arrests warrants and charges are handed down.”

“Before I go to bed, can I ask you a question?” she asked him.

“I’ll answer what I can for you.” He took her hand and stroked it with his thumb.

“Did you happen to find another body that might account for my latest ghost?” She returned the favor to his hand with her thumb.

“Yes, another young woman. Her name was Aspen D’Anna.”

"Oh, my." She blew out her breath. "I've heard that name before."

"Where?" Jaxon's brows rose.

"Emily mentioned her to me. She was her mentor, and I remember her mumbling something about her missing and no one cared." Peyton glanced at Jaxon. "You're tired. We can talk more tomorrow."

"I talked to Emily a bit today but will interview her more tomorrow." He pulled her into his arms and kissed her good night. He took her hand, pulled her up, and walked her to her room. "Sweet dreams, sweet lady. I love you." He opened the door and nudged her into the room. "I'm giving you fair warning there will come a time when I walk you to a door and follow you in and my home will be yours. I don't give up easily. I got my job by being tenacious, and you're worth the work." He blew her a kiss and closed the door.

Peyton stared at the closed door with her mouth hanging open. *I love you too, but I can be persistent too. I may have a few surprises up my sleeve for you.* All someone had to do was tell her, and she could be as stubborn as her cousin. Still, she sighed—he had a romantic if not slightly archaic way about him. She got ready for bed and slipped beneath the covers. Her trusty fairy nightlight giving out a warm glow in the room.

Hearing they hadn't found Kelsey but found Aspen's body was a bit of a shock to her. She wanted to find out all she could about Aspen. How do you tell the story of a bright star snuffed out way too soon? Peyton was overwhelmed with how easily it seemed some could forget their humanity and destroy another life without regard for their family and those who loved them. Murder destroys more than one life. A whole world changes in a moment. At least for now, as far as she knew, Kelsey was alive, but for how long she had no idea.

She rolled onto her side, tucking the covers under her chin. Peyton closed her eyes. When she dwelt for a moment longer on the scene at the door, she sighed. The man sure could kiss.

****

Jaxon stretched out on the bed. Damn, but it felt good. He smiled. The bed and finally saying the words out loud that he had been thinking about for months. In truth, since the first day he looked into her beautiful green eyes. She left him feeling off kilter whenever she was around him. Not unlike his early days when he wanted to ask a girl out. Thank goodness, his palms didn't sweat, nor his face break out. That wasn't a good look.

The investigation was moving forward, and they were close to connecting all the dots. No matter how he tried, he couldn't figure how Lewis fit into the whole scheme of the case. He wasn't a student or professor. He wouldn't have known who Peyton was if she hadn't been the one to find the body. Maybe he was simply an opportunist, taking advantage of a criminal situation. The problem for him was the man was nothing like the missing Lewis Buckner, or this would be another place where the case made him think outside of the box. That was Peyton's department not his. He closed his eyes. For his part, he had a couple of people who would keep their eyes on her for the next few days because of Buckner. No, he didn't tell her and wasn't about to. But he knew he could worry less if someone was watching out for her when he couldn't be.

When Jaxon opened his eyes again, the clock said six thirty. He groaned out loud, then pushed up. As tired as his body felt, his gut told him today, there would be a break in the case. He couldn't wait to get to the campus and continue their investigation. He wondered if Frank had the same impression. He was up early, letting Carlene out, and if his nose was working right, he had made coffee already.

Jaxon rushed through his morning routine and walked into the kitchen.

"I thought I heard you earlier, and I know I smelled coffee." He poured himself a cup of the dark brew.

"The sooner we get Carlene in action when she's fresh the better. I have a good feeling about the day. I think we were close yesterday, and I sure want to find that girl. She was calling to me in my dreams."

"I'm with you." He handed a mug with a lid to Frank. "Fill her up, and we'll get on the road. What do you need for Carlene? It's liable to be another long day for us."

"I've already put her food, treats, and water in the car. As long as she can rest in her crate once in a while, she'll be one happy dog."

"Good morning." Peyton walked into the kitchen. "You fellas are getting an early start."

"Hoping for a bit of luck for the good guys, and to find Kelsey alive and well."

"That sounds good to me. I'll hope with you." Peyton pulled a mug out of the cupboard and poured the coffee in with some cream. "Have a successful day."

Jaxon headed for the door after Frank but turned around. He pulled her into his arms and kissed her soundly. "I meant what I said last night. See you later."

"You'll hear my reply soon enough."
"I can't wait." He closed the door on his way out.

Chapter 44

A quick glance at the clock told her it was still early. Peyton took her time getting ready for work. She spent time on her hair and figuring out what she wanted to wear. She opted for some navy slacks and a green shirt. Usually, she had to rush off to work. This morning came as a luxury she rarely had these days. She even had the time to make a fresh pot of coffee and take her time to eat a bagel. She got up early and didn't need to rush out the door.

She often sacrificed a slower-paced morning for extra minutes of sleep. She was scrolling through her messages on her phone when she came across a simple text. —*Don't think I'm done with you by any means. We shall meet on my terms and my time.*—

Tell me something I don't know. You had to ruin a perfectly good morning. She frowned and trashed his message. Jaxon wouldn't like what she did. He'd call the message evidence, but she didn't want the message on her phone. He had found a way around her block.

Peyton left for work. The day should be fairly simple. The kids had an assembly this morning, which should take up quite a bit of class time. When the assembly was over, her only plans for the rest of the morning were to have a story hour and a no-mess art project. No mess wasn't a hundred percent foolproof though. Her class could find a way to cause chaos with paper and crayons. She loved to watch them at work and the joy that shone on their faces when they showed her their creations.

She arrived at the school and went straight to the office. Taking the papers from her teacher's mailbox, she greeted the office staff and headed for her classroom.

Hmm, what do we have here? She fingered the envelope with her name written in bold black letters. She took a letter opener and slit the envelope. The message inside was clear and simple.

No one gets away from me and lives to tell the story. I know where you work, and I know where you are staying. Are you afraid yet?

Funny, she wasn't. Maybe she should be. Although, she did have a sense he would try to do something different, and desperate this time. He didn't have Emily to hold over her, but he had some new tactical surprise if his past record held true. He was a traveler, and if anyone epitomized the spirit of one of the three brothers, it was what lived in Lewis Buckner's body. She found the whole sordid story sad that a man who lived a generous life and had done a lot of good for others would be blamed and his reputation destroyed for something he didn't do. If there was any justice, maybe she could exonerate the real Lewis Buckner somehow.

The dark web was his perfect hiding spot to find his next victim, and the college offered a place to hide among the others while he committed his crimes. His darkness spread across the campus and pulled in displaced, unhappy young men. Plus, someone posted the photos of girls along with their names on the dark web site operating somewhere on campus. Jeremy had sent her examples that he had found. She wondered if

Emily's photo was put on there. He found her somewhere and Mary too. She wouldn't rest easy until she found the answer. Hopefully, Jaxon would discover the truth. If not, she would. Her busy mind was pulled back into the moment when the first student was wheeled into class. She wouldn't stop to think on the subject again until she left for the bookstore and enjoyed a morning of laughter with her precious students. Those little people were the perfect cure for the thoughts that had plagued her since receiving his messages. No, she wasn't afraid, but she was mad.

By the time she arrived at the bookstore sometime after noon, she wished she could see the guy face-to-face. "Hi, Audrey." She waved when she walked in the door. "As soon as you get a break, go to lunch, and I'll take over for you."

"Sounds good. Molly is supposed to bring her little guy in to show the staff. I can't wait to see him."

"How exciting. I can't wait to see him too. I've heard from Kenny that he has his dark curly hair and his mommy's pretty eyes."

"I bet he's one pretty baby. He has good-looking parents." Audrey handed the customer back her card along with her purchase. "If you take the next customer, I'll hurry back."

"I'd be happy to." Peyton noticed the ghosts were agitated. She couldn't see a reason for their sudden activity, but they were moving back and forth from Joe's and the bookstore. The guardian didn't seem happy either.

Reba walked through the door, followed by a lot of noise in the coffee shop. Molly had walked in with her baby, and everyone wanted a peek at the new arrival.

Peyton wanted to join in with the others, but the ghosts seemed to be more agitated than before. She hesitated—something was about to go down.

The doors into Joe's slammed shut without anyone near them, and at the same time her phone rang. Peyton didn't want to answer the darn thing. She already knew who was on the other end.

"I told you we would meet again, and if you don't want them all dead, you'll do exactly what I tell you to do. It's a case of your life for theirs. Think of that baby who is just beginning his life."

"What do you want me to do?" Peyton put the phone on speaker for Reba to hear. She mouthed the words. "Call the police." She saw Reba nod.

"I want you to go outside and walk down to the corner. Stand there until you hear from me." Peyton could see the guardian move when she did, but when she went to go out the door, he shook his head and blocked her move.

"Listen to him, dear. He knows something we don't." Reba mouthed.

Her phone rang again. "I told you what to do. You'll be responsible for their deaths."

"I think not, you will be. Come in here to get me if you're not afraid." She actually thought she saw the warrior smile. He handed her the dagger and stood behind her while the five ghosts went to circle around her, but the guardian motioned them behind him.

"If you don't obey me, you'll pay for your insolence to me with the death of your friends."

"We'll see who is right. It's your end that is in sight. You have a few friends waiting to see you and give you a big send off. I'm sure you remember Mary. She's here along with a few of her friends, and more are on their way. Including the baby's father. He'll rip you from Lewis' body before you can travel again if you touch one hair on his son's head."

When he hung up, Peyton directed Reba to move to the stairs. She didn't want her to be harmed. She was on her own. This was between the two of them, and of course the lives he had hurt since bringing his darkness into the area. The time had come for him to leave.

Sadie had told her yesterday to sing an old Celtic song. The words would come from her ancestors when the time arrived. She hummed the tune that came into her head. The line she kept repeating was *the night is darkest before the morn.* When the front door opened and bounced off the wall, Lewis Buckner rushed in and stopped dead in his tracks. Peyton stood staring him down humming her song, speaking the words repeatedly in her mind.

****

She faced him without fear. Not intimidated, stare for stare, and matched his snarl with a smile. A horrendous light shone around her, hurting his eyes and making chinks in the darkness in his heart. He tried to leave, but he was stuck in place, and couldn't move. He swatted at whatever buzzed around his head.

The phone in his hand flew across the room, and he ducked before a book hit him in the head. What the hell was happening to him?

When he saw the dagger in her hand, and the shield hanging in midair with the Celtic cross—light shining through the center, he knew he was done here. He had seen that shield many times before when he faced defeat. He had felt the same strength from a woman in his past.

"Dub, go and return no more." She roared at him. Before he could move, she raised her leg and gave him a well-placed kick to the side of his head. He staggered backwards. Another kick buckled his knees. Knowing he could not win this battle, wounded and defeated, he jumped from the body he used and let it hit the ground.

Without the restraints of the cumbersome human he had inhabited, he could see what he was up against and shook with fear. A foreign emotion for him, one he hadn't felt in generations. At least, not since the curse on his family. He tried to flee on the spot except the warrior with the shield took him by his neck. Dub had no idea where he was being taken. They flew for what seemed a long time over water and land, into an area where he had never been before. Desolate, isolated, and dark like him. In the language of his homeland the warrior vanquished him to wander there alone. If his brothers got wind of what had happened, he would never live it down. He wouldn't tell them that's all. He only hoped his brothers would search for him. He was the charming one after all. He needed them. Like it or not darkness alone wasn't enough to fight the power of light.

****

Reba walked down the steps and stood beside Peyton. "If I hadn't seen it with my own eyes, I would have never believed it. I need to sit down."

"You and me both." Peyton sat beside her.

The doors opened going into Joe's. "Is everything okay in here? When did you shut the door?" Agent Huddle walked in. "Jaxon wanted me to watch you, and not long after the door closed, the cops swarmed the place over there. Who's the dude on the ground?"

"It's a long story. Tell them to search for a bomb. I

have the phone that I think was meant to detonate it. As far as that dude, he was used as a shield by another guy who left him for dead and fled the scene."

"The police will probably have a lot of questions for you both."

"Tell them I said to bring them on. We aren't going anywhere."

The police found the bomb in the car he had left behind which they had to disarm. They also found a huge scrapbook of photos of women whom he had killed. Some dating back many years and some were crude drawings.

Peyton and Reba spent a couple of hours answering questions. When everything settled down, she found herself back at the table sitting next to Reba, still trying to comprehend what she had witnessed.

"I've come in here and told you girls what I think many times, but I've never had to face what you've faced. I admit I wouldn't want to stare down what you did without a lot of help. Your story is the one that I will continue to repeat. There is no reason to equate those crimes with that young man. I don't believe for a moment that he was guilty." Reba reached for a tissue.

"He wasn't. Lewis was simply a body for the traveler to use. Not that it's any consolation for his loved ones, but at least they'll find a measure of closure."

When her phone rang, Peyton said, "I need to take this."

"Go ahead, dear. I think I'll call Lawrence. I could use a meal out tonight."

"Huddle called me. Are you okay?" Jaxon asked. "He told me about the bomb but didn't seem to have many details about what happened."

"I'm fine, but I'm sure Huddle didn't tell you half the story because he didn't know all the details. We'll talk later. I'm still processing the whole sordid event. I hope you're having a good day. Did you find Kelsey?"

"Better than yours, I think. And yes, we did. We can talk later."

"All right. I should be able to go home to my cottage."

"We'll talk about that too when I get back to the house. Okay?"

"Works for me." She disconnected the call. "Is Lawrence taking you out to dinner?"

"Yes, he is. You can join us if you want." Reba's hand shook as she reached for her purse.

"I think I'll take something home from Joe's." She hugged Reba. "Will you be okay?"

"I should be. I admit I've heard about travelers but never actually seen one except for here."

"What would I do without you? Have a nice dinner. Be careful driving home. You're still a bit shaky."

"I promise to take it nice and slow. I love you, my dear girl."

"I love you too." Peyton walked her to the door.

Peyton had told Audrey to go home, and she would close up. Doing the closing routine normalized her day. The coroner had removed Lewis's body, and his family would soon be notified. At least they would hear a decent story about how he died. He wasn't a criminal but a shield for one. Of course, they might continue to wonder where he had been all this time. Amnesia seemed like a plausible story worth repeating. When her order was ready at five, she headed for the house. Hopefully, she would be back at her own home soon. First though, she had to get the Parker house clean and ready for the returning honeymoon couple. She couldn't wait to hear the details of their trip.

Chapter 45

When Jaxon got home, he filled her in on the details that he could from the college investigation. Kelsey was in bad shape and in the hospital. She would survive, but she was on IV drips and sedation meds, and it would be morning before he could even begin to question her. He learned from Emily about Aspen, Leo, and Vance and their work on the college paper. They also found the operator of the web page, and he would reveal a few more surprises as soon as he could let the details out. He had to play it by the book.

She told him the details of her run in with Dub. "He had big plans to make this his legacy to impress his brothers. With him out of the way for now, I think it's time for me to go home tomorrow. I will clean the house and get the premises ready to welcome the happy couple home. Is that all right with you?"

"Yes. Frank and I will stay at my place tomorrow. I'll change the bedding and wash the sheets in the morning."

"I'm looking forward to being back in my place and having my cousin home." She leaned back on the couch. "I got a text from Emily. She is going to stop by the store tomorrow for a visit. I'm excited to see her under better circumstances."

"If she gives you any information that you think will be helpful, be sure to let me know."

"You know I will."

"The next few days will be busy as we bring this case to a close. I'll be by as often as I can but not as much as I would want." He put his arm around her. "Do you mind if we sit here together and watch TV? My mind needs a break. I've seen how ugly people can be to others for whatever their faulty reasoning, and my mind can use a break. Let me say there are a lot of good folks out there, but there is an extremely dark side to some too."

"One more question what time did the biggest break in the case come?"

"I'm sure that's documented somewhere, why?"

"Because the moment Lewis's body fell to the ground, the guardian took the dark spirit somewhere. I don't know where, but I believe his hold over the college was broken."

"Well, sweetheart, that will forever be our little secret." He kissed her and turned on the TV.

****

Peyton had a great visit with Emily. Emily spoke about the story that Aspen had started, and she inherited when Aspen disappeared. Leo and Vance were working with her. Their photos were all over the dark web with slurs and calls to stop them. Theirs was considered a hate crime because of a note found on the body of Leo. Emily told her that her abductor must have seen her photo online because he never mentioned her article. And she had a feeling Aspen was murdered because of her work on the article. They were all close to finding out the operator of the web site who pushed the narrative only certain people and especially males were the real Americans.

Peyton recalled the last words Emily said before she

left the store.

"Thank you for saving my life. I know he was going to kill me. He talked to himself while he thought I was sleeping. He didn't always make sense. Most of what he said sounded like a foreign language to me. Especially when he spoke over the charm. I have no idea why he took you, but I will be forever grateful that he did."

Emily would finish her story, and the college would be going through some major changes because of what happened. Peyton thoughts flew as she hung the welcome-home banner and scattered the paper hearts around the house. On Friday there would be a bouquet of roses from Sadie, ballons from her, and a stocked refrigerator. Of course, she wouldn't forget Matt's favorite, brownies from Joe's.

"Home at last," Peyton mused as she walked through the door to her cottage.

She hoped her cousin's honeymoon was as interesting as her past few weeks had been. She sat down on the couch and took a deep breath, then scrolled through her phone and caught up on all her emails.

****

Jaxon had been right when he told Peyton he wouldn't see her as much as he wanted. He had to go on the few stolen moments from their last night at Matt's. He texted and called her but hadn't been able to see her. Tonight, he finally was walking the familiar path to her cottage. Frank left a couple of days ago, and Matt and Jessie were home and enjoying married life in their home. Matt had already got caught up on what happened while he was gone. It's now Peyton's turn to hear all the details because as Matt said they wouldn't have solved the case as quickly as they had without her.

"Hi, beautiful," he said when she opened the door. He handed her a perfect white rose.

"What's this for?"

"I know when Mary was found, she had a charm and a white rose. I don't want the symbol to be corrupted by him. This perfect bloom symbolizes purity, new beginnings, and I was told it was suitable for honoring someone." He pulled her into his arms and kissed her as he walked near her.

"How sweet. Nice to see you too," she whispered in his ear as he held her. "Why me?"

"Your help was invaluable, and I want to honor the gift of you. Let's sit for now. I want to bring you up-to-date on what's happening. You will be called to testify about what took place in that shack. I'm not sure how you're going to do that though."

"The same way I've answered the police, truthfully. Lewis was a human shield for the bad person who fled when Lewis fell to the ground. I told them I never got a good look at the man, but I heard him and would recognize his voice. Emily said she never saw the man clearly because she was always drugged."

"Each of the places you told us we needed to visit, we found something sinister going on. At the dorm with all the guys, we found the web site and podcast hidden in the basement. The operator was a computer geek angry at the world. He was a rising star in one of the political parties which I'm sure will come out in court. The computers gave us a bonanza of information. Drug sales, porn, and chat rooms filled with braggarts and real scenes of murder which are being investigated." Jaxon shook his head. "I'm telling you, Peyton, the threats and vile posts in the chat room were beyond what I could image. Add the comments and podcast shows, and we have a whole society that is a breeding ground for hate and resentment. Aspen was on the assassination hit list and we are following the web footprint to her killer. The other girls were victims of some sick male initiation to prove their manhood."

"Emily told me her photo along with her friends' were on the site."

"They were, and another shocker is her boyfriend put it there. He's been arrested."

"Gregory?"

"Yes, he had a hand in Kelsey's abduction. What's worse was Kelsey was being guarded by a professor's female assistant. She is being charged also along with Terrance Haraway."

"Professor's Blatner's assistant?"

"Yes, but a strange twist is Blatner was clueless, but his colleague a tenured professor Joseph Muller was up to his neck in the secret society. They were collecting ancient artifacts for supposed educational purposes but selling them on the black market. All the members were making a tidy sum of money. Of course, some more than others. An operation which had been going on for some time. Among the people who benefited the most were the town mayor and a state representative. They were all turning their eyes and cashing in on their pretend ignorance. They're all being charged. A large cache of illegal weapons were found among the other treasures. We have yet to discover their purpose. One of the kids computers talked about a civil uprising."

"That's a bit scary. What's next?" She held his hand.

"The agency will be untangling who is guilty and who isn't on campus for a while. We need to answer who knew what and when. But thanks to an informant, at least, we now know where to begin looking for the murderer of Aspen and the other girls. A group of young men were pointed out to us, who think of themselves as the protectors of the secret society. I swear the whole thing is like some strange video game. These guys had no remorse and didn't see what they were doing as wrong. They were protecting something bigger than themselves was their same response. You can't make this stuff up."

"In the meantime, I've learned some truths that may seem ancient and foreign to most but are still real today. The invisible world impacts the visible world every day. We may have to fight crime on both levels. For now, I hope that the three brothers don't meet up in my lifetime. Darkness was enough to handle for me."

"Do you have any questions? I'm sure we will be learning more for a long time to come," Jaxon told her.

"What about the traveler's scrapbook?"

"Let's just say we took the most recent photos to see if we could identify the women in the book. The older photos and drawings are locked away and out of the report. A lot like our suspect Dub."

"Do you know who shot at you and Robert Craft?"

"Not yet. It seems the campus society may be a part of a bigger crime syndicate. Only time and a broader investigation will tell."

The rest of the evening was filled with intimate conversation, and more than a few stolen glances and kisses. "I guess I should leave. My family is at the house for Thanksgiving."

"What time do we need to be there? Madison is coming in the morning."

"Dinner is at two, and dessert is at the inn with all our friends at five."

"I realized something important during this time."

"Oh, yeah, what's that?"

"I love you and want to spend my life showing you how much. Think about what I've said, will you?"

"I always do." She kissed him good night. "I hope you know I love you too."

****

She closed the door and leaned against the frame. What would she do if he asked her to marry him? She wanted to say yes, but she wasn't sure if she was ready to be a wife at this point. Although, holding Molly's little fella yesterday, she could see the possibility in her future. But she wouldn't keep him waiting forever. No, she wouldn't do that. She loved him.

Chapter 46

Peyton was happy to see her sister when she arrived. They spent the morning chatting until the time came for them to get ready for dinner with Jaxon's family. Peyton dressed with care. She really did love his family. They were fun to be with, and she knew Madi would love them too.

Jaxon's house was filled with laughter and noise when they arrived. A holiday should sound like this and not like the ones Peyton grew up with. Sadie, Matt, and Jessie were already there and getting to know Jaxon's family. Jessie was playing with Emma, and Peyton snapped a picture. She couldn't help herself. Her cousin glowed with happiness, which bode well for Matt. He was taking good care of her.

"Hey, cous." Peyton sat down beside Jessie.

"Isn't she the sweetest little girl." Jessie smiled at Emma's antics.

"She is. You look happy."

"I am happier than I ever thought possible. Imagine me, the one who worried about a love that could last a lifetime. The last few weeks have been so wonderful, and at this point I'm simply content to have experienced the time with Matt."

"I'm glad you're happy."

"Matt told me you've had a rough few weeks. We'll get together, and you can fill me in."

"Sounds good. I look forward to working at the store while you are there."

"How's it going with your handsome agent man?"

"Fine, simply fine." She sighed. "He's everything I've ever dreamed of."

Jaxon's mother had cooked a feast, which they all contributed a side dish to. They laughed, ate until they were past full, and talked some more until someone said they could use something sweet. At that point they piled into the cars and headed to the inn for one of Katie's famous dessert tables.

Pumkin pie was on the table, but there was a whole lot more. From cream puffs, various pies, and even a chocolate cake, Peyton knew she would be running tomorrow after tasting a little of each.

Madison had a few of the single young officers keeping her company, Emma was sleeping contently in her daddy's arms, and Matt and Jessie said their goodbyes because a tired Sadie was ready to go home. As the evening wore on, the crowd began to thin out, and Madi told her Kip was going to show her around town. Each one left with promises to see each other again at Christmas.

When Jaxon's family headed back to his house, he took her hand. "I'll walk you home." He helped her with her jacket. "This was a nice day."

"One of the best Thanksgivings ever for me." She shivered when the chilly night air hit her.

"My family loves you just like I do." He slipped his jacket around her shoulders.

"Your family is the best, and I like your sister's future husband. She asked me to be in her wedding."

"She told me she wanted to ask you. I want them to

be your family too, you know. They all agree you fit right in."

"That's nice to know. I wouldn't mind if they were my family too."

"I didn't tell you and I should have. During this last case when we found Kelsey, I put myself between Frank and the defendant holding a gun. She shot at me, but her hand was shaking too much, and the bullet went to the side of me, narrowly missing my head. The one area that wasn't protected. I realized then I wasn't going to waste any more time. I want to marry you, Peyton. I know you are still figuring things out, but will you consider getting engaged?"

"I'm glad you told me. I've been thinking too. I can't imagine anyone else for me but you. I would be happy to consider your request when you propose to me."

"Really, you mean it?" Jaxon swung her around into his arms.

"Of course." She gazed into his incredible eyes.

"I guess that means the next move will be up to me." He kissed her soundly.

"I guess it is, unless I follow in the path of my cousin and ask you first." She smiled at his expression and sauntered away.

He rushed after her and pulled her into his arms and kissed her soundly. "I guess we'll see who is first, but either way we both will win."

"You've got that right." She kissed him again.

A word about the author...

I am a multi-published, award-winning Amazon best-selling author who writes romantic suspense with a touch of the paranormal. I enjoy writing fiction. I'm hooked from the first words on the paper, and I have to keep writing to see how the story ends. Layer by layer I build it until I come to the happy conclusion.

I live in Colorado with my family. I am a member of the RMFWPAL (Rocky Mountain Fiction Writers Published Authors League) and the Colorado Authors League. I have enjoyed becoming involved in my community as one of the many authors living in Colorado. I invite you to read one of my Blue Cove Mysteries and see for yourself why Blue Cove is a special and unusual place.

http://www.ionamorrison.com

Thank you for purchasing
this publication of The Wild Rose Press, Inc.

For questions or more information
contact us at
info@thewildrosepress.com.

The Wild Rose Press, Inc.
www.thewildrosepress.com

www.ingramcontent.com/pod-product-compliance
Lightning Source LLC
LaVergne TN
LVHW020529100826
845148LV00010B/1397

* 9 7 8 1 5 0 9 2 6 3 9 6 7 *